THE BLACK CAPE SAGA
BOOK TWO

ARCHER THORN

First edition 2025

Published by Everwatch Books

Book Cover Design and Interior Formatting by 100Covers.

ISBN 979-8-9899620-4-4

For everyone who said I'd never be a writer.

Actually, now that I think about it,
everyone's been really supportive.
But it would be so much more satisfying to
prove someone wrong, you know?
Wait. If they believed in me all along, did I just prove them right?
Not sure I care for that.

Do they think they're better than me?

Well, look, you already bought the book.
Might as well go ahead and read it.

ONE

Thirteen Years Ago

IT had all happened so fast. An adrenaline-fueled blur, followed by lights and sirens. Jimmy's hands still trembled from the rush of it. They had confronted real bad guys face-to-face.

And they had won. And Jimmy had loved every minute.

Now the Riven siblings stood at the mouth of an alley, watching from the shadows as the Twisted Pair gang was hand-cuffed and loaded into a police transport. Their costumes grew slick with the heavy mist that hung thick in the air—rare for a desert city. But this was a rare kind of night. Some heroes went out on their first night and never came back. Jimmy and Summer had busted a ring of high-tech thieves and lived to celebrate it.

Jimmy grinned. This was just the beginning.

"You did good in there," Summer said, blue lights illuminating her smile. "Kept your cool, got the win."

"And had fun."

"Oh yeah, that's our style. Let the boring heroes do all the brooding. It just leaves more fun for us."

They had a style. Jimmy liked that. Soon they would have a name, too. A name that people knew, that brought them hope.

With the last criminal loaded, the detective on duty closed and latched the transport and slapped the side twice. The engine roared and the transport sped off.

Then the detective turned toward the alley and stared right at them.

Jimmy gasped and fell back a step. He'd thought these shadows hid them better.

Summer caught his arm. "We knew this was coming. It's part of the job, Jimmy. Heroes and cops need to work together."

"Sorry." Jimmy swallowed hard, regaining some of his nerve. "It's just, I can't go back to the joint, man. I seen too many things, and I promised Stinky Pete I'd stay clean."

Summer laughed. "Okay, no more cop shows for a while."

Jimmy adjusted his mask, self-conscious as the detective drew near. He was middle-aged, short and stocky, and weathered in a way that said he'd seen a thing or two in his time. The mist was slowly collecting in his dark, curly hair. He stopped at the edge of the shadows, hands in his trench coat pockets.

"Hey," he said, his voice gravelly with a heavy East Coast accent. He nodded toward the transport. "Your handiwork, I assume?"

Summer stood taller, shoulders back. "Yes, Detective."

Jimmy mirrored her posture. His sister was right—this was part of the job. But that didn't mean every cop liked it.

This one gave a curt nod. "Pretty solid work. You left enough evidence to prosecute, maybe get some actual convictions. Not every hero has that attention to detail. But those of us who walk on the ground gotta deal with stuff like due process. Y'know what I mean?" He stepped forward, offering a hand. "Detective Stills."

Summer visibly stifled her glee, working to appear professional. She accepted the hand. "Just glad we could help, Detective."

Jimmy couldn't help adding something. "Yes, that's one less gang of thieves in our city."

Summer eyed the receding police lights. "Maybe it's naïve, but I hope this is a wake-up call for some of them."

"Naïve? Maybe." Stills shrugged. "But sometimes you need a little blind faith to do this job. And you never know, maybe it'll set one or two of 'em straight. Happens more'n you might think."

"Really?" Jimmy said. "I thought that only happened in movies."

Stills chuckled. "Ain't saying it's a nightly occurrence, but yeah, I've seen it." He trailed off. Brow furrowed, he pulled a hand from his pocket and grasped at something unseen. A way of gathering his thoughts, maybe. "There are career criminals who do it by choice, and there are villains who like being evil. But there are others, too—the ones who still have something good inside. Deep down, they want us to stop 'em. They want good to win. *Those* bad guys, they're the ones that might turn around."

"And they need our help, too," Summer said, as if she understood and agreed with all her heart. "Help to find a better way. So they don't go back."

Stills nodded. "Once they've paid their debt to society, absolutely. That's part of the job, too. It's just, no one really talks about it." He glanced over one shoulder and then the other. His head seemed to be constantly on a swivel, always watching. "Don't get your hopes up for the leader of this gang, though. Career criminal. He's in the wind for now, but we have some leads, thanks to you two."

Jimmy tensed. "We missed the leader?"

"Yeah. Bell—the guy running the Twisted Pair—we know him. Calls himself Overclock, and this ain't the first gang he's put together."

So, this wasn't a total victory after all. Jimmy's heart sank. He looked down in shame.

"I'm sorry, Detective," Summer said heavily.

Stills shrugged. "Ah, don't feel bad. Way it goes sometimes, and he's real slippery. Even if we can't track him down, it'll take time to build another gang. May not be a perfect game, but it's a win." He eyed the Riven siblings. "You're both new, right? Ain't seen you around before."

"We are," Summer said.

Jimmy recovered enough bravado to add, "And here to stay."

Stills wore an amused grin. "What are your names?"

"Ji–" Jimmy said, then clamped his mouth shut.

Great, first day and you almost give your real name.

"I'm Lock," Summer said quickly, covering his mistake. "He's Lode."

"L-O-D-E," Jimmy added.

Stills eyed them both. Then he nodded as if they'd passed some kind of test, and handed Summer his card. "Alright, then. You make any more collars, gimme a call. I'll get 'em booked for ya."

Summer brightened. "Looking forward to working with you."

"You got it." Stills turned to follow the transport.

Jimmy thrilled inside, pride and elation replacing the momentary disappointment. Thieves bagged, cops befriended, city safer. Even counting the overlooked gang leader, this was a night to celebrate.

"For Highreach," he said, offering his fist.

Beaming, Summer bumped it. "Always."

Now

A wide section of the wall slid silently open.

"Whoa," Zoe breathed.

The light from the Reliquary only penetrated a few feet, and then whatever lay beyond was shrouded in darkness. No matter how ominous it appeared, though, Jim knew it must lead where they needed to go. Where *he* needed to go. Whatever was going to happen next, it waited for them beyond those shadows.

Summer would have loved this.

Despite their grim situation, Jim couldn't help wearing a private little smile at the thought. Riddles? Secret doors? Some faceless evil pulling the strings? She would have eaten this up, and she would definitely have been the first to step through a mysterious doorway into the unknown.

"For Highreach," he whispered. "Always."

"What was that?" Eli said.

"Nothing." Jim put thoughts of Summer away for the moment. He needed to focus on whatever was about to happen here. With a deep, settling breath that didn't work at all, he made himself move. "Okay. Here we go."

One step. Then another. Slowly, he crossed the threshold with the team at his back.

The wall slid shut behind them. Jim kept moving forward.

The darkness enveloped him.

He tried to stay in the moment, alert and ready for whatever was about to happen. Unfortunately, his mind had other plans. Multiple streams of thought vied for his attention.

And they were all interrupted by a commotion behind him.

"Nope no way no thank you this is where I get off!"

"Right on, I'll take my chances here. Where's that door?"

With a scuffle and a thump, the secret wall reopened. Once again, there was enough light to illuminate them but not penetrate the darkness beyond. Clutching each other, visibly trembling, Tweak and Penumbra stumbled through the opening and back into the Reliquary. Kalliope watched them and shook her head in embarrassment.

Jim almost felt annoyed. Then he remembered how young they were, and how they'd nearly been fried by Geometron's little game in the atrium. Jim and his team had rescued them with literal seconds to spare. Anyone would be shaken by that.

"Come on, Kalli," Tweak said, beckoning. "We need you."

"Sorry." Kalliope eyed Jim. "I feel like we kinda ruined a moment here."

"Hey, as an expert in hiding until the scary stuff is over, I get it," Kelvin said.

"You guys almost died up there," Natalie said. "You're allowed to freak out."

"*Everyone* almost died up there." Kalliope gave a frustrated huff, then whispered to herself, "I thought we were better than this."

"You shot Geometron in the face," Jim said. "You've got nothing to be ashamed of. Go. Look after your friends."

Though he didn't say that it would be better this way, he felt it deeply. Whatever they were about to face, they couldn't do it at their best while looking after a group of shellshocked kids. Better for them to hide and recover and live to fight another day. One of them seemed to be holding together, at least—Kalliope would keep them safe.

She hovered at the edge of the doorway. "I wish I could help you finish this."

"Now's not your moment," Eli said. "Survive the day and it will come, I promise you."

Reluctantly, she nodded and stepped back into the Reliquary. As she gave them a last parting nod, the wall slid shut again, and the darkness returned.

With no choice but to trust that they would stay safe, Jim worked to put them out of his mind and focus forward again. Immediately, there was too much to consider.

He had found the green line, but only after awakening a power he never knew was there. Lord Neon must have counted on him discovering it, which means he was aware of Jim's potential all along. But how could that be, even for a legendary hero who supposedly knew everything? Jim fully intended to ask the next time they crossed paths. If the hero was capable of saying anything that wasn't a riddle wrapped in a puzzle.

Apparently, Jim's newfound Vessel ability also came with its own perception. The green orb he could now see glowing inside each of his friends suggested this green line wasn't anything physical, but an extension of a parahuman's power—one that stretched all the way to the deepest level of the Lighthouse, presumably where the Dare ended.

And hey, what *was* the deal with his powers? All his life, he'd believed he was a simple Electric Controller with one complication of being a Vessel. But if there were still more aspects of his power that hadn't emerged, what kind of controller was he really? Did he also have a full Sensor power, not merely an augment? He'd always assumed the ability to "see" electrical fields was part of being a Controller, but was it? Or did the emergence of this ability to see Faraday energy mean that he'd never truly understood what he was?

After working so hard to find the clues that led him here, while also not dying at the hand of Earth's finest heroes, Jim found he had more questions now than when he'd started. Which, when he thought about it, seemed pretty on-brand for the worst hero ever.

It also looked increasingly likely that the truth about Summer, and the finish line for this twisted game, were waiting in the same place. That didn't feel like coincidence, although Jim only had wild guesses why. But if they confronted whatever lurked down there, it might give them a chance to free the Spectrum from the power corrupting their minds.

"Ah, so *this* is how I die," Zoe muttered. "In total darkness, inside a wall. Glorious."

Jim snapped back to the present. "At least you know. They say not knowing is the worst part."

"I don't know, I think I'd embrace ignorance, given a choice," Kelvin said.

"If they can't see us, maybe they can't kill us," Natalie offered.

A light switched on.

7

"Oh, no!" Natalie froze, as if waiting for the end. When it didn't come, she relaxed. "Whew."

They stood in a twelve-by-twelve cube, a solid gray surface on all sides. Perfectly sealed with no apparent way in or out and no apparent source of the light.

"Uh," Kelvin said. "So, what now?"

All eyes turned to Jim.

He held up his hands. "I've never been here before."

"But you found this place," Kelvin said.

"And you witnessed my one good idea for the day, congratulations." Jim looked to Eli. "Have you ever, uh, custodian'd this place? Sorry, I don't know the verb form of custodian."

Eli was already turning, casting his gaze in all directions as if trying to see through the walls. What chilled Jim inside was the thing missing from Eli's expression. The Custodian had moved through the deadly maze of the Lighthouse with confidence, as if he knew what and where everything was—or at least where it should be. Now, though, when Eli met Jim's gaze, he looked utterly lost.

"I . . . have no memory of this."

"That doesn't seem like great news," Kelvin said.

"Believe me, Delete," Eli said. "No one is more troubled by it than I."

That felt like Jim's cue to do his own scan with, well, whatever his Sensor powers really were. If he could at least determine that the green line still . . .

Wait. The green line was gone. Electrical currents—also gone. Alarmed, he glanced at his team. Their green orbs were gone.

"Hey." Frowning, Natalie pressed a hand to her midsection. "You guys feel weird? I-I feel weird."

"I'm craving chicken parmesan. That's a little weird," Jim said. "Also, my powers are gone."

A wave of nausea and fatigue washed over him. He felt as if he were a battery with its charge being sucked away. The others must have felt it too—they reacted in unison, groaning and shrinking in on themselves.

Eli spoke through gritted teeth. "The important thing is to stay calm and–"

"I've gotta get out of here!" Natalie formed a stone shell over her fist and punched the wall. The stone turned out to be paper thin and shattered on impact. She yelped in pain.

Sheathed in inky blackness, Zoe leapt for the ceiling. The Aethyr puffed away too quickly and she fell in a heap.

"What's happening?" Kelvin turned translucent, failed to go invisible, and fell back to huddle against the wall. "*What's happening?*"

"Quiet!" Eli said. "And settle down. Just give me a moment."

That got their attention. As the team got ahold of themselves, Eli knelt and closed his eyes, fingers pressed to his temples. His breaths came slow and steady as if he were meditating. When he opened his eyes, they brimmed with recognition. And fear.

"Arbiter."

With a mechanical rumble, the room began to move.

TWO

"WHAT'S an Arbiter?" Zoe asked.

"She's a longtime Prism hero," Eli said. "Very well-re-spected, though most paras were uneasy around her because of her ability."

"Which is?" Zoe prompted.

"She's a Suppressor—the strongest I've ever seen. Instead of merely dampening abilities, she shuts down Faraday energy itself. Most Suppressors can only weaken a parahuman. Arbiter can switch their power *off*, and not just with low level-paras. I saw her do it to Anchor once, when he was alive."

Kelvin whistled. "No wonder people get nervous around her."

"That's the thing," Eli said. "You don't even have to be around her. She can find you at a distance and shut you down. So, for all of us at once to be suppressed by something we can't even see? No one I know could do that, except Arbiter."

"Hmm," Jim mused. "Then maybe the green line is an extension of Arbiter's power."

"Sorry, green line?" Kelvin said.

Ah, right. He hadn't told them about that.

He hesitated. "Uh, yeah. So, I guess I can sense parahuman power now. Lord Neon told me to hunt for something called 'the green line.' When I fought Geometron, I saw the first glimpse of it. Then when Millennia attacked, and I sort of, ahem, absorbed some of her power," Jim rushed through that last part, hoping no one would dwell on it, "I think maybe the whole Vessel thing made my power level spike higher than it ever has, which woke up some dormant, uh, talents. So yeah, that's how I found the hidden door. There was this line of green energy, and it stretches all the way to the bottom of the station. If Eli's right, maybe it's coming from Arbiter. Sooooo how's everyone else doing? Feeling good? Anyone hungry?"

Zoe looked to Eli. "Ever seen anyone who can do that?"

Eli glanced aside, as if peering into the past. "Once." He didn't elaborate.

"Wow," Kelvin said. "You're a para-power-sensing-*and*-absorbing Vessel, and you didn't even know before now? That's . . . wow."

"Yeah, it's been a strange day."

"It's kinda scary," Natalie said.

"I'll change my moniker to Boogeyman for the five minutes I'm a hero," Jim said. "Though people could think I'm the master of boogers, which may undermine my authority."

"No," Natalie said, her eyes going soft when she looked at Jim. "I mean scary for you."

"Nat's right," Zoe warned. "That is something I'd keep to myself. You think people get weird around a Suppressor? How do you think they'd be with someone who can *take* their power?"

Was she talking about herself?

You're already deep into this. Might as well just ask and deal with it.

Good point, Me. I'm glad you're here.

Yes, I'm very wise.

Okay, not that glad. Settle down.

Jim looked Zoe in the eye. "Will it be a problem?"

Natalie answered first. "No way, Jim! We're like brother and sister now. You won't get rid of me that easily."

"Far as I'm concerned," Kelvin said. "You're still my friend who cried at the end of *To Kill a Mockingbird* in fourth grade. We're all good."

"Pretty sure there was something in my eye," Jim said. "But thanks."

He kept attention on Zoe.

She turned away from him, toward Eli. "You seem more worried about Arbiter than the others. Why?"

"Because she's dead. Or she's supposed to be dead. At least, I thought so, but . . . could it be . . . if so, then how . . . ?" Eli cupped a hand to his forehead, his face slack and weary. "The closer we get to our destination, the more confused I feel, and the less I'm remembering. Things I *know* that I should know."

"So, on top of the truth about my sister, and the end of the Dare, there's a hero that can suppress our power who's supposed to be dead but maybe isn't," Jim said. "And we're riding this microwave oven until it spits us out at her doorstep. Did I miss anything?"

In the moment of silence that followed, Kelvin rubbed the patched wound on his chest. "New powers, corrupted heroes, secrets, lies, bombs in people's chests." He inclined his chin toward Zoe. "Villains turning good. Don't know about you guys, but I'm having a little trouble keeping up with everything."

Natalie nudged him playfully. "Kelvin, we should rename you the Understater. And I think it's okay if we feel overwhelmed."

Jim couldn't agree more. In the years to come, if he ever started wondering why he got out of this life, he could just think about today and say, "Oh. Right."

Eli glanced at Jim. "Wouldn't mind a sip of that top shelf scotch right now."

"You read my mind," Jim said, feeling a sudden longing to be back behind his weathered old bar. Versus may have been long past its prime, but it was his, and the only surprise was when they accidentally made decent chicken wings. "When this is all over, first round's on the house. That goes for all of you."

"Do you make good piña coladas?" Natalie asked.

"Nope."

"Oh," she said, crestfallen. Then she brightened. "What about–"

"Nothing that requires a blender."

"Oh. I guess I'll have a soda, then."

"You don't actually have to give me your order now," Jim said. "Maybe if we survive, though."

"Right, survive a mysterious villain," Zoe said. "Or heroes that are supposed to be dead. Or a lethal fight to get a job here, working for the people trying to kill us. Or all of them."

"Don't forget Jim's chicken parm," Kelvin said. "The way today's going, that's just as likely."

"Only if it's turned evil," Zoe said.

"Not possible," Jim said. "Chicken parm is incorruptible."

Natalie huffed. "It sucks in here!"

With a wordless shout, she jabbed her outstretched hand at the wall. A sliver of stone extended from her fingertips like a blade. There was a metallic screech and the stone shattered, leaving a scratch on the wall.

"Gravel! It didn't go through." Natalie sagged. "Sorry, guys. I can't do it."

Eli bent to examine the scratch. "You were more successful than you realized. Part of this scratch is actually a hair-thin cut. You sliced through, if only slightly."

"Do that a thousand more times and we're home free," Jim said.

"Make even one light bulb flicker and you've got a deal," Natalie teased back.

"Wait." Zoe grinned at Natalie. "Did you use *gravel* as a curse?"

Natalie turned red. "Uh, I guess so."

"Aw." Zoe put a hand on the tiny woman's shoulder. "You're the most adorable little destructo-doll ever."

Natalie giggled. "I prefer *action figure*, thank you very much."

"An ambitious one, too, trying to cut through metal with stone," Kelvin said.

"Well, my stone isn't exactly normal," Natalie said. "Because of my power level, and because the earthy stuff I make is a manifestation of my ability, it's sort of an amped-up version of stone. Except right now, of course, being suppressed and all."

There was a moment of quiet while the group absorbed another in what seemed like a never-ending string of surprise revelations. Compared to everything else, this almost felt routine.

"Well," Jim said. "Anyone else want to reveal some shocking truth? A surprise power? Maybe a secret agenda? Might as well say it while we're stuck in the Laundry Chute of Destiny."

"If I had secret powers, right now I could only describe them to you." Zoe breathed out and sagged against a wall. "Haven't been this exhausted in years. Is this how normal people feel all the time?"

"I'll ask my Nana when I see her," Kelvin said.

Shaking her head, Zoe pulled herself upright. "Well, even when powers fail, one thing never will."

"Right." Natalie pumped her fist. "The human spirit!"

"Nope. Gadgets."

She tapped a button behind her ear, and the mask-and-goggles unfolded across her face. She reached inside her trench coat and produced a small, square-ish device with a blinking red light. Kneeling, she stuck her device to the wall beside Natalie's tiny cut.

"We're moving downward in something like an elevator shaft. Hard to tell more through such a small opening." She tapped her device. Its blinking light, and the glow from her goggles, went from red to purple. "This may look like a solid cube, but an echo pulse reveals microscopic seams in the structure."

She produced a silver sphere the size of a tangerine and tossed it over her shoulder. The gadget hovered at the center of the cube. Its shell twisted and separated into segments, emitting laser beams that highlighted the seams.

"That might work," Zoe muttered to herself. Standing, she detached her device from the wall and stepped beneath the floating sphere. "I don't intend to just sit in this box and wait to be delivered to whatever's waiting for us. That's a good way to never be heard from again." She retracted her mask and eyed Natalie. "Can you make something a couple of feet long and hard enough to survive an impact?"

Natalie pursed her lips. "Maybe. But it'll take everything I've got left."

"Do it."

Zoe slipped a hand into her costume again. In went the square device, and with a subtle metallic rasp, out came Dark Sympathy.

Eli's eyes widened. "What have you *done*?"

THREE

"THAT does not belong to you!" Eli snapped.

Zoe shrugged, unaffected. "I thought you knew, with your Sensor powers. And I used it when I fought Royal Justice."

"I have focused my powers on keeping us alive," Eli said. "That sword belonged to the Chaos Merchant. Even the Spectrum does not know its true nature, or everything it can do." He shook his head, rueful. "You assured us you had reformed, and we believed you."

That seemed to land. Zoe looked at the floor.

"I do regret the theft," she said. "But I don't regret that it's been useful. Right now, the Aethyr layered into this blade is the only reason I can touch Aethyr at all. Like it's . . . connecting me to the source, somehow. Call me a villain if you need to, but if it takes *all* our skills to survive, that's a price I'll pay."

"That . . . that . . ." Eli drilled an accusing glare into Zoe. But as the moment passed, his jaw unclenched. ". . . that is a reasonable argument. We will discuss this at a later time. However, for now . . ." Hands up in acquiescence, he stepped back.

Zoe gave him a small nod, tinged with gratitude. Then she pointed at the tiny slice on the wall. "Get ready, Nat."

"On it!" Natalie pressed her palms together and stared down at them, brow furrowed in concentration.

Zoe produced yet another gadget. She held it in her left hand, Dark Sympathy in her right, and squared her shoulders.

"What else do you keep under that costume?" Jim asked. "The One Ring? The Ark of the Covenant? The Colonel's secret recipe?"

"Trade secret," Zoe said. "Become a retrieval specialist and we'll talk."

"In eighth grade, I tried to steal April Henley's heart. Does that count?"

"Nat," Zoe said. "Now!"

Natalie gave a cry of effort, and a length of shimmering diamond-like stone sprouted from between her palms. She shoved with all her might, driving it through the sliver she'd created earlier and punching into the wall outside their cage.

Zoe faced the opposite wall. Inky blackness flowed from Dark Sympathy to cover her arm up to the shoulder. She drew back, her entire body twisting, and flung the weapon with a shout. The blade pierced through a seam highlighted by her lasers and bit into the wall beyond.

With the sounds of groaning metal and stone, their mysterious elevator ground to a reluctant halt.

Natalie collapsed.

"Oh, dear!" Kelvin reached out, just managing to catch her before she hit the floor. "Uh, does CPR work on Smashers?"

Natalie gave a soft moan. Her eyes fluttered open and found Kelvin.

"Hey," she said dreamily. "You saved me."

"Oh. Heh, right." Kelvin blushed. "Good thing ol' Delete was here, or you might've . . . uh, sustained a minor bruise."

Natalie grinned. "Thanks, buddy."

"Hey, anytime."

"Nice work, Nat," Zoe said.

Natalie replied with a weary salute. "Back at ya."

Jim glanced at Zoe, who leaned heavily against the wall next to Dark Sympathy, looking spent. Steam wafted from her arm. Remarkably, her costume was undamaged.

"You good?" he asked.

She gave a slow nod, as if her head had gotten heavier.

He couldn't resist asking. "What is that suit made of, anyway?"

Zoe hesitated.

"Let me guess," Jim said. "Become a thief and we'll talk?"

"A girl has to have her secrets."

"Fine." Jim turned his nose up, feigning offense. "Then forget about learning the secret to the perfect gin and tonic. No no, it's too late. Become a bartender and we'll talk."

Zoe shook her head, but she wore that smile again. Gathering herself, she redeployed the mask and goggles. "Whew. Okay. Time for the next step." With one hand raised, she moved her fingers through the air.

"Hey, neat, invisible orchestra," Kelvin said.

Zoe chuckled. "It's an augmented reality HUD. Just sit tight for a . . . there."

Her floating sphere closed its shell. Then it rose until it touched the ceiling and split open again. This time, a thin arm extended eighteen inches and placed its tip against the surface, then unfolded to reveal two emitters.

The sphere rotated, spinning the arm clockwise. As it moved, the first emitter fired a cutting laser that melted a circle into the metal. Then the second emitter released some sort of cold ray that cooled the molten edges.

The device spun a full circle, folded back into a sphere, and dropped into Zoe's waiting hand. She stepped aside as the manhole cover-sized circle of metal dropped out of the ceiling, revealing darkness beyond.

Once again, Zoe tossed her sphere upward. This time it floated through the hole and deployed a ring of LEDs. Soft light revealed the shaft, and the absence of any gears or cables. The cube appeared to be floating on nothing.

But the magical flying box didn't have their attention. Everyone gaped at Zoe, then up at the hole, then back at her.

"You are the coolest person I've ever met," Natalie said, awestruck.

"I agree," Kelvin said. "No offense, Jim."

"Just honored to have made the list," Jim said lightly.

"I've seen better," Eli grumbled.

"Don't pout. You'll get your sword back," Zoe said. "Eventually."

One by one, they climbed through the hole to stand on top of the cube. Zoe set her echo device against one wall, then a second. On the third wall, it indicated a thinner bulkhead with no obstructions on the other side. She proceeded to cut another hole and send her sphere into the darkness ahead.

A random empty space, slightly smaller than the elevator, with odd sloping angles—one of those awkward corners inside a structure that no one ever saw once the walls were in place. But it was off the obvious path down, which hopefully gave them an advantage.

As the last of them climbed through, the elevator shifted as if trying to shake loose of its restraints.

"Oh hey, the sword!" Natalie said. "Aw, are you going to have to leave it?"

"Pity," Eli said, not bothering to hide his pleasure.

Zoe shrugged, feigning indifference. But then she peered back at the hole, closed her eyes and reached out. Her arm tensed. There was a distant rattling, then a screech, followed by a series of clunks and clangs.

Dark Sympathy flew through the hole and into her waiting hand. She gaped at the weapon in disbelief.

"Ha!" Kelvin clapped. "Nice."

"I did that once," Jim said. "But with a slice of cake."

Eli looked taken aback, which for him qualified as shock. "We . . . did not know it could do that. Perhaps your kinship with Aethyr . . ."

With an echoing *groan*, the elevator shuddered.

"My stone's about to give out." Natalie stared at the team defensively. "If I had my full power, it would *not* do that."

"We believe you, buddy," Kelvin said.

"Speaking of," Jim said. "Anyone else feel that?"

Vitality flowed back into him. His senses sharpened and his muscles wanted to move again. He blinked hard and his perceptions returned like a light bulb slowly brightening. Blue-white flows of electricity surrounded him once again, and the green line glowed in the elevator shaft. It didn't touch them here.

Everyone breathed a sigh of relief.

"Now that's more like it," Kelvin said.

"Let's never do that again," Zoe said.

Natalie conjured two stone fists and kissed them both. "Oh, yeah! This rocks."

Jim grimaced. "If puns are part of your power, we're getting back in the elevator."

"I had forgotten how unpleasant that was." Eli placed his hand on the wall opposite the hole, eyes unfocused. "I should be able to steer us around the worst of it now."

That sobered them all, reminding them what they were in the middle of. The team held its collective breath, hoping for good news. But when Eli took his hand from the wall, he gave a frustrated huff.

"Uh-oh," Natalie said.

"Let me guess," Jim said. "We're next to a secret aquarium for sharks with lasers and a taste for human flesh?"

"Possibly worse," Eli said. "Or possibly not. That's the trouble, Jim, we won't know until we're there. It's the Whetstone."

Kelvin leaned away. "Yikes."

"Gotta admit, I've always wanted a crack at it," Zoe said. "Just not like this."

Natalie looked confused. "What's a whetstone?"

"Their training chamber. Colloquially, most of the heroes call it Study Hall," Eli explained. "Currently, it's inactive, just a cavernous space taking up most of the Lighthouse's lower half. We could descend quickly in there."

Natalie brightened. "Oh!"

"Wait for the punchline," Jim warned.

"If, however, it activates with us inside," Eli continued, "there are layers of tech, such as particle emitters that can build near limitless varieties of challenges. There are difficulty levels ranging from *break a mild sweat* to *run for your life*. Given the . . . unpredictable state of the Spectrum, we have an equal chance of encountering nothing or mortal danger."

"There it is," Jim said.

"As punchlines go," Kelvin said. "That one's not my favorite."

"So, take the unexpected path through Study Hall, and maybe die," Zoe said. "Or go back to the elevator, lose our powers, and maybe die."

Eli nodded. As he said his next words, he met each of their eyes. "I provide this information, and whatever path you choose, I will help as I can. But I will not decide for you. You must do so, as a team." He paused, letting it all sink in. "So. What will it be?"

FOUR

EVERYONE processed the dilemma in their own way. Wide-eyed, Natalie rung her hands, tiny waves of stone unconsciously rippling up her arms. Kelvin turned his head from side to side and muttered under his breath, as if debating with himself. Zoe just waited, looking resigned. Eli stood still, hands behind his back.

When no one spoke, Jim realized no one wanted to go first. Maybe none of them wanted to choose a path that could end up hurting a friend. But the truth about Summer lay on the other side of this choice, and someone had to speak up.

"Well, either way sounds just great," he said. "Dying in the Spectrum's playpen may not be better, but it *will* be funnier. I vote Study Hall."

In an unreal, funhouse mirror way that matched the day's events, it kind of made sense. To him, anyway.

"I would choose what gives us a fighting chance," Zoe said. "Which means keeping our powers. I vote Study Hall."

Natalie nodded emphatically. "You said it, sister. Point me at the Study Hall and give me something to smash!"

"As an expert on hiding from danger, and as a recently double-crossed person," Kelvin said. "I'm not a fan of being stuck on a path that was given to us by a stranger. Harder to track, harder to kill, I say. Study Hall."

They looked to Eli, who simply nodded. "Well, then. Shall we?"

"Guess that's my cue." Zoe moved to the wall. "Just sit tight."

"This one will be heavily armored," Eli warned.

"Don't worry, I've got something for that," Zoe said.

"Don't tell me," Jim said. "This time it's a lightsaber?"

"Nah, Jedi have too many rules," Zoe said, fishing around inside her coat.

Kelvin chuckled. "She said to a room full of heroes."

"Not sure who you're talking about," Jim said. "I'm a bad man."

"You keep saying that." Natalie thumped him playfully on the shoulder. "I don't think I believe you."

"That's how I get you. Just wait. I'm going to be bad any minute now."

Zoe produced something like a laser pointer. "This will get very bright and very hot. Just so you're ready."

"Proceed," Eli said.

As the others backed away, Zoe deployed her goggles but left the face mask off. The device in her hand ignited with a loud hiss. She aimed one end at the wall and a yellow-white beam lanced out.

Instead of zipping along like her sphere had done, she moved slowly, inch by inch. It became clear how much thicker they had built this wall. Which made sense—if the Whetstone was so dangerous, the Spectrum would want to prevent anything that happened in there from punching into other parts of the station. Or into space.

While the others settled in to wait, talking amongst themselves, Jim only had eyes for the woman driving a fire lance through the Spectrum's precious base. He found himself drifting toward her as if she were the moon and he the tide.

"So, why *Moxie*?" he said. "I mean, if I were a villain, I feel like I'd be tempted to go with something diabolical, like Deathblade or Doomfate or Karen."

Zoe's cheeks turned red. "I started pulling jobs as an edgy teenager, and I wanted something with attitude. It was right around the time when swing dancing and stuff from that era made a comeback."

"I remember those thirty seconds."

"Right? So I chose the name and made the whole period-piece gangster costume to match. I regretted it fairly quickly, but by then I was building a rep and needed to stick with it. Changing the name would've meant starting over."

"Like when Tastee Cakes changed to Flavor Bombs and sales plummeted." Jim shook his head ruefully. "They eventually changed it back, but I could never trust them again."

Zoe laughed. "Something like that."

"So, now that you switched sides and joined Team Boring, why keep the old name?"

Zoe bit her bottom lip and continued cutting. Jim tried to concentrate on waiting for her response . . . but oh, that lip bite.

Focus, man.

She is dangerously cute.

Yes, we all know that. Survive first, then you can try to get a date.

Hey, I can do both.

I doubt it.

Just watch me, idiot.

. . . you realize you just called yourself a–

Can't hear you, I'm going through a tunnel.

"I guess I wanted to show people like me that it's possible," Zoe said. "Villains who aren't truly evil, I mean. I want them to have proof that there's a way out. That they can choose to be something more, and the hero community will embrace them. I mean, I know it's not the case with *every* hero. You saw that yourself."

"I miss Captain Eggplant."

Zoe smiled. "But enough of them will. The ones that matter will. Inviting me for the Dare is proof of that."

"If you don't count them trying to kill you now."

"Yeah, but they're trying to kill everyone. Which, weirdly, makes me feel better."

Jim chuckled. "Solid point."

"I've been meaning to ask. With what you can do, why not just switch off the Spectrum's communicators? It might cut off whatever's corrupting them, right?"

"Or it might fry their brains. I had no way of knowing which way it would go."

"Oh. So, you made a choice that actually *protected* the heroes?"

Jim held up his hands in protest. "If you're suggesting I did something good on purpose, I'll have you know it was completely selfish. A dead Spectrum would be more trouble for *me* in the long run."

"Well, that's a relief." Zoe grinned, shaking her head. Then her grin faded, and she turned hesitant. "Hey, I . . . I'm sorry about before. When you talked about your Vessel power, I was kind of cold. I don't like feeling vulnerable, and I didn't react well." She glanced at him, then quickly away. "But I trust you. We've known each other for like three minutes, I know. Still . . . I do."

Everything inside Jim went quiet. The team's conversation behind him, even the sound of Zoe's cutting beam, all became background whispers. It was like he'd been treading water in a roiling sea that suddenly went calm like glass, and all he felt now was . . . warmth.

"Accepted," he said. "Unnecessary—I get it, really—but still accepted."

Zoe smiled with relief, then quickly wiped it off her face. She cleared her throat awkwardly. "So, um, what about your original name, and your sister's? They don't match your abilities."

"That's true. But we were young, too, and wanted names that fit together like a team. Summer figured Lock could mean locking others out of computer control, and it was just too tempting to use Load, like carrying an electrical load. Then Summer suggested changing it from L-O-A-D to L-O-D-E, since magnetism relates to electricity."

"And a little misdirection with your names might not have been such a bad thing."

"Yeah, they made it harder for enemies to guess our powers. But that was a happy accident, and I take no credit for any cleverness. As young as I was, I'm just glad I didn't choose FighterJetKarateChopExplosion3000."

Zoe laughed. "Imagine them calling that out at Java Justice. *Large latte for Mr. FighterJetKarateChopExplosion3000.*"

"Please, just call me Explosion. Mr. FighterJetKarate ChopExplosion3000 is my father," Jim chuckled. "I know it's fashionable to hate that place. It's kitschy, and it goes way too hard at the hero theme. But they actually make the best Mex–"

"Mexican chocolate mochas." Zoe's red-goggled eyes whipped toward him as they said the same thing. "Jinx. And yeah, I'll admit it. I love that place. Wouldn't it be crazy if we've been there at the same time and never knew it?"

"Doubtful," Jim said. "I'm pretty sure I would've noticed you."

She looked at him again, and this time she didn't look away. He held her gaze, almost seeing her real eyes through the red lenses, appreciating and lamenting the fact that there was a layer between them. It felt liberating and limiting all at once.

Was he crazy to be thinking about this now, of all times?

A little crazy now and then is good for the soul.

Good point, Me.

I'm just telling you what you want to hear.

I'm okay with it.

"I, um," Zoe said. "I really should focus on this."

"Got it. Carry on."

Jim stepped back to join the rest of the team, relaxing while Eli and Kelvin debated the merits of scones versus muffins. Perhaps the biggest shock of the day was Eli staunchly defending Team Muffin. Jim would've bet every bottle behind his bar that Eli was a scone man.

He felt eyes on him and glanced over to see Natalie watching him with the biggest grin her face could make.

"What?"

She shook her head, but her eyes flicked from him to Zoe, and somehow her grin got even wider.

"You know I can melt you with my brain, right?" Jim said.

Natalie giggled, unintimidated by the depths of his evil.

Jim narrowed his eyes. "Okay, Marble. That was a lie, you caught me. But I'm still watching you." He pointed two fingers at his eyes, then at her.

She covered her mouth, laughing harder.

"Try your best to behave, Jim," Eli said.

"What, no lectures for Chuckles McGhee over there? We're in mortal danger and she's laughing and I have *no* idea why—"

The walls shivered around them, rocked by a distant explosion. Was it Jim's imagination, or did he hear a scream?

It must have been real, because the mood in their little space turned serious, the moment of peace squashed by the reminder—not just of their situation, but everyone's. People were fighting for their lives out there.

Jim's gaze returned to Zoe. Her shoulders had bunched up, going tense at the sounds. Beyond her, as Jim's abilities continued to reawaken, the Whetstone glowed brighter in his perceptions. There was a lot of power in that place.

And that power felt *weird*, unlike any source he'd encountered. Whatever exotic system controlled the Whetstone, it drank rivers of electricity, but beyond that Jim couldn't tell much. He reached out to touch a corner of it with his mind and felt a sensation almost like vertigo. As if all that power wasn't really where it appeared to be, and didn't flow where it seemed like it should.

"Got it," Zoe said.

With the smooth motions of a hand magician—or a master thief—Zoe pocketed the cutter and opened her palm just in time for the little sphere to emit its cold ray. Steam wafted from the cooling layers of metal and ceramic, curling around Zoe to create a dramatic scene, like an old world hard-boiled detective suddenly transported here from a foggy night.

The sphere completed its work. Zoe gripped a melted edge, and with a heavy grunt she pulled. A surprisingly thick plug slipped out of the wall and *thunked* to the floor.

Beyond the hole, there was only darkness.

Eli stepped forward. "Remain quiet. Diminish the light, please."

Zoe raised her hand and closed it into a loose fist. In response, the sphere's LEDs dimmed to a faint glow.

The team held its collective breath as Eli moved to the opening, hand out toward the Whetstone, no doubt extending his Sensor powers into the cavernous space. He closed his eyes.

"It appears to be inactive." He tilted his head. "Curious. I imagined the Spectrum, in their current state, would want it turned to max lethal. My powers are still recovering from the suppression, so I want to make extra sure . . . wait." He leaned closer, his arm stretching through the opening. "Even if the entire system were dormant, it still should not be this dark or *oof-*"

Something yanked Eli through the opening, into the pitch black of the Whetstone.

FIVE

THE thing about screaming is *someone* has to do it when their friend disappears through a hole into pitch darkness. So if Jim screamed along with his friends, isn't that heroic in its own way?

Shut up.

"Where did he go?!" Kelvin cried, sticking his face into the hole. "Give us back our friend!"

Then he was taken, too.

Shock and fear are natural reactions to a second friend disappearing through a hole into pitch darkness. If those remaining didn't scream, it really would have been insensitive to Kelvin's predicament, wouldn't it? Jim was just being a good friend.

"Uh, guys . . . . ?" Natalie called, her voice quavering. "Something's happening!"

Jim and Zoe turned from the Whetstone hole and faced the far wall. Except the far wall wasn't there anymore. Natalie backed away, staring in wide-eyed terror at what replaced it.

Darkness. A wall of absolute darkness had overtaken that side of the room and was slowly advancing toward them, swallowing the space inch by inch.

"So," Jim said. "Who had *Eaten by Shadows* next on their Certain Death Bingo card?"

"*I SEEEE YOUR FEEEEAR,*" a harsh, disembodied voice whispered. The words bounced off the walls, coming from everywhere and nowhere. "*I SMEEEELLLLL YOUR DESPAAAAIR.*"

Zoe raised a fist and opened it. Her sphere turned its LEDs so bright that Jim couldn't look directly at it. Every shadow in every corner disappeared—except for the black wall that continued to swallow the room.

"Oh, no!" Natalie exclaimed. "Should we go through the hole?"

"We don't know what's out there," Zoe said.

"*YOOOOU HAVE ENTERED MY NIGHTFALL KINGDOOOOM.*"

"But-but-but," Natalie stuttered, on the verge of panic. "We're running out of time!"

"*I WILL FEEEEAST ON YOUR SOOOOULS.*"

Jim tilted his head. Wait. . . had he really just heard that?

"Uh, hey, creepy disembodied voice?" Jim called. "Are you Canadian?"

The wall stopped.

"*I . . . AM YOUR DOOOOOM!*"

"Yep, definitely Canadian," Jim said.

"I hear it now," Zoe said. "When he says the *oooh* sound. Hey, wait—didn't we fight once, when I retrieved that prototype battery? You came after me with the cutest little shadow monsters."

"*AAAAAAAAAAAAAAAAHHH!*" the voice raged.

Dark beams lanced from the wall of shadow, slamming into Jim, Zoe, and Natalie, hurling them backward. Jim clutched his aching side, surprised. Whoever this guy was, his shadows hit impressively hard. If Jim hadn't absorbed some of their power, they might have knocked him out.

He should have expected this. The Spectrum didn't recruit just anyone.

"Ow," Natalie gasped.

"I agree," Zoe said, rattling her head.

Jim spoke hurriedly. "Take our chances with Study Hall?"

"You ready my mind," Zoe said. "On three, we–"

The wall burst into a mass of creeping black vines that surged forward with inhuman speed. In a blink, all three were bound tight from head to toe. Jim watched with rising fear as the vines tossed Natalie and then Zoe through the hole and into the black of the Whetstone.

Total darkness enveloped him. He felt a swift motion and his stomach leapt into his chest. Without seeing it, he knew the vines were hurling him through the hole. Now was his chance. If he played this right, he could save his team before hitting the bottom far below. Kicking his senses into overdrive, he searched for nearby sources of–

"HURGH!"

Jim realized he could see again just before crashing onto a wide platform only a few feet beneath the hole. He rolled and skidded to a stop on his back. The black vines dissipated like mist.

Apparently, the darkness they'd seen in the Whetstone had only been a small illusion placed over the hole. Now Jim could see the space, and *cavernous* hardly described it. This was more like an airplane hangar tipped vertically.

Scanning with his eyes and Controller senses, Jim confirmed the Whetstone was mostly dormant, except for basic lighting and the particle engine that had built this platform. So, why was this shadow-controlling hero determined to get them in here?

"Everyone okay?" Natalie said.

Zoe groaned. "Does embarrassment count as damage?"

"Only at certain levels," Jim said, picking himself up. "Giving a class presentation with spinach in your teeth, no. Asking Keri Davenport to the prom and having her only response be *ew*, definitely yes." He glanced around. "Where are Eli and Kelvin?"

"*YOUR END IS NEEEEEEAAR!*" the voice boomed from everywhere at once.

Jim winced. "That is the most violently Canadian accent I've ever heard."

"Yeah, now I can't *not* hear it," Zoe said.

"*HEEERE IN MYYYY DOMAIN, YOU WILL KNOW PAAAAAIIIIN.*"

The last *pain-pain-pain* echoed and then there was silence, as if the voice were pausing to create drama, or in case they wanted to beg for their lives. Instead, they shared a look and laughed.

"Will there also be rain?" Zoe asked.

"Will it leave a stain?" Natalie added.

Jim pretended to wipe away tears. "I've never been prouder of you two."

"*RAAAAAAAAAAAAAHHHH!*"

Shadows rocketed through the hole in the wall like a firehose. They collected around the opening, building into a mountain of darkness that towered over the team. The voluminous mass resolved into a nightmarish giant with fangs and bat-like wings billowing out in black waves.

"*I AM GLOOOOOM, THE DOOOOOM FROM SASKETOOOOON!*"

"Okay, that's it." Squaring off with the monster, Jim pointed up at it. "Start being nice, give us back our friends, or I will personally destroy all the maple syrup on the planet. We all know it's the source of your power."

"*DIIIIIIIIIIEEEEEEEE!*"

The monster raised its gigantic fists and slammed them down. The platform shook with a resounding *boom*, and the monster became a wave of darkness that rushed forward and enveloped them all.

Then the Whetstone woke up.

SIX

IF darkness could be a storm, Jim stood inside it. The black tempest raged all around him like tornado winds. Currents of shadow separated for mere instants before crashing back over him. He only caught glimpses of his friends through the shifting dark.

Expanding his senses, he tried to wrap his thoughts around the Whetstone. If he could feel the entire system, he might find a way to bend the power flow. But it kept slipping from his grasp as if this place was some kind of mirage.

He should keep moving, make himself harder to pin down. But what was the right play here? Find his friends and assist, or give them space to fight?

As Natalie came into view, she lost her footing and toppled over sideways. That made Jim's decision for him. Burying his fears, he moved in her direction. But then a darker, more solid shadow melted up through the platform to block his way. Jim darted aside, and it shifted to meet him. He dove, rolling past it. When he somersaulted to his feet, the shadow was nowhere to be found.

Until those creepy vines reached from behind and clamped over him. He found himself lifted off the floor, arms trapped at his sides.

"*Your friends will find you in pieces!*" Gloom whispered raggedly into his ear.

"Ah, Maple Man," Jim gasped, straining against his bonds. "Thank Canada you're here. We have a pancake emergency."

"*So funny. Let's see if you bleed jokes.*"

Something stirred in Jim's awareness. One current of the Whetstone's slippery, unpredictable power shifted toward him. As it drew closer, the power resolved in Jim's senses. He felt and saw a new form taking shape—Gloom had commanded this place to build something.

The pile of amorphous particles coalesced into an eight-foot-tall gunmetal gray robot, with a beam cannon for a head and a gleaming chainsaw for a right arm. It probably had a left arm, too, but the GIANT CHAINSAW ARM occupied Jim's attention.

"Well," he said. "I see someone learned villainy from Saturday morning cartoons."

He could hear his friends struggling out there. Gloom's darkness roiled and parted, revealing Zoe swarmed by flying drones. She was a symphony of destruction, carving swathes through the machines and leaving piles of wreckage in her wake. But there were so many, and the Whetstone kept making more. Jim watched her take one hit, then another, before the shadows closed around her.

He tried again to wrap his will around the Whetstone, and again it slithered out of his grasp.

The shadows revealed Natalie as a turret grew from the platform and loosed a thick gout of flame at her face. She formed a stone shield in one hand to block the attack, a huge cartoon mallet in the other, and swung with a shout. The turret shattered back into particles. Then three more formed at her back.

"Nat, behind you!" Jim shouted.

She whipped around just in time to be engulfed in flame. The shadows closed again and Jim lost sight of her.

An angry red light burned through the shadows. A mechanical scream like metal-on-metal pierced the howling dark. The robot—the only construct of the Whetstone that Jim could sense clearly—appeared through the maelstrom, beam cannon ablaze, chainsaw raised high.

"*This will hurt,*" Gloom taunted. "*And it will not end quickly.*"

Too fast, this was all happening too fast. Ever since Eli disappeared through that hole, they'd only been reacting, barely defending themselves, and losing ground. If they were going to survive, Jim couldn't just change the game. He had to flip the table.

But how? Suppression had revealed how taxed and over-drawn he was. In one day, Jim had stretched his abilities beyond what he'd thought were their limits, discovered new powers, and fought other parahumans for the first time. He was drained, his concentration fractured, and he'd never encountered anything like the Whetstone before. It felt like learning to use a computer for the first time after days without sleep, while someone tried to strangle him.

From the robot's shoulder, a targeting laser locked onto Jim. There was a high-pitched whine as the cannon charged up. Jim's heart pounded like a drum. What an embarrassing way to die.

But then it struck him—why was he trying to control this whole place when it had handed him a perfectly good murderbot?

The robot simultaneously swung the chainsaw to cut through his chest and fired its cannon to vaporize his face.

Jim took all the para senses he'd expanded around the Whetstone and shrank them down to a single point, aimed at the robot like his own kind of targeting laser. Suddenly he *knew* the machine. Every component, every pulse of power flowing through it, everything it could do.

And how to command it.

He flicked his left hand. The chainsaw veered away and chewed into the floor, sending out sparks. He flicked his right hand. The cannon lurched, and the beam fired over his shoulder. Gloom shrieked. The vines holding Jim puffed away and the shadow storm abated. Dropping to his feet, Jim spun to face his attacker, only to see the hero melt through the floor and disappear.

His friends were still fighting. Gloom may have had a setback, but the Whetstone still obeyed him. Now that Jim had deciphered one of its projections, though, it was time to expand his focus.

"Jim, it's not over," Eli spoke into his ear.

Jim gave a cry of righteous anger, definitely not a yelp of shock. "Why? Just *why* would you do that?"

"Delete is keeping me and himself invisible."

"Hey, buddy," Kelvin said.

"Listen," Eli continued. "Gloom is a Darkness Controller of unparalleled skill."

"You don't say."

"He's also a Phaser. That's how he escapes through solid surfaces. Those powers together are formidable. Though you've wounded him, finding and neutralizing him will be difficult."

"I'm getting that."

"Remember, you now carry within yourself both keys to defeating him."

"I'm so glad you've chosen now to be cryptic," Jim said. "As always, your timing is . . . you're already gone, aren't you?"

There was no response.

"Perfect."

Eli may have been right, but Jim had more immediate concerns. He started toward his friends.

Then Gloom made his next move. Pillars of shadow sprang up from the floor—dozens of them, several meters tall and thick as tree trunks. They coiled and writhed like cobras. Two struck at Zoe while she was mid-leap, catching her in the shoulder and the hip. She spun in the air and slammed down hard.

Several clustered around Natalie. Dancing around the fire turrets, they darted in and out to pick away at her defenses, disrupting her balance and shoving her into the path of the flames. After being knocked back and forth, she closed herself inside a cocoon of stone.

As for Gloom, the shadows were big enough that he could be inside any of them, or–

OOF!

Jim went down hard, struck by three shadow vipers that now loomed overhead. He flicked both hands and his trusty murderbot charged in. Chainsaw whirling, beam cannon ablaze, it cut and burned through the attacking darkness, keeping it at bay while Jim collected himself.

Eli said that Jim already possessed both keys to winning. He also said *you now carry*, and as deliberate as Eli was, the choice of words could not be accidental. Which suggested that Jim should focus on newly discovered talents. Although, he'd have to find Gloom first.

Wait.

Idiot! He mentally kicked himself in the face. *The green!*

In his defense, Jim had only discovered the talent like half an hour ago. But now that he remembered . . .

As the murderbot defended him, Jim rolled over into a crouch and stared across the platform with half-focused eyes. He peered past the shadow monsters and the death machines to focus instead on what his eyes couldn't see.

And there they were. Little green orbs of energy, visible to Jim even through the thick, undulating shadows. That one to the left was Zoe, and over to the right was Natalie. The two clustered together in a corner must be Eli and Kelvin. Which meant *that* one—the orb moving beneath the surface of the platform—must belong to Gloom.

But tracking Gloom was only the first key. What was the second?

Jim thought he knew. If he tried and failed, though, it would leave him vulnerable to Gloom's counterattack. Even scarier, if he succeeded . . . well, that was an ability any sane person would be afraid to have.

Zoe hit the floor, the cloud of attack drones swarming her like a hornet's nest. Flame turrets bathed Natalie's stone shell in waves of fire, as if trying to bake her inside it. Jim's doubts didn't matter anymore. He had to try.

He focused on his murderbot, then used it as a doorway to broadcast his senses into the system controlling the Whetstone. Those massive energy flows tried to slip away again, but now he had them figured out. He reached out, locked them in his grip, and mentally shouted a single command.

OFF!

The lights shut down and everything created by the Whetstone disappeared. The murderbot. The drone swarm. The fire turrets.

And the platform beneath them.

SEVEN

CRIES echoed in the pitch black as the platform disappeared and everyone dropped.

Mid-plummet, Jim grinned. Now Gloom was blind like the rest of them, he had no floor to escape through, and Jim could see his green orb as clear as day. He commanded the Whetstone to form a new platform beneath them, which they would reach in three . . . two . . . one . . .

Thuds and groans as bodies hit the new platform thirty feet down. They would walk away with bruises, but they would walk away. Parahumans could take the fall—Jim had counted on it. He'd also counted on being the only one who knew when it would happen. Legs coiled beneath him, he rolled as soon as he hit the platform and broke into a sprint.

On the far side, a falling green orb suddenly stopped. There was a heavy grunt like someone had been punched in the gut. Jim rushed to close the distance before his quarry recovered.

The green orb began to move. Jim leapt.

"Lights!" he shouted.

The Whetstone's ambient lighting switched back on to reveal a vaguely person-shaped shadow. Jim tackled Gloom full-force. He punched once, twice, and connected with some-thing fleshy as they rolled across the floor. Coming to a stop, he pinned Gloom down and reached into the shadow, grasping for something human to cling to—anything to prevent him from melting through the platform.

Arms of formless black swung at Jim. Nails scratched at him. He slapped them away and kept up the pressure, clamping his knees around what he hoped was a rib cage. Finally, his hands found purchase around a familiar shape, and when he squeezed, Gloom gave a desperate gurgle. Jim's hands were now locked firmly around the man's throat.

Now for the scary part. Jim thought back to the moment Millennia had attacked. When he soaked up the para energy she used against him. He focused hard on what it had felt like to be *that* Vessel, to drink in her power.

Now, instead of waiting for that power to be directed at him, he reached toward the green orb inside Gloom. Wrapping his senses around it, feeling the pulse of that energy, he *pulled*.

Gloom gasped as if he'd been dunked in icy water. In Jim's eyes, the green glow inside the hero began to roil and distort, and finally to stretch until it flowed into Jim. He kept pulling, willing that mysterious place inside himself to take it all in.

"Please," Gloom breathed. His shadows collapsed, leaving only a man in a cloak. He stared up at Jim in abject terror. "Please . . . have mercy."

Jim's fear ignited, becoming rage. Seething, he leaned closer. "I'm fresh out."

Gloom's back arched. He gave a last cry and went limp, unconscious.

Jim let go and scrambled away from the hero. Head bowed, arms wrapped around himself, he closed his eyes and tried to expel the red mist of anger wreathing his brain, searing it like hot barbed wire. But every cell in his body vibrated with power and rage and there was nowhere for it to go. He realized he was shivering and muttering and couldn't stop.

A gentle hand gripped his shoulder.

"Jim," Eli said softly. "It's okay. You're going to be okay. This will pass."

Jim shook his head. The red mist would not dissipate.

"It will," Eli said. "I've seen this before. Or something like it, anyway. What you're able to do . . . sometimes there are consequences. Consider it the Price for your unique gifts, and for your potential power level."

The Price? It was the first thought that truly broke through the red mist. Only high-level paras had a Price, didn't they? That didn't describe Jim, so he'd never given it a second thought. But if he absorbed enough power . . .

"Just breathe," Eli continued. "In and out, again, and again. Breeeeeathe with me, Jim."

Jim latched onto Eli's voice, the soothing rhythm of his speech, and that red mist abated just enough for him to listen, to breathe with his friend. In and out ten times, twenty.

Then, as quickly as it had appeared, the red mist dissipated.

Jim sighed. Opening his eyes, he slowly turned until he sat facing his team. They had grown quiet, each gazing at him with their own mix of sympathy and trepidation.

Well. Might as well just say it.

"So," Jim said. "Anyone strong enough to lift this elephant in the room?"

They looked away, shuffling as if uncertain what to do next. Jim felt like the guy in a horror movie who just got bitten by a zombie, and his friends were trying to figure out how to tell him they had to shoot him in the head.

He could be at Versus right now, serving drinks and smiles. Everyone liked the guy who served drinks. They almost never tried to kill him. In fact, they gave him money and then left. If he'd told Lord Neon to take a flying leap, he could be that guy right now.

That guy was no closer to the truth about Summer.

Jim tried to shove that internal voice away, but it wouldn't let up.

After all this, do you really think you can go back to being him? Does Jim the Bartender and Nothing Else even exist anymore?

He mentally turned his back on the voice. Introspection was for poets and vegetarians.

Zoe eyed him warily. "What happened just now?"

"I took some of his power. Like with Millennia . . . except, on purpose this time. But there was some kind of blowback or aftershock or something. For a minute there, I didn't quite feel like me." Looking up, Jim saw her expression. He sat straighter and stared right back at her. "We were losing. Someone had to do something."

Kelvin broke from the group and sat down next to Jim, hand on his shoulder. "I think you may have just saved our lives. Thanks, buddy." Eyeing the rest of the group, he raised an eyebrow. "Whatever you can do, you'd never use it against your friends, right?"

Jim considered, then set his hand over Kelvin's. "Actually, I'm kinda tired. If I could just take a little bit . . ."

Kelvin played along and started shaking. "Oh dear lord in heaven, he's turned on us! Jim was the real villain all along. Guys, this super sucks."

He collapsed onto his side, and his laughter seemed to release a pressure valve. Tension ebbed, shoulders relaxed, and everyone appeared to remember that they were a team. The others sat now, too, clustered together in a tight circle.

"So," Kelvin gestured at Gloom. "What's that guy's deal?"

The unconscious hero's hood had tossed back in the struggle. He was a pudgy, middle-aged man with long, scraggly dark hair and dark rings around his eyes. A man who would intimidate no one if they bumped into him on the street. Maybe that was the best disguise of all for those who wanted private lives, separate from their hero personas.

"Darkness Controller and Phaser," Eli said. "Mid-level power. Parahumans like him are easy to under-estimate, but those with a smaller power set can sometimes be the bigger threat. They spend their whole lives honing one or two abilities."

"And the whole eater-of-souls persona?" Jim asked.

"It can be effective against enemies, sometimes comically so." Eli shook his head. "I must admit, being on the receiving end was somewhat tiresome."

Natalie sighed. "I was so excited to meet all my heroes. Never imagined I'd be meeting them like . . . this."

Jim saw more than just fatigue in Natalie. Her heart was weary, too. With all her strength, it was easy to forget that she was only seventeen. She'd come into this idolizing the Spectrum, aspiring to the romanticized life of legendary heroes. Eventually, she would have learned that this life was not always glory and primary colors. As jaded as Jim knew he was, though, he found himself wishing she could have learned it another way. If any of them were going to get through this alive, he secretly hoped it would be her.

"At least there's only one Prism on the Lighthouse," Jim said, offering small comfort. "Imagine facing all seven teams."

"Yikes," Kelvin said. "No, thanks."

Natalie looked to Eli. "You said something about a price. What did you mean?"

"The Price," Eli said, emphasizing it like a title with capital letters. "There are certain natural orders to the universe—a balance of power. That includes parahumans. At lower power levels, they have weaknesses common to everyone. Bullets, falling from great heights, sickness, car accidents, telepathic attack, extremes in temperature. Someone with a 3.0 rating, for instance, is unlikely to be bulletproof unless it's their only ability. You follow the concept?"

"Sure," Natalie said.

"But move up the power scale, and that begins to change," Eli continued. "In general, the higher someone's power level, the fewer mundane weaknesses they will have. All that energy inside them heightens their entire physical existence, not just their abilities. An 8.0 Runner may focus on super speed, but will likely also possess some level of bullet immunity."

"And that's when the Price becomes a thing?" Natalie asked.

"Yes. The universe wants to stay balanced. The more power you possess, the more likely you are to have a weakness which can bypass all your strength and shut you down. At extremely high levels, those parahumans are vulnerable to very few mundane threats, but their Price will be acute enough to incapacitate them if activated."

From the corner of his eye, Jim caught an odd motion. Tensing up, but not wanting to alarm anyone, he slowly turned his head. That's when he noticed Zoe. Eyelids drooping, head nodding, she wavered as if on the verge of passing out. Was someone else out there in the shadows, pushing her into unconsciousness?

"What is the Price?" Natalie asked. "I mean, what's the weakness?"

Eli gave a wry smile. "Asking someone about their Price is . . . not advisable. The specific weakness is different for each of them, and they guard that knowledge more than civilian identities, more than bank account numbers. Imagine if someone put an off switch somewhere on your body—would you want just anyone to know where it was?"

"It helps that they're random." Kelvin said. "They *are* random, right?"

"It appears so," Eli said. "However, that's only a theory based on limited evidence. To confirm it, high-level paras would have to reveal their Price and allow it to be studied. I do not see that happening."

"So a 9.0 para might be weak to meteor cannons, or bunny rabbits," Kelvin said. "There's really no way to know?"

"Not unless you happen to discover it," Eli said. "But if bunny rabbits are your weakness, 9.0 or not, they'll take you down."

Zoe's eyes were nearly closed. She swayed one way, then the other. Jim hovered on the verge of action, prepared to sound a warning.

"I hadn't thought of it like that." Natalie hesitated. "So, at my level will I . . . ?"

Eli regarded her, lips pursed, as if carefully considering what he should say.

Eyes fully closed now, Zoe swayed until she was leaning against Jim. Then she relaxed into him. Her breathing smoothed out, becoming rhythmic and constant. That's when Jim realized there were no threats in the shadows. Zoe Blake, the legendary thief, had fallen asleep on his shoulder.

Her hair smelled like flowers.

Tiny fireworks popped inside Jim, starting where Zoe pressed against him and spreading across his body, leaving gentle warmth in their wake. Is this how it would feel to fall asleep next to her, sharing space and time and breath that belonged only to them as the world outside drifted by unnoticed?

The Lighthouse shuddered. Zoe snapped awake.

"Whoa." Natalie looked up. "If that's from a fight, someone just got hit *really* hard."

Zoe blinked, eyes bleary as she slowly remembered where she was, and then realized what she was doing. She straightened, pulling away from Jim. They exchanged a glance and embarrassed smiles, then focused on looking at anything but each other.

Which is how Jim saw his team with fresh eyes and realized Zoe wasn't the only one on the verge of collapse.

"We need to rest," he said. "We may have powers, but we're still human."

Kelvin gave a relieved sigh. "Finally. I'm about to drop."

"I could use a nap," Natalie said. "But where can we rest that's safe?"

All eyes turned to Eli.

He gave a reluctant nod. "I know a place."

EIGHT

JIM commanded the platform to stop moving. It was at the lowest part of the Whetstone now, where an exit door awaited.

"What should we do with him?" Zoe inclined her chin at Gloom.

"He'll be out for hours," Eli said. "It would be dangerous to leave him here, exposed."

"Dangerous for who?" Jim said.

"Don't forget, he is not the one behind this," Eli reminded. "It's not his fault."

"No sweat." Natalie plucked the unconscious hero from the floor as if he were a bag of feathers. She slung him over her shoulder. "We can find somewhere to leave him, right? Like we did with Reverie."

It took her a moment to realize everyone was staring.

"What?" she said.

Kelvin shook his head in amazement. "Sometimes I forget about your power level. Gosh, that is neat."

"How easily could you bench press all of us at once?" Zoe asked.

"Oh, you guys," Natalie giggled. Then her smile took on a hint of mischief. "And I could bench press you with two fingers."

"No jar of pickles is safe," Jim said.

Eli cleared his throat. "Moving on?"

Following the Custodian through the exit, they descended to the next level down. One level closer to finishing the Dare. To confronting whoever was pulling the strings.

To learning the truth about Summer.

It wouldn't be long now, if they managed to survive. The Lighthouse didn't have that many levels left. Maybe a handful more, and then there was just outer space.

Jim tried to ignore the overlapping waves of anxiety and anticipation as they followed Eli through the twists and turns of this level. It clearly wasn't meant for public view, but it didn't have the industrial feel like some of the higher support levels. It felt more . . . sterile. The lighting was bright, the surfaces gleaming steel and white stone that had a faint sparkle.

"What's down here?" Jim whispered.

"The infirmary," Eli replied. "But that's not where we're going."

They turned a corner and came to an abrupt stop. Dead end. What had looked like it should be another hallway only went about twenty feet before ending at another wall.

"Oh, good, you found a quiet corner for them to kill us," Jim said. "That's convenient."

Eli almost smiled. "Oh ye of little faith. You're about to–"

He cut off, his head whipping toward the way they'd come. His eyes grew heavy with dread. "Be ready to move the very instant I say so."

He extended a hand toward the dead end wall and his body tensed. For the space of a breath, nothing happened.

Then Jim felt something. Not from Eli's dead end, but from the hallway they'd just left. It wasn't a sound or even a physical sensation, but it was there, imperceptible yet unmistakable. Every molecule in his body felt heightened, as if they'd been infused with energy and were now vibrating faster. A glance at his friends told him they were feeling it, too.

Eli drew in a sharp breath. His outstretched hand flexed. In the air between the team and the dead end wall, seven points began to warp.

The looming energy vibrations grew, becoming physical. A subtle hum. And then the scariest thing of all–footsteps. A parahuman was here, stalking the halls of the infirmary, and they were getting closer.

"Come on, come on," Eli muttered. "Cycle through. Why would you build so many layers?"

The seven points grew like starbursts, warping the space further as they stretched toward each other.

The sterile white light of the hallway shifted to red— faintly at first, but growing with each approaching footstep.

Zoe eyed the oncoming red light, bouncing on her toes. "Anytime now, Eli."

"Wait," he said through clenched teeth.

The energy pulsed, bathing the hallway in red. Everyone released an involuntary gasp.

"Whoa," Jim whispered. "So that's what my dinner feels like in the microwave."

"Should I make us invisible?" Kelvin asked.

"It won't help," Eli said. "Not with him."

"Not with who?" Zoe asked.

Natalie formed a spiked stone gauntlet around her fist. "Stay here. I'll buy you a few–"

"Now," Eli said.

The warping starbursts finally touched, all seven points intermingling and folding around each other. Jim got the sense it wasn't the air doing this, but dimensional space itself. The threads weaved together, forming tessellated layers. A sense of vertigo washed over Jim as he peered into the undulating shapes, like he was looking over the edge of a cliff into a cosmic kaleidoscope.

Eli glanced over his shoulder at them. "Go!"

Zoe moved first. Grabbing Jim's hand, she dashed forward with him in tow. He felt a surge of fear, followed quickly by acceptance. Die from whatever hero was coming, or fall forever while being clutched by a dangerously cute brunette? The choice was easier than deciding between cake or pie.

Fight me, it's cake, he thought to no one. *Frosting is forever.*

At the instant they leapt, as thoughts of cake and Zoe filled Jim's mind, the spatial patterns seemed to click into place. Chaos gave way to harmony. The layers spun together to form some kind of tunnel, through which they dove.

Everything twisted. Jim's entire being separated into threads and tumbled along the warping layers like a sock in a bottomless dryer. Then, before conscious thought could process what was happening, he toppled through the last layer and became himself again, just in time to avoid falling on his face. Zoe lurched forward a step and managed to keep her feet, too.

"Wow," Jim said. "The service in this place sucks. I told them specifically that my soul is dry clean only."

"Just be glad we're still wearing clothes," Zoe said.

She seemed about to say more, but stopped as she looked down at their hands. Which were still intertwined.

Oh, so that had actually happened before reality got all squiggly. Jim had forgotten about it while his very essence was unraveling. Before leaping into oblivion, Zoe had reached out and found him. Now she released his hand like it was a skillet she'd grabbed, only to realize was scorching hot.

Jim tried to be cool about it. He failed. "I'm still deciding whether to be touched, or to wonder if you just wanted me to die first."

Zoe cleared her throat, smoothing her suit jacket. "Stay sharp. We don't know–*oof!*"

The tunnel spat out a wall of bodies that collided with Jim and Zoe, casting them all to the floor in a jumbled heap.

"Oh, there you guys are," Jim groaned from the bottom of the pile.

"Blah!" Kelvin spat. "Someone's foot was in my mouth."

"Someone's hand is on my . . ." Zoe stopped. "Never mind, just move it."

"Sorry," Natalie said sheepishly.

Eli stood over them, the only one to come through with his dignity intact. "That was far too close."

Jim craned his neck to peer over the jumble of bodies. The tunnel created a kind of fisheye lens distortion, oddly stretching his view of what was on the other side. Still, he saw it clearly enough to be thankful they'd escaped.

A boot came into view. Then a costume.

Then a cape.

Red Plasma stopped where they had been standing only a moment ago, angry red light radiating from his eyes and the palms of his hands. Glowering, he studied every corner of the dead end like a predator who sensed he'd narrowly missed catching a meal.

"Oh my grandma's tea and biscuits," Kelvin breathed. "Did we almost get vaporized?"

Natalie's voice quavered. "He can't see us, right?"

"Not while we're in here," Eli assured. "But if he had . . ."

He trailed off, leaving the rest unsaid. But they all knew.

Most Blasters were "glass cannons," meaning they could deal out lots of damage but were less capable of taking it. Unless a Blaster had an uncommon power set, they had to be strategic in a fight, which usually meant firing from a distance while Smashers and Strikers handled the up-close stuff.

But there was a reason, beyond being a highly respected hero, that a Blaster made it onto the Spectrum. Red Plasma possessed a rare combination of abilities. Plasma Energy Blaster, Striker with a Brawler sub-class, and a rumored 8.8 on the Faraday scale. So even if someone got close without being relieved of their atomic structure, the hero could take some hits and still dismantle them with plasma-bomb fists.

As Jim had witnessed back in the Torch, this mind-con-trolled version of the hero wouldn't hesitate to unleash that power. Staring into those molten eyes, he felt deeply that if Red Plasma had discovered them in that corridor, there would have been no time for clever tricks. Some of them may have escaped, but not all.

"I think you just saved our lives, Eli," Jim said. "Also, I'd like to get up now."

"Seconded," Zoe said.

The team disentangled from each other and regained their feet. Natalie retrieved Gloom's limp form and tossed him over her shoulder again. Each kept one eye on Red Plasma until he huffed in frustration and moved on. When he left, a stifling shroud of tension went with him.

Only then did Jim have enough spare attention to take in their surroundings. His jaw fell open.

Kelvin said it perfectly. "Where in Great Aunt Sally's underpants are we?"

NINE

"WELCOME to Lord Neon's meditation chamber." Even with Eli's deadpan delivery, it sounded grandiose. That went away, though, when he added, "Do not touch anything."

"I'm not even sure what we'd be touching," Kelvin said. He turned in slow circles, mouth agape.

The smooth ground was some kind of stone stretching as far as the eye could see—either matte black or a very dark gray. Lines of dark purple light cut through the stone beneath their feet, criss-crossing in all directions. Some cut a straight line all the way to the horizon, while others curved and overlapped to create geometric shapes and complex patterns. Although the light wasn't especially bright, a bit of purple glow reflected off what appeared to be thick clouds hanging low in a night sky.

Eli stepped onto a cluster of glowing hexagons. The purple light there flashed brighter. A dozen hexagons of varying size rose from the floor, becoming short columns of stone in the shape of a huge armchair. Sitting, Eli traced the fingers of his right hand across the flat stone of the chair arm.

All around them, the air warped and hundreds of flat black shapes unfolded from nothing. Some were rectangular, some hexagonal, others were round, still others may have been spherical. The hovering shapes moved to form an overlapping dome all around them, at least fifty feet across.

Then they all switched on.

News feeds. Security cameras. Mobile phones. Social media. Public and private streams. Computer code. What looked like government surveillance. More, so many more sights and sounds from across the planet blasted Jim with pure information, as if he stood at the bottom of Niagara Falls while it dumped thousands of digital gallons onto his brain.

After five seconds, a kind of wave swept around the dome and every feed changed to something else. Five seconds later, it happened again.

Jim shook his head. "This takes ADHD to a whole new level."

Natalie practically shivered with glee. "This place is amazing! What . . . where . . . *how* is it?!"

"It's a kind of pocket dimension," Eli replied. "Don't ask me how it works. Lord Neon built it."

It made sense in a high-level-parahumans-are-super-weird kind of way. The motif of this place, with its blocky dark stone and purple light, looked as if Lord Neon's armor could have sprung fully formed out of the ground here. Not a stretch to imagine the same person designed both. And the screens were probably just one of many ways that Lord Neon, the hero who knew things, absorbed information about the world.

"Heh," Zoe said. "I went to a rave once, in a place that looked like this."

Jim raised an eyebrow at Eli. "Don't tell me. Lord Neon moonlights as a DJ?"

Eli pointedly ignored him and tapped on the stone. His chair spun to face a particular group of screens, which floated closer and expanded. He tapped again and those feeds changed in rapid succession, like a flip book. It seemed he was looking for something in particular.

"Never been to a rave," Kelvin said. "Too many people, too many eyes on me. What was it like?"

"Loud. Lots of lights. Smelled like sweat. I don't remember much else—I was there to do a job. Some heiress's engagement ring that her ex-fiancee wanted back."

"Ah," Kelvin said. "Wait, was she wearing the ring when you took it?"

Zoe gave a cryptic smile.

"Wow, you *must* be good," Kelvin said. "And I didn't realize you could hire a thief to, what, settle a grudge?"

"That's the super-rich," Zoe said. "A bunch of spoiled babies, and they spend cash like it's air. I got a nice bonus off that job for also taking the necklace her new boyfriend had given her. Don't feel bad, he was just as rich and an even bigger douche."

Eli breathed a sigh of relief and leaned back in the chair as if tension had gone out of his muscles. Jim tilted his head, puzzled. The Custodian had flipped through dozens of international news feeds, but none had focused on any particular story. What had he been looking for?

"Nobody won the Powerball yet, right?" Jim asked. "You've still got a shot."

"News of the Dare going wrong hasn't made it out. We managed to lock it down." Eli wiped sweat from his brow. "No news is very good news."

Zoe crossed her arms. "That seems a little callous. Should we worry about bad press when people are fighting for their lives?"

Eli faced her, brow furrowed. Before he spoke, though, his expression softened. "You're right. I apologize. But you must understand, it will do significant damage long-term if confidence in the Spectrum is shaken. People *need* to see them as beacons of hope. That's why they do their best to keep failures quiet. Not because of ego—because the world relies on them."

Zoe frowned as if not fully convinced, but didn't argue.

"I get it," Natalie said, surprising everyone. "My family runs, like, a top-level crime syndicate, but they're still crazy focused on their image. Seven Serpents can't just *be* strong, it has to *look* strong. If something made them seem weak, it would be like blood in the water. Other families would start poaching their territory, protected partners would stop paying dues. Reputation loss can be as bad as war with a rival syndicate." She rolled her eyes. "And they wear the most boring suits! Ugh! I tried to tell them you can wear something with color and still look tough, but nobody listened."

"Good point, Nat," Kelvin said. "Personally, I think organized crime could use a little more pizzazz."

Jim was about to reply when something caught his eye. He pointed across the dome at two screens hovering side-by-side just below eye level. "What's with those? They're the only ones that never change."

"Is that . . . ?" Zoe eyes widened. "Is that Framework?"

It was Framework. Of the two screens, the left displayed a never-ending loop of all the footage captured during the battle ten years ago. Over and over again, from dozens of cameras and multiple angles, downtown Sydney went from pristine to smoking ruins.

In her massive battle armor, Framework fought wave after wave of heroes, tossing them like toys. Which was amazing in itself, since the armor looked like a monstrosity hammered together on-the-fly from whatever machinery lay close at hand. Whenever a hero scored a hit and sheered off a piece of armor, something else ripped away from the city and melded with her to bring the armor back even stronger.

When numbers began to overwhelm her, Framework crashed into a skyscraper, which then animated and fought for her, as if the building itself had become her armor. Then it smashed into yet another skyscraper and incorporated that, too. The harder they fought, the more her powers seemed to expand, until the heroes had to battle an entire transformed city block while trying to get civilians out *and* locate Framework inside the behemoth. Some theorized that if the fight hadn't ended when it did, she would have eventually controlled all of Sydney. Or more.

Jim had watched the footage far too many times, studied it far too closely, desperate for some glimpse of his sister. Wherever Summer was fighting, though, she never appeared on camera. Eventually, he had come to believe it was for the best. His last memories of Summer were happy ones and should stay that way. So he'd stopped watching the recordings and never looked again.

From the moment Lord Neon knocked on his door, those long-buried feelings had been clawing back to the surface. Now they doubled their efforts. Jim knew he should look away, but couldn't bring himself to. Just like he couldn't stay away when the hero tempted him with some elusive truth about Summer. Teenage Jimmy Riven was still inside him, and he was desperate.

Jim swallowed hard. With effort, he looked away. It felt like gnawing off a leg to get free of a bear trap.

Puzzling over the second screen helped a little. He focused on that. It was still Framework-related, but at least there was no battle, and in the background Sydney was mostly rebuilt. This feed was current, a live image from one stationary camera.

Hyde Park, in the heart of Sydney's central business district—the oldest public park in Australia. Its vibrant trees and shady green spaces gave pedestrians a welcome respite from the bustling city around it.

Or, it had until ten years ago, when the Spike appeared. The claw-shaped monolith had ripped up through the ground, thirty feet of dark stone criss-crossed with veins of glowing silver that pulsed and undulated across the surface. Subzero cold radiated from the object, causing waves of misty fog to billow from it.

No one knew how Framework had created it, or why. They only knew that it was the first blow she struck, the opening salvo of that cataclysmic battle. At least one hero had died simply from touching it.

Even with Framework gone, the Spike endured to this day. Hyde Park was a scar of perpetual winter in the heart of Sydney, blocked off by tall, reinforced walls and purposely forgotten. The camera feed revealed the Spike, exactly the same today as it had been a decade ago. The silver veins still shimmered, the waves of perpetual fog continued unabated.

Jim couldn't help wondering, had Summer seen the Spike before it all went wrong? Had she gotten too close? Skypuncher never said how they'd lost her, only that it was during the battle. It had been years since Jim allowed himself to ask the question, but seeing the Spike again now . . . could Summer have been the hero who touched it? If so, had it actually killed her?

"Or something worse?"

"What was that, Jim?" Eli said.

Jim snapped back to the present. He'd been in his own world, only half-hearing the team talk about Framework and the Spike and the battle that had rocked the world. His own thoughts had stayed internal—except for the last one. Apparently, he'd spoken the question aloud, because now everyone was looking at him.

"Oh," Jim said. "I was just, uh, thinking about Versus. If they run out of fried ravioli tonight, they're going to have to serve something worse. Like the *other* fried ravioli that we don't talk about. I just hope everyone survives."

Kelvin placed a hand on his shoulder. "It's okay, buddy. You can tell us if you're thinking about Summer. I was. I mean, I only met her once when we were kids, but she was nice. She didn't deserve . . . whatever happened to her."

Peering up at his old friend, Jim swallowed the flippant response that tried to come out. "Thanks. I, um, may have also been wondering why Lord Neon would still watch these after a decade."

They looked to Eli, who shrugged. "Framework did things that no one has done before or since, and the mystery of the

Spike remains unsolved. Perhaps someone whose job it is to know things would want to figure them out."

"I don't know why," Zoe said. "But it's kind of annoying how much sense that makes."

"Maybe because so little here makes sense." Kelvin held up his hand. "Up top for confusion!"

It seemed like an odd thing to celebrate, but Zoe shrugged and returned the high-five.

"We're-in-this-together five?" Natalie offered her own hand, which Kelvin happily slapped, and the two of them giggled like the silly geese they were.

Eli raised an eyebrow. "I get the feeling we could all use some rest. Choose a place to bed down. The stones will adjust for you. They are more comfortable than they look."

That, too, made an annoying level of sense, so they acquiesced. With nothing resembling a bed, everyone picked a random-ish spot on the ground and did their best to settle in. Everyone except Jim.

"I'll keep Gloom with me," Natalie volunteered. "Don't worry. If he wakes up, I'll knock him into next Tuesday."

"You're my hero, Nat," Kelvin said.

Jim waited for his friends' eyes to close and their breathing to even out. Then he quietly approached Eli in the stone chair.

"You have questions," Eli said.

"I'm guessing you have answers," Jim replied.

"You want to know about that rage you felt. If it will happen again."

"Unless you want to talk about the next trend in hero fashion." Jim crossed his fingers. "Personally, I'm hoping bell bottoms make a comeback."

Amusement flitted across Eli's face. Then he recovered his stoicism and tapped the armrest. Another chair rose from the stone.

"Sit down, James."

"James? I feel like I'm about to be grounded."

Jim slid into the seat and leaned back, willing his muscles to relax as much as possible. The stone *was* actually more comfortable than it looked.

Eli steepled his fingers and peered over them at Jim. "Ask your questions."

"The red mist—that rage I felt—you said it was my Price. But I've never been powerful enough to have a Price."

"That's true. You're a mid-range parahuman."

"Well, don't flatter me too hard."

Eli held up a finger. "At rest, anyway. But you and I both know that a Vessel's power level is . . . malleable. It's what sets you apart. It's also the reason you have a Price—one that appears to activate conditionally."

"You mean when I take enough of another para's energy."

"Very likely. You've used the Vessel ability before, absorbing electricity to boost your Faraday rating. But unless I'm mistaken, you have not used the *other* aspect until today."

"Didn't even know I could, until Millennia punched me. I was as shocked as anyone. Well, maybe not as shocked as she was. Heh, the look on her face, totally worth it."

"Be cautious about using it outside of a controlled environment. At least, until you learn the extent of your weakness."

Jim's brow furrowed. "You think there's more to it?"

"I cannot say for sure, but a Price which activates conditionally, and which is tied to a rare and unpredictable power, may not produce just one effect. There may be an element of variability to how and when that weakness manifests. Be mindful and be careful." Eli hesitated. "The story you told us . . . Summer's fate and what it did to your family. To you. Could it be that you rejected heroes so deeply, with such bitterness, that you actually suppressed your own powers? Stopped their development before they could grow? It would explain why, at your age, you are only now discovering your true potential."

Memories flashed unbidden through Jim's mind. Sad times, dark days, tragedy and loss—all the ingredients of a classic hero's origin story. A difficult past that would lead ultimately to something epic. Pain transmuted into valor.

Except, young Jimmy Riven had rejected that path. If the life of a hero was a room, he had doused that room in gasoline, set it on fire and walked away while it burned, never once looking back. It hadn't felt like resentment or anger, but resolve—a conviction that went so deep it filled every cell in his body. Maybe it hadn't left space for anything else. Including his true self, fully realized.

If things had been different, what might that James Riven have become?

"Losing Summer defined you," Eli said softly. "But it doesn't have to *keep* defining you."

Jim realized tears had gathered at the corners of his eyes. He scrubbed them away before they could fall.

"Wow," he said. "Thanks, Oprah. Tell Dr. Phil I'm ready to start the healing process."

Eli wore a knowing smile. "One day, Jim, you're going to take off that armor. When you do, I look forward to meeting the man underneath it."

Jim slid out of the chair. "I'll think about . . . well, all of it. For now, I should go pretend to sleep."

"One more thing." Eli held up a staying hand. "Even your core Vessel ability comes with risks. Absorb too much energy too quickly and you could injure or even kill yourself. It would be like never lifting weights and then trying to lift a thousand pounds. Take it slow, expand what you absorb gradually. Caution will keep you–"

Kelvin suddenly gasped and sat up. "No more tacos for dinner!"

He looked around bleary-eyed, seeing nothing, then lay back down as if nothing had happened. He was snoring in seconds.

Jim eyed his friend, then Eli. "I can't imagine why you thought we needed rest."

Eli chuckled. "Good night, Jim."

Jim nodded, then found his own spot on the ground. As he crooked an arm under his head, he felt the hexagons rearrange beneath him, conforming to his body shape. Was it his imagination, or were they getting warmer?

Eli was right, they needed this respite. But, in the midst of battling for survival, how could they relax enough to actually rest? Personally, Jim was grateful for the break, but there was no way he expected to get even one second of genuine sle–

TEN

Thirteen Years Ago

FROM the outside, 116 Washburne Avenue looked like just another house at the end of a cul-de-sac. The citizens of Highreach would never know the epic secret hiding inside.

Two heroes lived here now, and they'd just snuck back home after winning their first victory. Striking their first blow against the forces of darkness. Announcing their arrival at the battle for good. Kicking evil square in the . . . okay, that was enough for one night. Besides, there would be many more to come.

Jimmy Riven posed in front of his closet door. Standing tall, hands on hips, he gazed proudly at his costumed form in the mirror.

It was a simple outfit. A knee-length jacket, all black except for the sleeves, which started black at the shoulder and faded gradually to dark blue, then light blue, then slashes of white, ending in white-and-blue gloves. Under the jacket, a dark gray canvas utility vest buckled across his torso. Then black pants and blue high-top sneakers. Summer had helped him cobble it together out of everyday materials. They couldn't afford duraweave or nanomesh—especially since Mom and Dad had no clue what they were doing.

His parents were asleep downstairs now. Tomorrow morning, Jimmy and Summer would reveal everything over breakfast, present themselves as successful heroes who'd already begun making a name for themselves. He hoped they would be more proud than scared.

Jimmy gave a satisfied nod and peeled off the black mask affixed to his face. The glue took a bit of skin with it. He'd have to learn how to avoid that in the future.

He moved to unzip the jacket, which would go into a box with the rest of the costume, tucked in the deepest corner of his closet. But he stopped with his hand on the zipper, not yet ready to take Lode off and hide him away.

Instead, he sat on the edge of his bed, unzipped a pocket inside the costume jacket, and pulled out a small object. His most prized possession—something he intended to carry with him every time Lode went out to defend the city. He stared down at the thing cradled in his hands, unable to contain a proud smile as he took in all its details yet again.

The hero coin wasn't as shiny as it used to be, but to Jimmy it gleamed. One side showed an outline of Thunderous, a street level hero who spent over five decades fighting for the regular people of Highreach before retiring. Jimmy flipped it over and, for what may have been the ten thousandth time, read the inscription on the back. The saying that Thunderous was famous for.

FOR HIGHREACH. ALWAYS.

The hometown hero had always been Jimmy's favorite. While little girls pretended to wear armor and battle like Millennia, and little boys pretended to fly through mountains like Skypuncher, Jimmy had wrapped his hands in strips of old t-shirts and pretended to brawl like Thunderous.

The hero had been a Striker Brawler with an Electrical augment, meaning he could imbue his punches with electricity.

He even had a signature move, the thunderboom, in which he bashed his fists together to create a shockwave.

Although Jimmy loved to see another electrical parahuman making a difference, that wasn't why Thunderous was his favorite. It was because he wasn't the strongest in the world—far from it, in fact—but he never gave up. Never walked away from a fight that needed fighting. With him out there, the little guy could feel a little safer.

Eighteen months ago, Jimmy and Summer had been walking home from school. Across the street, a purse snatcher stripped the bag from a frail old woman's shoulder, and her cries got Thunderous's attention. Then there he was—the Highreach hero, right there in front of them, chasing down a bad guy!

But as thrilled as Jimmy was to see him in the flesh, protecting the innocent, he quickly realized two things. First, the robber was too fast and Thunderous wouldn't be able to catch him. Second, the robber's escape path was about to take him right by two school children that he obviously didn't consider a threat.

Dropping to a crouch, Jimmy stuck out his leg and spun. The motion caught the robber's foot mid-stride and sent him tumbling to the pavement. Before he could recover, Thunderous was there, and the fight was over.

The hero flipped the bad guy around like it was nothing, clipping restraints around his arms and legs. Jimmy watched in awe, knowing he would treasure this moment and wanting to remember every single detail.

Then it got even better. In the middle of working, Thunderous looked right at him and grinned. "Nice takedown, kid."

He pulled something from a pocket and flicked his thumb. There was a metallic ping and a glint of reflected light. Jimmy reached out and the little object slapped onto his palm. When he saw what it was, his jaw fell open.

A Thunderous hero coin.

Not every hero used coins. Even those that did use them rarely gave one out. All of them respected the meaning, though. If someone received a coin, it meant they had done something special enough to earn a hero's admiration. The rarity made any coin a prized possession, so few people ever gave one up. But if they presented that coin to any hero, they could ask for help or a favor and receive it.

A few months later, Thunderous had retired. Ever since, Jimmy had wondered if this was the last coin he gave out. There would never be a way to know, but he liked thinking it.

He lay back on the bed and held the coin overhead. It glinted in the light of his bedside lamp. One day, Lode would have his own hero coin. He would make Highreach proud.

Clutching the coin to his chest, he closed his eyes and gave a contented sigh. He must have fallen asleep, because when he awakened, an hour had passed and he was still lying there in his costume.

And he wasn't alone.

Now

Jim snapped awake. It had been a dream, but also a memory—one he remembered like it was yesterday. He was just glad the dream had ended before . . .

Shaking it off, he clambered to his feet and had the best stretch of his life. The kind that only the truly exhausted could appreciate. Except, to his surprise, he no longer felt exhausted. Emotionally, he was still ragged, but his body felt like he'd slept a full day after a nourishing meal. It was ready to go.

There was movement at his feet. He glanced down to see a cluster of hexagons lowering until they were flush with the ground. How much had that feature cost? Surely it was a premium upgrade in the folded dimensional space market.

He studied the deeply weird place. The endless stone and glowing geometric purple veins, the floating virtual screens, the illusion of a cloudy night sky. *Was* it an illusion? What kind of knowledge—what kind of power—would it take to create something like this?

"Morning, friends." Natalie gave a pleasant growl as she stretched. "Hey, I feel great!"

"Morning, Nat," Kelvin said just as cheerfully. He lay curled up on his side. "Never thought I'd say this after sleeping on a bed of stone, but can I have five more minutes? I'm what the kids call *mad comfortable* right now."

"Is it really morning?" Zoe rubbed her eyes and yawned. "I can't tell in here."

"Yeah, this place is like a casino," Jim said. "No clocks, no windows, an old guy sitting in a chair and staring at a screen for hours."

"I heard that," Eli said. "You know I can vent you into space anytime I want, right?"

Gloom still lay in a heap near Natalie. He didn't stir—a small but welcome blessing. Though now they'd have to decide what to do with him.

Zoe gave a deep sigh and stretched, her back arched. Jim tried not to look, failed, then succeeded, then failed again, then decided there were certain failures he could live with.

Instead of ending the stretch, Zoe leaned back and twisted until her palms were on the ground. She kicked up her feet, and her entire body whirled and flipped. In a blink, she was standing. She stretched everything systematically now, as if testing for battle readiness.

"Remind me to thank Lord Neon for whatever this place did to us." Zoe tapped her chin in thought. "Actually, if we're getting close to the Big Bad, whoever they are, I should switch suits."

She reached inside the pinstriped suit jacket and tugged on something. With a zip-swish sound, her trench coat, suit pants, jacket, and hat split into segments and peeled away from her body. They whipped around behind her and disappeared into a small pouch on her back.

Now, instead of a bespoke costume out of an old gangster movie, Zoe stood sheathed in a sleek ultra-modern bodysuit. The general motif matched her other costume—a mix of blacks and dark grays and subtle red striping—but the similarities ended there.

This high-tech design matched her mask-and-goggles and her gloves, synthetic and lightly armored with a few pinpoints of red light. Jim noticed the lights flickering, so she could probably turn them off when it was time to be stealthy. Apart from the pockets hidden subtly around the waist and upper arms—no doubt for sneaking around with her many gadgets—the outfit hugged every one of Zoe's ample curves. As she twisted and flexed, the materials seemed to actively move with her.

Kelvin grinned and pointed. "Hey, cool, it's Space Ninja Moxie!"

Zoe chuckled. "I'm actually okay with that moniker. It's the next best thing to Master Thief Barbie."

Hefting Dark Sympathy, she pursed her lips at the sword as if pondering what to do with it now that there was no easy hiding place. Then she tapped the fingertips of her left hand together in quick succession. Her glove must have registered a pattern, because the suit material on her back shifted. With a flourish, she slid the blade into a newly formed sheathe.

"You look so awesome!" Natalie peered down at her own outfit—little more than an old spray-painted hoodie. "I can't wait to have a cool costume someday."

"I can help with that. You know, if we live." Zoe bumped shoulders with her friend. "And thanks. The other suit is fun, but it's more about branding. You know? People see it and think *Moxie*. But this is what I wore for the serious jobs."

Jim hadn't said anything. Zoe glanced his way at the perfect time to catch him . . . noticing. His eyes went wide, and she gave a smirk.

"And what are you looking at?" she teased.

"Your personality, obviously. Not sure what *you* were thinking, sicko."

Zoe laughed.

Kelvin was the last to stand. He stretched while emitting sounds of embarrassingly deep satisfaction. "I feel better, too. At least, my body does. Even the wound from the Chaos Merchant's little surprise." He frowned, eyes downcast. "The rest of me is, uh, kind of dreading leaving this place."

A knowing look passed between them all. They felt it, too. In here, for a few precious hours, they could rest and marvel at this surreal place and pretend their peers weren't unwilling pawns in a lethal game they would soon have to rejoin. But the fate of everyone left alive may depend on them doing just that.

"Well," Eli said. "I suppose it's back to work, then. Gather round, please."

Jim and the others surrounded the chair, which spun toward a tall, rectangular display that expanded to many times its original size. Eli tapped and a general map of the Lighthouse appeared, then zoomed until the bottom third of the facility filled the screen.

"You're like an expert with this place," Natalie said.

"Even secret pocket dimensions need maintenance," Eli said. "Lord Neon is extremely private, but occasionally he makes an exception."

"Like when he needs his inter-dimensional espresso machine fixed?" Jim asked.

"Something like that. Eyes on the screen, please. As you can see, only a handful of levels separate us from our goal."

A red dot appeared at the lowest level. Jim felt his anxiety ratchet up. He was so close to reaching the source of the green line. If Arbiter was actually there, did she know the truth about Summer? If so, would he survive the Dare long enough to learn it?

If he had to choose between ending the Dare or learning about Summer, would he have it in him to let her go?

A hero would have said yes immediately. But Jim wasn't that guy anymore. In many ways, Lode had died on the same day as Lock.

Jim shoved his doubts into a corner and tried to focus as the team hammered out a strategic path to the last level of the Lighthouse. Eventually, his friends seemed happy with their plan, and he contributed by nodding when anyone looked at him. At this point, he'd be willing to grease up and slide down the laundry chute, as long as it got him there. As long as this could all be over soon.

There was only one sticking point.

"What do we do with him?" Jim pointed at Gloom. "I assume we can't leave him here."

"We cannot," Eli confirmed. "Nor can we stash him in a closet like we did with Reverie. Upon waking, he would quickly get free."

"Right, he could just phase through anything we tie him up with," Kelvin said. "Gosh, what a neat trick. Must be a big help when he's not twisted by evil."

"I can rig something up," Zoe volunteered. "If he moves, it'll give him a nice little shock. Would that be enough to interrupt his phasing?"

Eli tilted his head, considering. "Possibly. His ability requires a measure of concentration. If there are no other options, we may . . ." He trailed off, then his head whipped toward the shadows. "Move!"

Eli tapped the chair and the pocket dimension collapsed with an all-encompassing *WHOOOSH*, depositing them back in the dead end hallway. The team had clustered around his chair and were still standing close together now, and this sudden shift caused a moment of disorientation.

Too late, they all heard the running footsteps. Jim had only an instant to realize what was happening, and to curse Lord Neon's secret clubhouse for being so relaxing. It made everyone drop their guard.

Roaring, Gloom leapt with arms and legs spread wide and crashed into all of them at once. Suddenly, the whole team was falling through the floor.

Something smacked into the back of Jim's head, and he saw stars.

ELEVEN

Thirteen Years Ago

LYING on his bed, Jimmy stared up in terror at the face glaring down at him.

He found me. How did he find me?!

"You oughta be more cautious going home, boy. Especially after playing hero." The man threw back his hood to reveal a face covered in tattoos that made his skin look like a circuit board. "Don't you know heroes make enemies?"

Overclock, leader of the Twisted Pair gang, was in his room. He had one knee on Jimmy's chest and a pistol pointed between his eyes.

Jimmy couldn't move or speak. Was he about to die after one night as a hero?

"Haven't killed a kid in a long time," Overclock said. "Should I make it quick? One shot to the brain?" With his free hand, he drew a long, a half-serrated knife. "Or should we get to know each other first?"

Jimmy shivered. He tried to speak, but couldn't feel his lips. Overclock took the gun away from his head, leaving a split second to act, to turn the tables. Jimmy did nothing. The moment passed, and as Overclock tucked the gun away, he set the tip of the blade against Jimmy's sternum.

"We'll do this the quiet way. Then, after I'm done with you, I can go from room to room and take my time getting to know your family. Your sister first, your mommy, then your daddy."

Overclock paused and looked aside, as if something had just occurred to him. Being sure to keep Jimmy pinned, he reached into a back pocket and pulled out his phone. Only now did Jimmy remember he had powers. But as he stared at the device in his attacker's hand, he couldn't think of a single thing to do with it.

"First, though, how about we post your identity online? It's not every day someone like me gets to kill a hero. A *family* of heroes. You're gonna send my rep through the roof. I'll get a new gang, a better gang." He unlocked the phone. The camera flash turned on. "Smile."

Then his phone emitted a squeal of digital distortion, and his screen became a blindingly bright pattern of coruscating lights. Overclock recoiled and fell back, dropping the phone and taking his knee off Jimmy's chest.

The bedroom door burst open. Summer charged in, decked out in fuzzy pajamas, a baseball bat in her hands.

She swung. The bat smashed into Overclock's knee. His leg crumpled, and he opened his mouth to scream. Before he could make a sound, she swung again and Jimmy heard ribs crack. The gang leader hunched over with a guttural moan. He looked up at Summer, tattooed face equal parts agony and rage, just in time for her to swing a third time. The bat connected with his jaw. His head jerked around, his body spun with it, and he dropped to the floor, unconscious.

Summer loomed over him, hefting the bat like she might swing again. As the terror faded, Jimmy found he could move. He slid off the bed and came to her side.

"I'm okay," he assured, gently prying the bat from her grip. He gazed up at her in wonder. "You saved my life. You saved *all* our lives."

And Jimmy had just laid there waiting to be murdered. Right now, as far as he was concerned, there was only one real hero in this house. A simple thank you didn't feel like enough.

He slipped his Thunderous coin into her hand. In this moment, it was the most significant thing he could think to offer. Summer didn't respond, but she clutched the coin tightly in her trembling hand.

Jimmy reached for his phone. "I'll call the police."

"No," Summer snapped. "Mom and Dad are still asleep. If they find out this happened, they'll never let us be heroes. I'll . . . call that detective from tonight. Detective Stills. I'll arrange to meet and hand *him* over." She took a deep breath, recovering more of herself. "This is a lesson, Jimmy. We have to be more careful, even after a victory. We won't make this mistake again."

Her voice had gone soft, but her expression was hard as steel. She turned her gaze back to Overclock's prone form, and it was like a shadow fell over her eyes.

"This will never happen again."

Now

Jim woke as they fell through another floor. Gloom was shouting. Someone else was screaming. Jim himself remained stoic and brave in the face of danger and there's really no one around to say different, so who are you going to believe?

The team phased through solid floor, then ceiling, then some kind of office furniture made of glass and stone, then floor again, while also phasing through each other as they fell. They may have been incorporeal, but that didn't stop Jim from feeling super icky as his arm passed through Kelvin's head and Natalie's leg plunged through his chest.

They tumbled together, falling through unfamiliar levels too quickly to catch details, unable to disentangle from Gloom. Jim feared what might happen if they even tried at the wrong moment.

When they hit the next floor, their descent slowed. Instead of plummeting through air, it felt like they were passing through thick clouds, or gelatin, or marshmallows. Except the marshmallows had tiny hooks that clung to their atoms and pulled in all directions hard enough to be thoroughly unpleasant. Momentum carried them through, and finally they passed into the next level down.

Even whirling and disoriented, Jim felt immediately that this place was different. The level was one large chamber with flows of electrical power so strong he could sense them physically, like warm static.

Then another thought occurred to him, and it chilled him to the bone. He was pretty sure this was the last level of the Lighthouse. Beyond it, there was only space. And they were about to fall right through the floor.

Their mission would end abruptly, with whatever the opposite of glory was. They would asphyxiate, boil, freeze, maybe implode? He wasn't sure what space did to a human body, but he knew it would happen silently and they would float away unnoticed in the black, never seen or heard from again.

There was a flash of green, and then his electrical senses went blank. His powers were being suppressed. Did that mean–?

WHAM!

Jim went solid just in time to smack into the floor, which then vibrated with five other impacts.

He groaned, mentally thanking the green line's power suppression while cursing gravity for its very existence. While he was at it, he wished a pox and a curse on the house of whomever had given this level metal floors.

Zoe wasted no time. Crawling over to Gloom, she peppered him with a volley of darts. They stuck into his skin, forming a line that went up his neck and onto the side of his face. He cried out in protest, reached for her, then his eyes rolled back and he collapsed. When he was out cold, Zoe whirled on Jim.

"You said you took his powers."

Sitting up, Jim held out his hands in protest. "I didn't *take* his powers. I just absorbed his energy, and not even all of it. For all I know, that would have killed him, and I don't even know if it can do that since *I just got this ability like twelve seconds ago!*"

"Well," Eli said, sounding frazzled and worn. "He'll be out now for sure."

Natalie frowned. "Guys, I feel funny again."

"Same," Kelvin said. "I think our powers are muted here, and thank heaven for that. It saved our lives."

Standing, Jim offered Zoe his hand. She eyed it for a moment, looking abashed, then seemed to accept it as a peace offering. She grabbed hold and let him pull her to her feet. Together, they turned in a slow circle and examined their surroundings, jaws mirroring each other as they fell open.

"Okay, someone has to say it," Jim said. There was no response. "Come on, in a room like this, someone *has* to say it."

An awestruck Natalie spoke first. "Guys, what is this place?"

Jim pumped his fist. "There it is! Good game, everyone."

The domed chamber was about a hundred feet across and fifty feet tall. Overlapping metal plates of smoky gray chrome covered every surface from floor to ceiling. Far to the right, one of those silver-hamster-ball pods that had brought the team to the Lighthouse sat docked. It appeared to have its own launching hatch, so whoever had access to this place could come and go directly from here without having to navigate through the station. But of everything in this place, that was the least interesting.

A dozen devices sat equally spaced along the circular wall. They were like nothing Jim had ever seen, resembling hazardous chemical tanks crossed with some kind of high-tech engines. Thick pipes and cables sprouted from the bottom of each device and trailed across the floor to meet in the center of the chamber.

Where, Jim suspected, the team had been heading all this time. It was a sphere about thirty feet across, with the bottom quarter sunk into the floor. The surface appeared to be heptagonal segments of frosted glass, glowing a soft white from the inside.

One device on the wall hummed to life. A wave of inky blackness washed over the white sphere, momentarily blotting out the glow. Then the machine went quiet, and the wave dissipated.

"That felt like Aethyr," Zoe said, her voice subdued.

"I didn't realize machines could manipulate it," Kelvin said.

"It's mindblowingly difficult," Zoe replied. "And I've never seen it done on this scale."

The next machine in line hummed, and a different kind of wave coated the sphere. This one shimmered, reminding Jim of Gloom's phase effect, as if for a moment the entire sphere became incorporeal.

The pattern continued this way, with the next machine switching on, followed by some kind of effect applying to the sphere. There were four wave types—Aethyr, Phaser, a third one that made the sphere look much older for an instant, and then one he guessed was electromagnetic but couldn't be sure with his perception muted. Based on his glimpse of this chamber before his abilities had been suppressed, there was a staggering amount of power running whatever this was.

"Is . . . is this the end?" Natalie gestured at the glass sphere. "Is that what we've been searching for?"

All eyes turned to Eli.

He didn't respond right away, staring unfocused into the middle distance. Then he nodded heavily. "Yes. This is where the Dare ends."

"Are those waves some kind of security system?" Kelvin offered. "One last obstacle keeping us out."

"Or keeping something in," Zoe said darkly.

The implication sent a shiver through them all. Either reality was equally possible. The source of the Spectrum's corruption, of the Dare going horribly wrong, may very well be waiting inside that sphere. Jim eyed this team of misfits and wondered privately if he and they had what it took to stop this. To save everyone who could be saved.

"Hey, look." Natalie pointed. "Bottom left of the sphere. Is that a door?"

It was a door. Or, rather, a faint door-shaped outline in the frosted glass. There was no handle.

Kelvin indicated the Gauge on his wrist. "I imagine this is the key."

Zoe and Natalie each had their own thoughts on that. The three of them began to strategize about how to get inside between the waves, while also considering whether they were supposed to get inside at all. They didn't really know what this thing was, after all, and . . .

While the others debated, Jim backed away from the team and closer to Eli, watching him from the corner of his eye. The Custodian looked deeply troubled, frown lines creasing his face as he gazed at the sphere.

"Something on your mind?" Jim asked.

Eli pursed his lips. "The path we took following your green line. This chamber. I knew them once. But this whole time, I've only remembered them vaguely. I suspect I was made to forget key details. But now . . ." He turned to face Jim fully, lowering his voice for only them to hear. "I remember now why you were brought here. Why you were guided to me. Things are about to get much more difficult for you, and it is imperative–"

"Whoa, hey, something's changing," Natalie said.

The last machined hummed, the last wave passed over the sphere, and then all went still.

Zoe raised an eyebrow. "Well. Anyone feel like knocking on the door?"

Kelvin made a face. "Personally, I hope there's no one home and it's just a big red button that says *Stop Murdering Us.*"

Their discussion went on. It seemed, now that they were facing the end, no one wanted to take that first step toward it.

"Jim." Eli grabbed his arm and leaned in, eyes lit with internal fire. "Whatever you discover in there, you must be prepared. There will be a hard decision to make—the hardest of your life—but I believe you will do the right thing. No matter the cost."

Jim narrowed his eyes at the Custodian. He was definitely sure of one thing now, above all—he had had enough.

"Okay, that's it. Who and what are you *really*? I never bought for a second that you were just some trash-sweeping oracle we happened to rescue, but I went along with it. Every time you knew too much about a place, or about one of us, I let it go because you were helping us stay alive. But now we're at the end, and I'm not playing anymore." He twisted his arm free of Eli's grip. "Tell me what you really are and why you're really here, or go away so I can figure this out myself. Because right now, I don't trust you to go in there with me."

Eli stared hard at Jim. Not with a glare or a look of aggression, but with the face of someone waging a war within himself. A look that said if he chose wrong, the consequences would be broad-sweeping and dire. A choice in one hand, a world in the other.

Shoulders sagging, Eli sighed. "Alright, Jim, you win. We're all going to need each other before the end. I need you to trust me, and if this is what it takes . . ." For another moment, he stared into space as if fighting the last remnants of that battle within. Then he nodded to himself, the decision made. "I truly am the Custodian. But I'm also more than that."

"Then what are you? Some Prism hero? The Lighthouse barista?"

Eli locked eyes with Jim, and for the first time, his gaze felt infinite. "I'm Lord Neon."

TWELVE

JIM stared at Eli, cycling rapid-fire between bewilderment, disbelief, frustration, anger, a sudden and intense craving for cinnamon rolls, and finally acceptance. Not the kind of acceptance that came with peace. The kind that resembled resignation, as if it say *I've already fallen into this pit of boiling acid, so sure, fill the pit with sharks, too.*

"Back in that weird dimensional space, you said you didn't know how it worked."

"No, I said don't ask me how it works," Eli said. "There's a difference."

"And I saw Lord Neon in the Torch," Jim continued. "He was there when everything went wrong."

"Lord Neon, as the world knows him, is a . . . projection."

"You mean like a hologram?"

"No. The truth is deeper and far stranger than that."

"Of course," Jim said, shaking his head. "Of course you'd tell me this now, when there's no time to ask follow-up questions."

"You demanded to know."

"First of all, don't try to distract me with facts. Second, I didn't think you could unmask a Spectrum hero just by asking. And third, will there be cinnamon rolls in that sphere?"

"I promise, in time, you'll receive all the answers you seek. I just can't answer them all here and now."

Jim stared expectantly, eyebrows raised.

Eli sighed. "There are no cinnamon rolls."

Jim tossed up his hands with an exasperated huff. "I knew it. This place sucks!"

"The most important thing right now is for you to trust what I'm telling you," Eli said. "The fact that I chose to reveal myself should impress upon you how critical this moment is. I'm the hero who knows things, Jim. Trust that I know what's ahead of you, and how you can help save . . ." He trailed off, his eyes darting to the sphere. "They know we're here."

"They?"

"You will have to choose. Both sides needed you to be here, but for opposite reasons. Just know that I have faith in you. Despite what you claim, Jim, you're a good man. I know it. I've *seen* it."

"What a weird time to try to hurt me. We both know I'm a bad man."

Despite the tension, Eli smiled.

Jim tried to process it all, but kept coming up short. He only understood ten percent of what was going on here—or at least it felt that way. Now he was supposed to step inside a weird glowing ball and make some kind of important decision about something mysterious while other big, mysterious stuff hung in the balance. And apparently there were two opposite sides counting on him. But two sides of what?

With a growl of frustration, Jim mentally shoved it all aside. As far as he was concerned, there was only one reason he stood here. "The truth about Summer is in there?"

Eli nodded.

Jim turned and walked toward the sphere.

He heard the others scrambling to follow. They sounded surprised that he was taking the lead, but did their best to line up with him. No way of knowing if that was a good thing or not—

for them—but Jim surprised himself by feeling comforted that they were here. If he was marching toward his last moments, at least he would face them knowing the truth about Summer, and surrounded by people who had earned his trust.

He pursed his lips, disappointed in himself. *If you tell me the real truth about Summer was the friends I made along the way, I will turn this after-school special around and find an airlock to fling myself out of.*

When he came within a few paces of the sphere, the edges of the doorway glowed brighter. To the right of it, a pinpoint of light traced a small rectangle that resolved into an access panel with a speaker, a screen, and a scanner.

"Hello, Jim," the panel said pleasantly. "Scan your Gauge, please."

"Uh . . ." Jim glanced at his wrist, where the Gauge had been before it melted during their little adventure in the Torch. "Would you accept a Diner's Club card?"

"They still make those?" Kelvin said.

"How did it know Jim's name?" Natalie asked. "Why is it only talking to him?"

Working to hide how much his insides were trembling, Jim turned to her with a grin. "Hey, no intelligent questions. You know that's not how we operate."

Zoe produced a slim dagger and sliced cleanly through the strap of her Gauge. Taking Jim's hand, she pressed the device into his open palm.

She locked eyes with him and whispered, "Whatever's going on, you've got this."

She let go and stepped back. Jim couldn't help holding her gaze for a moment. Before it got weird, he made himself nod in thanks, then held her Gauge to his wrist and stepped up to the door.

He let the Gauge read his vitals and load his information, then waved it over the panel. The screen flashed blue and disappeared behind frosted glass. The light around the door winked out, followed by a hiss of air pressure releasing, like a seal being broken. The outline of a door became a door for real, which cracked open and swung inward a few inches, revealing a glimpse of ambient white glow inside.

Jim took a deep breath. Ten years. He'd been dreaming of this for ten years, and now at the threshold he felt less sure than ever.

But Summer deserved for the truth to be known. If nothing else in the world was true, that always had been.

Jim steeled himself, pushed the door open, and stepped inside.

The floor and the curved walls were made of the same frosted glass-like substance. The ambient glow seemed to come from everywhere and nowhere, much like the hidden elevator they had found in the Reliquary.

To the right, there was a large, blocky white chair bolted to the floor, facing inward. Masses of intertwined metal tubes sprouted from the back, sides, and thick base of the chair, pulsing and humming with energy like the chair was alive. They snaked every which way before sinking into the floor.

To the left, a transparent cylinder big enough to contain Jim and his whole team dominated the side opposite the chair. Its base was the same smoky chrome-like metal as the chamber outside, and the heptagonal pattern etched into the cylinder's clear surface suggested it was the Spectrum's special brand of invisalloy. The tubes that began at the white chair, with their pulsing energy, sprouted from the floor to plug into the cylinder's base.

The design of this whole place shouted *put the thing you're most afraid of in here.* Whatever it was, Jim figured it was in that cylinder. He couldn't be sure, though. Continuous waves of gauzy, misty energy roiled inside it, starting at the base and rising like the icy flames of some otherworldly bonfire.

Whatever was inside, the energy obscured it, and Jim had only seconds to wonder before motion drew his attention back to the chair on the right. Or rather, its occupant, who'd been sitting so still that Jim hadn't noticed her on his first cursory glance around the room.

The old woman had braided her white hair on one side and left it free-flowing on the other. She wore layers of flowing robes in soft earth tones, intricate designs covering the wide belt and sash. If Jim had to describe the style, he'd have gone with *space monk*. Even her posture and expressionless face projected focus and serenity.

"James Riven?" she said.

Jim nodded and made a guess. "Arbiter?"

The woman stared at him as if trying to see into his soul. Then her facade of serenity dissipated. With a sigh of relief, she sagged back in the chair and her face went slack, as if sitting straight had taken everything she had.

"Took you long enough," she growled. "Well, get in here. I haven't got all day."

Jim glanced back at his friends, who offered a collective shrug, which summed up this whole experience nicely. He gave his own shrug and stepped closer to Arbiter. At least he was about to get the one answer that mattered.

"I'm here for–"

"You are here to stop Framework," Arbiter said.

Behind Jim, someone gasped.

There are few occasions in life when the word *flabbergasted* can perfectly describe a person's state of mind. Personally, Jim found it showy and old-timey and didn't care for it much. He preferred terms like dumbstruck, perplexed, mystified, and on special occasions, befuddled.

Today, though, he was flabbergasted.

"Uh, what?" he said.

"I'm so tired. I've battled to keep her contained for so long," Arbiter said. "But she's too strong. Soon, she will be free. James, that cannot happen. You must take my place!"

"Whoa, whoa," Jim spluttered. "Take your place? I'm here for the truth about Summer Riven."

Kelvin tapped his shoulder and whispered, "The Dare."

"Oh, right. If we could pull the plug on the Dare and stop the Spectrum from killing everyone, that would be good, too, I guess."

Arbiter shot a hard glare at Eli. "You did not prepare him."

Eli cleared his throat and looked at the floor, embarrassed. "There was limited opportunity. My memories . . ."

Arbiter's anger turned to dread. "So she did get to everyone."

Eli nodded heavily.

"Then all is nearly lost." Arbiter beckoned to Jim. "Come closer, James. We haven't long."

"I don't want to sit in your weird chair, lady," Jim said. "Tell me what I want to know."

She waved dismissively. "Yes, yes, your answers will come soon enough."

"No, you'll tell me now."

"We do not have time for this, boy!"

"Speak for yourself. I have all the time in the world."

Arbiter clenched her fists, trembling with effort or frustration—or both—but her next words were clear. "If you do not take my place, every living thing on Earth will perish."

Looking to Eli, Jim shrugged and crossed his arms. He couldn't let any of this manipulation sway him. Not when he was so close to the answer. "I warned you. I told you I'm not a hero."

Kelvin stepped forward. "I was a lost cause before you all took me in. At least I can give something back. I'll sit in the chair."

"You can't," Eli said. "None of you can. Only Jim has what we need."

Jim glowered at Eli and Arbiter in turn. "Then *give me what I want*."

They stared back but said nothing more. Then Jim realized something, and his heart sank. If they would not tell him even now, when they claimed there was so much to lose, maybe there was nothing to tell. Maybe there had never been some hidden truth about Summer. Maybe Skypuncher hadn't lied ten years ago, and "missing, presumed dead" was all anyone ever knew.

With a bitter grimace, Jim turned toward the door.

"Please," Eli said. "We all need you."

Jim whirled on the hero. "If you are who you *say* you are, then you should've seen this coming. Did you really think you could lie to bring me here and still get what you want? Sorry, I'm not built that way. And if you did use Summer against me, as far as I'm concerned, you can all burn."

"I didn't lie," Eli said. "But . . . I also didn't give you the whole truth."

"Why? Only days ago, I was nobody, and I liked it that way. What could possibly make me so important now?"

Arbiter gasped, her whole body shuddering. "Please. I can barely hold on . . ."

"But Framework is dead," Natalie said. "Isn't she?"

The white energy inside the cylinder slowed, moving less like flames and more like a languid, swirling fog. And then everyone saw it. All this time, they had focused on Arbiter and her chair and cryptic message. Now, through that waning energy, they caught a hint of movement. Someone *was* in there.

"Oh, dear Lord." Kelvin fell back a step. "Is that really Framework?"

"Nat's right, she's dead." Zoe tilted her head. "At least, that's what they told everyone."

As the energy continued to fade, going from white to dull gray, the misty veil parted to reveal the outline of a woman floating in the heart of the cylinder. She wore a simple white leotard with metal bracers around wrists and ankles. She had long brown hair, and her eyes were closed. Mist obscured all but the general outline of her face.

"Eli?" Natalie said. "*Is* it Framework?"

Eli didn't respond, his focus divided between watching Jim and the woman in the mist. For the first time since they had met him, he looked genuinely afraid. "Jim, I'm begging you. Please don't let this happen."

Jim could only stare at the woman, thunderstruck. Though he could see little more than a silhouette, it was all he needed. "That's not Framework."

"How do you know?" Kelvin asked. "That armor she wore always hid her face."

Zoe drew Dark Sympathy. "If it *is* her, get ready for the fight of your lives."

Jim's insides were numb. When he spoke, it felt like someone else's mouth saying the words. "It's not Framework."

"How. Do. You. Know?" Zoe challenged.

Arbiter let out a sound, half weary moan, half desperate wail. "She knows you're here. It's happening . . ."

Jim barely heard, every cell in his body trained on that cylinder. Eli had been right all along—he *was* needed here. But the heroes wouldn't like what was about to happen. All this time, all those years he grieved, and every single day of it had been a lie.

"I know it's not Framework," he said. "Because it's my sister."

THIRTEEN

QUESTIONS peppered Jim from all sides.

What do you mean, that's your sister?

Didn't the Spectrum tell you she was dead?

So, that's *not* Framework?

Arbiter said it was Framework, right?

Do you see now, Jim, why I did not reveal everything at the start?

Wait. Is your sister Framework?

They bounced off him. His entire existence narrowed to a single beam of focus, a straight line from Jim to Summer as she hovered there in the Spectrum's secret orbital prison cell. Since she'd come into view, her eyes had stayed closed. Now they fluttered as if she were waking.

Jim had a question of his own. "Has she been here all this time?" No answer came. He half-glanced at Eli. "Have you kept her for *ten years*, knowing she's alive while her family thought she was dead?"

Eli at least had the decency to look ashamed. "It was necessary, Jim. Given the choice between one family and the entire world, what would you do?"

"She's not Framework," Jim insisted again. "I saw what that woman did—the entire world saw it—and Summer was never that powerful. You don't actually know everything, Eli. You made a mistake."

"The Summer you knew was not that powerful," Arbiter said. "Not until she went Apex after–"

Arbiter gave a strangled cry, lurching and spasming. Then she went limp. Jim's friends made sounds of alarm, but he was too full of his own feelings to react. As Arbiter slid out of the chair, Kelvin rushed over to catch her before she slumped to the floor.

"Don't worry, I've got her. Carry on with, uh, whatever's going on here."

Zoe looked on with a haunted expression. "Did she say Apex?"

Natalie tilted her head, puzzled. "What does that mean?"

"It's when someone exceeds the Faraday scale," Zoe explained. "Their power level literally goes off the charts. It almost never happens. Almost."

There was a pause, a moment of heavy silence. Then . . .

"Jim?"

There was a hollow echo to the voice that spoke his name. But he would know that voice anywhere.

Eyes open, feet on the floor, Summer had her hands pressed against the invisalloy. Her eyes, wide with elation, drank in the sight of her brother. A tear slid down her cheek as she cried out in relief.

"I knew you'd come. I knew it!"

She studied her prison. The cylinder hadn't deactivated— wisps of energy still wafted up from the floor. Arbiter's chair must have been feeding some kind of battery. The containment's power was diminishing, but apparently only enough for her to wake, not enough to break free.

"They won't let me out," Summer pleaded. "Help me."

"You must not," Eli said. "It is imperative that you hear me now."

Summer's chest and shoulders heaved with emotion. "I've been trapped here for so long. They won't believe anything I tell them. Please, I just want to go home!"

Jim stepped toward her. Eli caught his arm.

"She's behind everything, Jim. The Framework battle in Sydney. This Dare now. Destruction beyond imagining. She spent ten years slowly weaving her power into our systems, creeping into our minds, corrupting, planning for this day. Building up to this moment. And she will not stop here."

Jim shook his head. "If that's true, then Lord Neon's a part of it, isn't he? He's the one who brought me here. So, how could I trust his motives at all?"

A knowing look passed between them. Of those in the room, only they and Arbiter knew Lord Neon's true identity, and it seemed they were both in silent agreement to keep it that way. Jim didn't fully understand why he kept the secret of the man who'd done nothing but trick and use him, but right now, all he had to go on was instinct.

Eli pursed his lips, considering before he spoke again. "Because of the nature of his gifts, Lord Neon only fell halfway to Framework's influence. The other half has been battling her in secret, but she has been slowly winning. I . . . cannot speak for Lord Neon, but this much I can tell you. When he determined he could not defeat Framework, could not stop the Dare or prevent her from bringing you here, he decided instead to intercept you. He . . . sent me to guide you, prepare you to make the right decision when the moment came. *This* moment, when you would come face to face with the hardest choice of your life." He leaned in, looking more earnest and determined and uncertain than ever. "Framework gambled everything on the belief that you would set her free. Lord Neon gambled everything that you, after learning the truth, would stop her and save the world. A world that, though no one knew it, has remained in peril these past ten years."

Jim rocked back. So many words. So much . . . so much *everything* . . . all dropped on his head at once. He rubbed his temple, trying to absorb it all, to make sense of it.

"And now you have a story about her going Apex to explain it all. Convenient." Jim narrowed his eyes. "Tell me, Eli, would *you* trust you right now?"

Eli gave a resigned sigh. "There are facts about that day in Sydney, at the Spike, that only those who were there know. We kept it that way on purpose to protect the world."

"I thought they were my friends," Summer said, her voice thick with emotion. "I thought we would save the world together. Then they turned on me, trapped me here."

Desperate need surged within Jim. He studied the containment apparatus, searching for weaknesses, something that would help him breach it. Eli must have sensed his intention—his grip on Jim's arm tightened and his voice grew more insistent.

"The Spectrum does not hold hostages. They contain threats. You know this!"

"I know you lied for a decade. I know that lie destroyed my family."

"I stopped the threat, protected everyone, and they feared me for it!" Summer cried out, on the verge of tears.

"That is *not* what happened," Eli countered.

"Then what did happen? Tell me," Jim challenged. "What would make my sister do all of this? What could possibly turn Lock, a Prism hero, into Framework?"

"She went Apex, not gradually, but in an instant. You know what that can do to a person."

"Not enough. You didn't really know Summer. I see that now. You don't know everything she did to protect me, our family, our city. We fought so much darkness and corruption, but she never once got numb to it. One time, a gangster shot at us and ended up hitting a dog. She cried over that dog for two days. That's Summer. That's Lock."

"That *was* Summer," Eli said. "But when she went Apex–"

Summer fell to her knees, forehead pressed against the invisalloy. Her voice cracked pitifully. "It hurts in here. I'm so tired. Please."

Eli spoke again. Someone behind Jim spoke, too, maybe Kelvin. He wasn't listening anymore.

Arbiter's chair still powered the cylinder. But when she fell unconscious, her power dampening field faded. The green line was no more. From that moment, Jim had been buying time, keeping the discussion going while his power recovered. But not one word of Eli's excuses and obfuscations mattered. They never had.

Ripping free of the hero's grip, Jim lunged forward and slapped both hands against the invisalloy.

"Jim, no–!"

With a connection established, he found the river of power coursing between the chair and the cylinder. He placed himself inside it like a dam, immersed in that energy flow, and *pulled*. There was a high-pitched whine as he sucked power away from the machines, then a grinding groan as he turned that power back on itself and *pushed*.

The chair rumbled and sparked and tipped over onto its side. The tubes connected to the cylinder burst and the metal base fractured.

The invisalloy shattered.

"Jim," Summer breathed.

She tried to get to her feet and collapsed halfway there, stumbling forward. Jim rushed in and caught her. Wrapping his sister's limp form in both arms, he held on tight. Behind him, there were momentary flares of intense electrical power. He ignored them, focused fully on what he had in his arms—a dream that had lulled him to sleep every night for a decade.

"Summer . . ." Overwhelmed, Jim swallowed a lump in his throat. Then he realized he had no idea what to say. Every thought and feeling from every day of those ten years seemed to collide in his head. Finally, his shellshocked mind had to spit out something, anything. "Hi!"

Wow, profound. Ask if she had a good weekend. What's it like at work these days?

At least his inner monologue was intact. Jim rattled his head to clear the overlapping thoughts. He had to grab hold of himself, or getting what he wanted might just be the thing that broke him.

With a soft sigh, Summer opened her eyes again. They were glazed as she looked up at Jim, like she'd only half-awakened. She gave a languid, peaceful smile.

"You saved me."

He returned the smile with a heavy dose of wryness. "Well, that's in progress. We're not exactly home yet. But . . . wow. You're really real, aren't you?"

She was. He knew it in every cell of his body. Summer was alive—his sister, not the world-ending threat Eli tried to paint her to be—and soon she would be safe. Soon, they would both be home. Gazing down at her, he felt a decade-old knot inside him untangle and fall away.

"I'm real," she said, putting a hand to his cheek. "And you— *look* at you. You're all grown up. I knew you'd be strong enough to get to me. I just knew it."

Jim blinked. ". . . you knew I was coming?"

She didn't answer. Instead, she turned her head to look behind him, and her voice took on a bitter tone. "Framework. I've always hated that name."

He peered over his shoulder, following her eyes. His team hung limply like marionettes. No one moved or spoke or even appeared to see him, as if they were frozen in time. Jim recalled the electrical flares. He'd ignored them before, but now he wondered . . .

"It was the only way," Summer said. "Eli wanted to put me back in that cage, and eventually they would have tried to help him. They would never have given us the time we need. And we need to talk."

Ice slithered up Jim's spine. "What did you do?"

"They're fine, just . . . paused. I've had a long time in here with nothing but my own thoughts. At some point, I realized the human brain isn't so different from a computer—at least when it comes to my powers. So I found a way to use any device with a computer to tunnel into the central nervous system. From there, it's a short path to the brain, and to creating or interrupting any signal I need to."

Staring at his friends, Jim tried not to feel horrified. Everyone had something computerized on them, whether it was a Gauge or a phone or tech built into their costumes. Which, apparently, now provided Summer a way to access their minds. He made himself look away, pointedly not allowing himself to recall Eli's explanation. But when he returned attention to Summer, he saw something and that icy feeling spread into his veins.

A Spectrum comm unit—the very thing that had driven all the heroes mad. It had nestled hidden under her hair, but now, with her head turning, the strands parted to reveal the communicator affixed to Summer's right ear. And if she could use her powers on the human mind . . .

No. This was Summer. There had to be another reason for all this. He was just in too much shock to figure out what.

She patted his arm. "I think I'm okay now."

"You're sure?"

"It'll take time to recover fully, but I can at least stand."

They stood, and despite Jim's belief in his sister, he took an unconscious step back. "They're not in pain, are they? My team."

"You know I wouldn't do that. They're only stunned. I owe them, too, since they got you here."

Jim hesitated. "Yeah. About that."

"You have questions." Summer nodded as if answering for him. "Long ago, a sympathetic hero slipped me one of their communicators, and I knew there was only one person I could reach out to. Only one who would believe in me enough. My one hope for freedom." She gave an affectionate smile. "It was always you, Jim. It took years, but I used the comm as a gateway into the Lighthouse computers. I wanted to take over as many systems as possible and then find a way to reach you. But there were roadblocks. All the system AI's united, and we fought to a stalemate. So I searched for another solution, and that's when I discovered my powers had grown, and I was no longer limited to technology. I couldn't fully overthrow the Lighthouse or the minds of the Spectrum, but I finally gained enough ground with each to make my move."

"So, you did create this new Dare. Why?"

"They controlled enough that I still couldn't act directly. I had to come at everything sideways. So instead of just plucking you from Highreach, I used a smokescreen for the Spectrum and bait for you." She glanced down, embarrassed. "I hadn't realized how much you changed. How much you'd grown to hate heroes. My little brother Jimmy would have beaten down the door until they let him try out. Jim Riven, though, wasn't so simple. I have to admit, I wasn't sure what to do to get you here. Even sending those OmniBots to pretend to stop you didn't work."

Jim made the connection. "Then Lord Neon made his move, brought me himself."

Summer nodded, pride in her eyes. "But he underestimated you. And now here we are."

Why are the heroes hunting everyone? Is that part of her plan, too?

That's ridiculous. Why would she do that?

Why would the Spectrum?

Jim shoved the voice away. It wouldn't leave. *You're ignoring the questions that matter.*

It's Summer. She wouldn't–

Ask her about Sydney, you coward.

He mentally turned his back on the voice. The lingering questions didn't matter when Summer stood here, alive against all odds, and they were a family again. It was time now to plan their exit and get moving.

But when he spoke, the very words he'd rejected came out. "Sydney. What really happened? Why . . . why did they call you Framework and blame you for everything?"

A shadow fell over Summer's eyes. "When Lock . . . when I arrived, the heroes were already losing badly."

"They told us Framework made the Spike and started the fight."

"No. I was in the Lighthouse when the Spike appeared. They sent another Prism to check it out, and things went wrong. My Prism was the second wave. By the time we arrived, two heroes were already dead and more wounded. I . . . I can still hear their cries. It felt like we were all going to die."

"What were they fighting? Who put the Spike there? What does it even do?"

Summer didn't answer. She stared into the middle distance, as if reliving the memory. "I had to do something. I *had* to. So, I . . ."

Jim's insides shivered. He couldn't stop now. "What, Summer? What did you do?"

"I reached out and–"

She cut off, her eyes sharpening on something over his shoulder, and she snarled. Jim whipped around. Quaking with effort, Natalie gave a shout and smashed her forearms together. The Gauge on her wrist shattered, and then she was free.

Summer backpedaled until she was standing on the broken remains of her prison. Hand on the comm, she whispered, "Defend me!"

Natalie raised her fists and wrapped them in granite. "Jim, get away from her!"

Jim held out his hands. "No, please! She just–"

With a rapid-fire series of booms and crashes, something ripped through the top of the sphere and slammed down hard enough to buckle the floor and send out a spiderweb of cracks.

When the dust cleared, Skypuncher stood there, glaring at them.

FOURTEEN

YELLOW cape. White suit—normally bright and clean, now smeared across the chest with the dark brown of dried blood. Skypuncher's eyes, normally clear and friendly, were blood-shot and intense. The good-natured grin was gone, square jaw clenched so hard that Jim could hear his powered jaw grinding those indestructible teeth.

He turned that frenzied glare on Natalie. She fell back a step, eyes wide.

"Summer, no. Call him off!" Jim said. "These are my friends. They're just confused. They don't know you like I do." He pointed at Skypuncher. "And for a decade, *he's* told every-one you're the most dangerous villain in the world. I know that's a lie."

Summer's eyes brimmed with panicky tears. "I can't go back inside that thing. I won't!"

Skypuncher took an ominous step forward.

If she's controlling him like this, then the Dare . . . this hunt . . .

Hard questions later. Survival now.

"You won't go back," Jim promised. "We can fix this together, show everyone the truth. Just calm down or they'll never listen to us."

Summer was shivering now. She gave a desperate, pleading gasp. "Jim . . ."

He could see the war going on inside her head. The fear of being caged again ran so deep that she clung to her control of Skypuncher like a lifeline. As if Summer Riven trusted Jim and wanted to let go, but Framework wouldn't budge. He held out his hand as if trying to calm a wild horse and gestured to his team with the other.

"At least let them leave. Show them who you really are."

He flicked his hand and every electrical device touching them switched off, interrupting Summer's connection to their minds. They lurched with a collective gasp, coming back to themselves.

"The Dare is over," he said over his shoulder. "Go home."

His team didn't move. Jim studied them, puzzled, before realizing why. The way they glanced between him and Skypuncher and the woman they saw as Framework . . .

"Summer and I, we've got this now," he assured them. "Don't worry about me. Just go."

His friends shared a look. Then Zoe nodded, and Kelvin and Natalie mirrored her. Last of all, his face inscrutable, Eli gave a nod of his own. His superhuman mind must have been using those mountains of knowledge to craft a hundred different plans of action. But he had built the machine that brought them to this moment, set it into motion, and it seemed now he was trusting Jim to take the wheel.

"Okay, Jim," he said, backing away toward the door. "We'll see you both again soon."

A blur of motion. A streak of yellow and white. Skypuncher appeared between them and the door, pointing at Eli.

"Not him," Summer hissed. "He stays, or no one leaves."

Jim frowned, considering how to protest while keeping things calm. Then Zoe took one step too close, and Skypuncher shoved her.

From a normal person, the shove would have been casual, almost playful. From Skypuncher, it was like a wrecking ball. Zoe rocketed across the sphere and bounced off the frosted glass. The wind burst from her lungs as she fell to her hands and knees.

Kelvin made a shocked noise. Skypuncher turned on him and his eyes began to glow.

"SUMMER!" Jim cried.

She didn't respond. The air around Skypuncher's eyes burned bright. Jim hovered on the edge of action, close to doing something he and Summer would both regret.

. . . but, could he actually do it? He hesitated a moment too long.

Natalie rushed in, terror on her face as she threw herself at Skypuncher and drew his attention. He loosed twin beams of crackling yellow energy at her. She tried blocking the blast, but it shattered her stone gloves and kept going past her. Zoe tackled Kelvin and Arbiter as the beams sliced through the air where they'd just been.

Natalie formed new gloves. Skypuncher fired again and they shattered, too. But this time they took the full force of the blast and the energy dissipated.

Fists clenched, Skypuncher growled. The light in his eyes went blinding bright. The air around his head sizzled and popped as he powered up.

Natalie stood her ground and made a shield of prismatic stone in her left hand. The stone spread across her body, forming chunky blocks of sparkling armor. She raised the shield as Skypuncher loosed a giant blast.

With a heavy grunt, she caught the energy and slid back. The shield absorbed the twin beams, glowing from the inside now. Her stone boots sprouted claws and dug into the floor to halt the slide. Shoulders hunched, head tucked, she held fast under the barrage.

Then her armor changed shape. The light absorbed by the shield refracted across her chest and shoulders. As the prismatic stone continued to morph, it channeled all that burning light into her right arm, where it collected until her fist blazed like the sun.

Shouting, Natalie sent Skypuncher's beams right back at him. The devastating blast struck him square in the chest. He flew back and crashed into the wall, sending heavy splits and cracks through the dome.

Every jaw in the room fell open. This young, upstart wannabe had just scored a hit on the most famous hero on the planet, and he'd actually felt it. No one was more shocked than Natalie, who burst into panicked laughter as Skypuncher shook his head to clear away stars.

But Jim knew this man. On the rare occasion someone managed to ring his bell, his counterattacks were devastating, leaving no question as to why he led the Spectrum.

Jim moved in, his thoughts flashing back to Millennia—taking those punches and absorbing her Faraday energy with his newfound Vessel power. Skypuncher was orders of magnitude stronger, so this would probably turn Jim into a crimson stain on the floor, but he couldn't leave Natalie alone to–

Natalie charged. Hands clasped, she drew back and her armor morphed to form a giant club. She swung with all her might.

Skypuncher delivered a single left hook. His fist intercepted hers, stopping her attack cold and smashing the giant club. As if it had hit nothing, his fist kept going until it collided with her jaw. With an echoing *boom*, Natalie's body armor shattered like a pane of glass. She slammed face-down onto the floor and lay still.

A shadow streaked at Skypuncher. There was a glint and a metallic screech. He swung, but the shadow bounced out of reach. Zoe skidded to a halt as the blackness receded, Dark

Sympathy vibrating in her hand. She had scored a hit with the mysterious weapon, but hadn't left a mark.

"Summer, stop this now!" Jim said.

His sister said nothing. He grabbed her arm and shook. When her eyes met his, he let go and stepped back in revulsion, a black pit forming in his stomach. Those were not Summer's eyes. Something in them was dark, ominous. And . . . excited? Was she enjoying this?

The first shadow of real doubt grew in Jim's mind. What *had* happened that day in Sydney? Too much was happening too fast to process. Ten years of nothing, and now Jim faced every possible thing in one moment.

He beckoned to Eli. "Do something, man!"

The Custodian was shaking with effort. He spoke through gritted teeth. "I'm trying. My *other half* is largely under her control—I only retain my Sensor powers. And she is so strong."

Groaning, Natalie rolled onto her back. She opened her eyes, and they went wide as saucers. Skypuncher stood above her, fists clenched. He drew back to strike.

His head disappeared.

"Go, Nat!" Kelvin called.

Sitting up, Natalie pounded her fists onto Skypuncher's feet. The force drove his feet through the floor, up to his knees. She stood, eye level with the hero now, and drew back both arms. Spiked gauntlets grew around her fists and a spiked helmet covered her face. As Skypuncher's head reappeared, she smashed her fists into his temples twice in quick succession.

Then, clutching the sides of his head, she shouted something in Mandarin and head-butted once, twice, three times. The spiked helmet crushed to rubble between their foreheads. She cocked both fists back to strike again.

Skypuncher caught them and held tight. The two of them locked together, face to face.

"I'll break us both before I let you touch them!" Natalie snapped.

Skypuncher smirked. "I'll beat them to death with your corpse."

He squeezed her fists, and she cried out in pain. But then her cry turned to one of rage. Enormous stone plates stacked layer after layer across her body until she was twice her opponent's size. Lunging, Natalie grabbed Skypuncher in a crushing hug and heaved him out of the hole in the floor. Then she twisted and hurled them both through the wall. They tumbled into the main chamber and out of view.

As much as Jim wanted to rush after Natalie, he understood what she'd done and made himself stop. She was buying them a window to end the Dare for real. To deal with the person really in control. Jim couldn't waste it.

He faced Summer, for the first time truly uncertain who he was talking to. He took a deep breath to steady himself. There was a crashing sound outside the sphere—Natalie was fighting for her life. For all their lives.

"Summer, look at me."

She did, and once again he met a stranger's eyes.

"He'll kill her. Don't let him kill my friend. Stop now and we'll figure this out together."

Summer's face was a roiling sea of emotion. Sadness, resignation, bitter vengeance, and more, all colliding and flashing by like a storm. For an instant there was fear, and then regret. The regret gave Jim hope.

But then the resignation came back. She shook her head, and her eyes hardened. "I guess you should start calling me Framework."

The ice in Jim's veins finally reached his heart.

FIFTEEN

NATALIE'S mind raced as she and Skypuncher crashed through the sphere in a tangled mass. Mid-air, she did some quick and dirty math.

Okay, Marble. You're tough, but 7.8 is a LONG way from Skypuncher's rumored mid-9s. If you give this guy an inch, you're dead.

Which meant doing something Natalie Yu rarely made herself do. She had to let go of her smile and summon every ounce of rage inside her tiny body. She had to make up for weakness with sheer ferocity.

Their flight crested and arced down toward the chamber floor. Still clutching Skypuncher, Natalie rolled so that she was on top with the hero between her and the floor.

Oh, there was one more thing—something Jim had taught her without realizing it.

Don't forget to have fun!

They smashed down hard and bounced. Natalie rolled them over and smashed down again, crunching Skypuncher halfway through the floor's metal plates. Momentum carried them forward, still flying and tumbling. On the next roll, she smashed down again, making another crater in the floor with the hero's body.

Halfway through the next roll, Natalie was winding up for a fourth go when Skypuncher flexed his grip. The arms of her stone battle suit shattered. He fired eye beams and sliced the head clean off. As he landed on his back, he punched upward and caught the armor square in the chest. Half the suit blew away, becoming scattered gravel.

This left Natalie exposed but unharmed. She gave a sigh of relief that she'd made the suit big enough to hide in the lower torso.

Skypuncher didn't reach for her. Instead, he wrapped arms around as much of the remaining suit as he could and squeezed. The rock buckled under the bearhug that would surely crush Natalie inside it.

She closed her eyes and clenched every muscle. Spikes of glassy black stone lanced out from her, turning her into a human porcupine. Skypuncher made a pained noise and let go. They separated and stood.

As they faced each other, the hero swiped under his left eye. Natalie noticed a drop of blood on his finger, and a scratch on his cheekbone. He gave her a reappraising look—one with a sliver of grudging respect.

Don't think about that. Don't stop for anything. Keep him off balance!

She dashed in, forming long spears and tossing them with every step. Skypuncher knocked them away, that flash of respect replaced by murder. As they closed the distance, Natalie formed a comically huge cartoon mallet, spun and swung with an aggressive shout. Skypuncher smacked the head and the mallet disintegrated mid-swing.

Which was exactly what Natalie wanted. As stone chunks filled the air like confetti—a momentary distraction—she leapt high while forming spiked armor across her thighs. Reaching through the flying debris, she grabbed the large man's head and smashed it down onto the spikes. As he recoiled from the blow, she held on and placed her knees on his shoulders. Stone spread from her to envelop him from the neck down and tighten like shrink-wrap.

This will only buy you a moment. Make it count!

Wielding thick stone gauntlets, she rained down blows on Skypuncher's head with the force of a wrecking ball. The surrounding air shook with rapid-fire *boom boom boom* concussions. Natalie finished with an overhead double-fisted slam that drove the hero to his knees. She powered up again, aiming to punch him through the floor and into space.

I'm doing it!

She may not have a real suit, or a name people knew, but right now she was doing what heroes did. Protecting the innocent.

Skypuncher caught her arms, stopping her as if he'd plucked a tiny bird out of the air with no effort at all. Their eyes met, and he flashed a dark grin.

Natalie's insides went cold.

Oh, sh–

In a blur of motion, Skypuncher released one of her arms and struck her in the solar plexus. It felt like getting hit with the living embodiment of a thunderclap. The reverberating blow knocked the breath from her lungs.

Then he clutched her face with the iron grip of his giant hand, spun, and hurled her like a baseball.

Natalie flew up like she'd been fired from a cannon and smashed through the ceiling, leaving wreckage in her wake. Then she smashed through the next ceiling. And the next.

Bouncing off the fourth ceiling, she left a Natalie-shaped imprint before pinballing off several other hard surfaces in the room. She rolled to a stop on the half-collapsed floor.

A wave of delayed pain crashed down on her. With a gasp, she deflated. Her vision swam. For a moment, she didn't know who or where she was. She just knew everything hurt.

Jim stood between Summer and his friends, hands out to both sides in a staying motion. He'd need an industrial laser to slice through this tension.

"Get a leash on her, Jim," Zoe warned. "Or I'll–"

"Wait," Jim said.

"Just say the word, Zoe," Kelvin said.

"Wait!" Jim implored.

Everything was going to pieces. He had to try something different. Facing Summer, he let his desperation turn to frustration. Pleading with her hadn't worked. Maybe shaming her would.

"Come on, Lock, are you a hero or not? Is Framework too strong for you to stop?"

He scrunched his face into a tough mask, while inside his heart was breaking. After so much, after so long, he found himself standing between the family he loved most in the world and the friends he was surprised to discover he cared this much about, begging them to let him fix this before it got any worse.

Summer hesitated. Jim could see the conflict in her eyes, pain and rage warring with the hero she used to be. The sister he'd known ten years ago—he could've perfectly predicted what she would do. This woman in front of him, though . . . he wished he could be sure.

"I know you're angry. So am I. The Spectrum will answer for what they did, I promise you." He gestured all around them. "But not like this."

He glanced at Eli, silently asking for help, a calm voice to help everyone simmer down. The Custodian stared blankly into the middle distance, apparently still struggling to retake control of Lord Neon, whatever that actually meant. Jim stifled a frustrated huff. So much for the Spectrum saving the day.

"We'll show the world how they've lied about you all along," he promised. "But first, you have to show them you're not a threat. Release the Spectrum. Save everyone."

Summer shook her head. "I can't. They want to stop me, Jim, and we can't let them. The world needs me—every single person. I *have* to help them." She got a faraway look in her eye. "You'll see. Once I'm back there, I can finish this. When I'm near it again."

"Near what?"

"Where it all started."

Natalie rattled her head and sat up. Though her sudden entrance had smashed some machinery, the large room she sat in still contained half a dozen functional FabriKaters—machines invented by the builder parahuman FabriKate to mimic a version of her atomic manipulation power. Among other things, parahumans used them to create costumes, specialized tools, and battle suit components.

She glanced down at herself, suddenly self-conscious. Her hoodie and pants were in tatters, reduced to rags that barely clung to her body. Street clothes and regular fabrics were not built for powered battles. But she was a long way from being able to afford materials like that.

Not that it mattered right now, amid fighting for survival. In fact, when Skypuncher showed his face, maybe she'd throw some FabriKaters at it. She climbed to her feet, recollecting herself for his inevitable arrival, which should happen any–

One instant she was alone, the next she was hoisted off the floor with his hand around her throat. On instinct, she sprouted a layer of form-fitting stone to sheathe her body.

Skypuncher lifted her until he was looking up into her eyes. He wore a smirk, but it was a thin veil over his anger.

"Maybe you haven't heard of me," he said. "But pebbles don't exactly slow me down. They just annoy me."

In the sheer insanity of this moment, Natalie had an insane thought to match it. *What would Zoe say right now?*

"Well," she gurgled, half-choking. "Good thing I'm a Marble, then."

His brow furrowed in confusion. Oh, right. He didn't know her moniker, so that would have sounded like gibberish.

But it bought Natalie an instant to spread her arms wide. Thicker stone gauntlets formed over the base layer of her armor. She extended them, treating the stone like extra long arms with extra large hands, which she shaped into scoops. Grabbing a FabriKater in each makeshift hand, she clapped with Skypuncher right in the middle. Heavy machinery and stone crunched together around him.

He gave her a flat look, sighed and shook his head. "Pathetic."

"Can't blame a rock for trying."

"And you thought you were Spectrum material?"

Even knowing he wasn't in his right mind, that hit Natalie harder than any punch. She squared her shoulders and worked to brush it off. Wounded pride should be the least of her concerns.

Especially now that her distractions and time-buying antics had run their course, and her actual attack was ready. All this time, she'd been hitting Skypuncher with diminished attacks and weaker stone constructs. Much of her power had been boiling under the surface, reserved for cooking up something special. It would leave her drained for a while, so she mentally crossed her fingers.

"Maybe I'm not," she said through gritted teeth. "But right now, neither are you."

While her fists had kept the hero distracted, Natalie had dedicated her insides to the parahuman version of extracting and refining ore from her own manifestations. Earth Smasher powers could mean a lot of things, and what was a large amount of the Earth's crust made of?

Metal.

Natalie gave a shout and flexed inside and out. A solid steel icosahedron enveloped them both. The shiny gray twenty-sided sphere engulfed Skypuncher completely, except for the arm that held Natalie in the air.

The steel encased her, too, up to the waist. She could step out of it anytime, of course, but chose to stay locked here with her quarry. The move had exhausted her—she could feel her body wanting to slump over. Still, she grabbed onto the hero's arm with what remained of her grip and held as tightly as she could.

The longer she held him here, the more time she bought her friends.

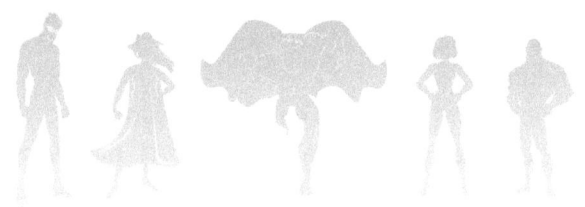

SIXTEEN

Twelve Years Ago

THE makeshift little robot, cobbled together from scrap and salvaged wires, danced like a marionette. The battery taped to its back had only a whisper of a charge remaining—time was running out.

Jimmy sat cross-legged on the dusty warehouse floor. His hand hovered over the little machine, fingers dancing with it, his Controller powers acting as the strings. Sweat coated his brow. Recently, he'd focused his training on holding the maximum control over an electrical device with minimum access to its electricity. It felt like bench pressing with two fingers. Still, he'd gotten better. A week ago, the robot would have slipped from his control by now.

He trembled with exertion. *A little longer, just a little longer . . .*

The little spark in the machine was fading, little more than the memory of an ember now. Still, he held on, and the robot danced.

BAM!

Jimmy flinched. His concentration splintered. The metal man clattered to the floor. He released a breath, part frustration and part relief.

Summer stood at the far end of the warehouse, lips pursed in annoyance. Her much larger construct had toppled over, too. Hands on her hips, she stared at the machine as if it had offended her.

"Thought I had that one," she muttered.

She'd been training a similar skill with her own power, controlling larger and more complex machines with smaller and weaker computer cores, stretching her abilities to increase their strength and endurance and fine control. Over the weeks, she'd improved faster than Jimmy, and now it seemed she'd found a new limit.

"That was loud. The neighbors will talk," Jimmy joked.

Summer laughed. "You mean that family of rats? Pretty sure they'll keep it to themselves."

This warehouse was long-abandoned. They'd stumble onto it in a forgotten corner of the Pendulum district after foiling an armored car heist. After weeks of careful observation, they'd concluded it was fair game, moved in, and adopted it as their secret training facility. Summer kept trying to name it the Kernel, after the computer program at the core of an operating system. Jimmy found that boring and never missed the chance to tease an overly-serious name, so he kept calling it the Air Popper. She did not like it.

She blew out a breath. "Well. That's why we train. Better to fail in here than out there."

Moving to join Jimmy, she opened her water bottle and took a long pull from it. He stood and did the same. The icy sensation flowed down his chest and out to his fingertips. He gave another sigh, this one of satisfaction. Abandoned warehouses didn't offer air conditioning.

"Wanna play Gotcha?" he asked.

Summer eyed him sidelong. "You sure . . . ?"

The look and her tone added the second half. *You sure you want to lose again?*

"Put up your dukes, Lock."

He flicked his fingers at one corner, and their game switched on. In their first week as the new stewards of the warehouse . . . er, headquarters . . . they had transformed the inner shell into a sort of life-sized game board—one suited to their particular brands of Controller powers. The corrugated metal walls and sloped roof were now crisscrossed with bundles of reclaimed electrical wiring.

At key points and junctions, those wires intersected with makeshift levers attached to actuators and a few other components Jimmy didn't quite understand, but Summer seemed perfectly comfortable with. Together they created Gotcha's three-dimensional maze of paths for electricity to follow—true paths and false paths and collapsible paths, along with switchable traps built from those levers and actuators.

The heart of the game sat in the corner Jimmy had motioned to—a bank of scavenged old car batteries festooned with yet more wires, and a modified stack of Raspberry Pi computers. He controlled the power flowing from the batteries while Summer controlled the signals from the computer.

His goal? Send an electrical pulse from the batteries, guide it through the maze, and return it home to the batteries once again. Summer's goal? Block or trap that pulse in the maze, preventing it from returning home. They had played at least three dozen times now.

And Summer had never lost.

"Ready, Lock?"

"Just say the word, Lode."

"Go!"

To anyone else, it would appear that nothing happened. To the Riven siblings, the chase was a fireworks show that moved at the speed of thought, Jimmy's electrical pulse blazing furiously along the paths he chose while Summer bent the computer processor and the game board itself to her will.

The game lasted 3.8 seconds. The chase ended with Jimmy's electricity hopelessly boxed in with nowhere to go.

"Curses!" Jimmy shook his fist at the sky in mock outrage. "We'll meet again, Lock!"

Summer laughed. "Take him away, boys."

Jimmy looked at the floor, his humor waning. "Hm. I think I might've actually done worse that time. Didn't I last five seconds before?"

"I do have a few years on you." Summer ruffled his hair. "Don't worry, Lode, you'll get there. The bad guys won't know what hit 'em. Remember, this is our house. They just rent a room."

He nodded, but didn't look up.

"Want to go again?" she said.

At first, Jimmy didn't react. Then he gave a sly grin.

Now

"Where it all started," Jim said. "You mean the Spike? That thing's just been sitting there for a decade. You don't have to save us from it."

Summer shook her head. Jim caught a look that reminded him of one she used when they were kids. A rueful *you don't understand anything* look. She wiped away a tear, looking frustrated, and a fresh one took its place.

Eli blinked hard, coming back to himself. "Tell him."

Summer's eyes darted warily to the Custodian. Lowering his arms, Jim shifted to place himself between his sister and his friends. There had been lots of unspoken meaning behind that look of hers, and something told him this was part of the truth he'd come here to find.

"Tell him, Summer Riven. Lock. Framework," Eli pushed. He wore a face that matched Summer's, full of history and implication. "Tell him everything. If anyone would understand, wouldn't it be him, your own blood?"

Summer hesitated.

Eli persisted. "Tell him how you want to save the world."

She squared her shoulders, chin up. "I will save it. I'll save *them.*"

"Save who? From what?"

"Everyone." She looked aside, her expression turning distant, as if she could peer through the walls and see down to the planet. Then she smiled as if this were all a peaceful dream. "I'll save them from their pain."

Alarm bells rang in Jim's head. "Uh, what exactly does that mean?"

Summer's gaze lingered on that distant place, whatever her mind's eye saw. "The moment it happened—when I went Apex—I connected with every computer-controlled device on the planet and instantly knew all the information they contained. The entire library of human knowledge, the full scope and history of our species. Every action, every discovery, down to the smallest moments ever recorded. Humanity's highest highs and our lowest lows. I saw the pieces all at once—the full jigsaw puzzle of our existence assembled in a flash. I came to know us, and the world we've built, like no one has before. And when I saw it, I realized what our existence really means. What everything we've ever done boils down to." She turned a haunted expression on Jim. "Do you know what it is?"

"What?"

"Nothing."

Jim's heart sank.

"It's all meaningless suffering. There's no endgame, no point to any of it. The only real constant in this world, the only thing we've created that never ends, is pain." Her darkened eyes showed a sliver of hope. "But I can save us from all that."

Jim could barely bring himself to do it. But someone had to ask. "How?"

She gave him a sympathetic look, as if sharing a hard truth with a child. "I think you know."

He wished to God that he didn't . . . but he did. And in that moment, Jim knew he was learning the whole truth—the curse of knowledge that Lord Neon had promised. The weight of his imploding heart made it difficult to breathe.

He should have stayed behind his bar.

"People can't feel this meaningless pain," Summer concluded. "If there are no people."

Kelvin gasped.

"That's it." Zoe deployed her mask.

Summer peered over Jim's shoulder, and her expression went from regretful to fierce. She reached toward his friends.

Jim put up his hands. "No!"

Eli grimaced. With a labored groan, he fell to one knee, hands clutching the sides of his head like he'd been stricken with a migraine. For an instant, the motion drew everyone's attention.

Long enough for Lord Neon to melt through the wall, float up behind Summer, and press his hands to either side of her head. His palms radiated purple light. Summer gasped and raised up on her toes, her whole body going taut.

"SUBMIT," Lord Neon commanded with that deep, echoing voice. "Your fight is over, Summer Riven. Be at peace."

Her eyes shut, mouth wide in a silent scream. Her knees buckled and she sank slowly toward the floor.

Jim's insides were on fire, every instinct raging at him to help his sister. Even hearing the truth from her own mouth, his mind could believe, but not his heart.

They'll put her in a cage again.

What would you do? Did you hear her version of saving the world? Sydney was just a preview. Skypuncher was right all along—Framework really is the world's most dangerous villain.

But . . . it's Summer. She was supposed to be its greatest hero.

"Don't fight, Summer," Jim said, hating himself as much as he hated every word. "Let go. I'm here, I promise. I won't leave you."

"Jim!" she sobbed like a child lost and desperate, blindly reaching for him as tears painted her face. "Please!"

Something inside him died. *You were supposed to save each other. Now you'll be the last one to betray her.*

Shut up shut up just SHUT UP

Summer's last shreds of resistance were draining. Wheezing, knees almost to the floor, she cried for Jim again. It was almost over now.

Then her knees stopped buckling, and Lord Neon flinched as if he'd been struck. Reaching up, she clutched the hero's hands. He made a sound of surprise, and then surprise became alarm.

Summer opened her eyes, and they may as well have been on fire. Fury had replaced fear. She loosed a growl that became a roar as their roles reversed—Summer regaining her feet while Lord Neon shrank back. He tried to pull away, but she held fast, commanding the situation now.

Oh crap oh crap this is bad

Jim had to do something, but what could he do without hurting his sister? Again he stood frozen, caught between head and heart.

Summer shrieked. Jim felt power surge through the comm unit she wore. A corresponding wave blasted through Lord Neon's comm, which exploded. Then the hero vaporized.

A dart flew over Jim's shoulder, latched onto Summer's comm, and emitted a powerful electrical burst. Summer cried out, as did Eli.

A second dart followed. There was a *pop*, and a tiny explosion shredded Summer's comm. She recoiled, scorch marks on her face. Eli screamed and collapsed in a heap. Then Summer's head disappeared.

"Go!" Kelvin said.

Zoe leapt at Summer, sword high.

Hands up, Summer curled her fingers as if they were claws. The entire sphere around them shattered into chunks of glass and steel and circuitry. They flew in and swirled around her like a tornado, knocking everyone back. With Kelvin's concentration broken, Summer's head reappeared.

She raised her arms and the maelstrom responded like a living thing. Piece by piece, the remains of the broken sphere collected around her until they formed a giant makeshift suit of armor. The thing towered over them with Summer hidden somewhere inside it.

Jim stared up at the behemoth in a wide-eyed mix of awe and horror. The Summer he knew could never have done that.

But Framework could. She had done it in Sydney.

It was all too crazy. Was it even possible to stop this before it escalated further? He tried to speak, searching for something to say that might calm his sister down.

Before he could find it, Summer turned and stomped away from them. Too late, Jim realized where she was heading. The transport orb sat in the corner, forgotten until this moment. Zoe chased after her, striking blow after blow, but nothing penetrated.

The world had no idea how much trouble it was in. Only the people in this room knew. Burying his doubts and his questions, Jim focused on what needed to happen right now, and reached toward his sister.

The debris comprising her armor still retained traces of electricity. So, wrapping his will around the hulking thing, he commanded it to dismantle. It resisted. He pushed harder and it resisted again. Then Jim remembered Gloom and all that parahuman energy he'd absorbed and never expended. Could it really work . . . ?

This was no time for theories. Reaching into that place inside him, Jim accessed his Vessel ability and shunted Gloom's energy into his struggle with Summer's armor. The force of his commands multiplied. Her armor began to peel away and fall to the ground like scales. Soon she would be exposed.

And then what?

Jim faltered at the thought.

After putting her back in the cage, this time they'll toss it down a hole she never comes back from. Summer will be gone, for good this time.

He pushed forward. Armor pieces fell like rain around Summer as she fled.

You came here to save her. You still can. She's still in there.

Are you willing to bet the world on that?

Even as he asked it, Jim knew the truth. For him, it wasn't about betting the world. It was about the real reason he held back even now, appearing to give it his all while letting his foot off the gas . . . just enough for his sister to reach the pod with her last layer of armor intact.

Because when he looked at Framework, all he could see was Summer.

Well. I did warn everyone I'm not a hero.

And so Jim stood there, reaching toward her with a trembling hand, ignoring a dozen electrical devices he could bring into the fight. He might even be able to shut down the pod itself before she got away. But as the hatch bloomed open and the last layer of her protection peeled away, Summer leapt into the craft and shut the hatch an instant before Zoe could reach her.

Countless times, Lock had risked her life to save others. Put herself on the line when it meant redeeming those that everyone else had written off. She had never let Jim down, never stopped protecting him.

Now, as the floor opened and the orb dropped away, he held his head in his hands, wondering if he'd just saved his sister or doomed the world.

SEVENTEEN

THE twenty-sided sphere shivered. Clearly, Skypuncher did not appreciate being encased in solid steel. Natalie felt it vibrate down to the molecular level as the hero flexed his power. The metal was already warping.

Then, from the inside out, it started getting hot. *Really* hot.

Yellow beams burst through the surface. The makeshift prison shredded and Skypuncher emerged, his face twisted with rage. He slammed Natalie down once, then again, driving her into the floor while metal plates buckled around her body.

His voice shook with fury. "I'm going to boil your brain."

He focused those glowing eyes on her forehead. Natalie fought to shake loose, but the hero's grip on her throat was unbreakable, and any blow she landed just glanced off him. It was getting harder to breathe.

A chill of panic snaked up her spine. Was she about to die?

The energy in his eyes built to a sizzling crescendo, as if he wanted to savor the moment before vaporizing her face. Natalie cried out, wrenching helplessly at his arm.

Skypuncher's comm blew to pieces. He lurched, the light fading from his eyes. His grip went slack as the remnants of the comm fell from his ear. He wavered, then collapsed on top of her, unconscious.

A sound of relief bubbled up from deep inside Natalie. Sliding out from under the hero's bulky frame, she crawled from the hole in the floor and breathed several sighs in a row. That had been way too close.

Okay, Marble. Okay. You survived.

Barely. But still.

If Jim were here, he'd try to convince her she technically won the fight. Natalie was just happy to be breathing.

She hoped her friends were okay. Her exhaustion didn't matter—she should get back to them. With a groan, she climbed to her feet . . . and stopped short when she saw her reflection in the broken sphere.

Her pants were in tatters, barely clinging to her. She'd lost one shoe. The hoodie was gone, leaving only the old sports bra she'd worn underneath, and one strap was broken. Even for a poor aspiring hero who lived in her car, this was pretty sad.

Her eyes wandered to the FabriKaters. Several were still intact. Natalie tilted her head, a gleam in her eye.

"Hmm."

The glass dome was a shattered mess, pieces strewn across the chamber. Natalie dropped back through the hole her body had created in the ceiling, and crunched down onto the debris. A mass of white and yellow was slung over her shoulder.

"Oh, thank God," Zoe said. "We were just regrouping to come back you up."

"Or at least stand at a distance and yell harsh criticisms until he surrendered," Kelvin said.

They helped her set Skypuncher down next to the unconscious forms of Eli and Arbiter. Then they embraced in a three-pointed hug, a tiny celebration of being not dead yet.

"I can't believe you survived a fight with Skypuncher," Kelvin said. "They should give you a cape just for that."

Natalie gave a tired smile. "I think they're all taken."

"Just one more reason to use Jim's idea—a black cape and a white cape. Right, Eli?" Kelvin glanced over his shoulder. "Oh, right. He's unconscious."

"What happened up there?" Zoe asked.

"I was finished," Natalie said. "But then his comm broke, and he just fell over. Is everyone okay here?"

Quickly, they filled her in on what she'd missed. There was plenty of incredulity to go around. These few minutes had been crazy enough to make the previous day seem like a stroll through a field of daisies.

When they released from the hug, Natalie's friends stepped back and examined her head-to-toe.

"Whoa," Kelvin said. "Sweet upgrade, Marble. Is that duraweave? How did this happen?"

Natalie's cheeks reddened. "Turns out hoodies aren't great in powered fights. But there are perks to almost dying in a FabriKater room." Bashfully, yet proudly, she spun to give them a full view. "You really like it?"

She wore a sleeveless bodysuit, revealing slim yet chiseled arms. The duraweave textile didn't reduce incoming damage like nanomesh did. Its purpose was to survive extreme punishment without taking damage itself—which was how parahumans got through fights without being naked at the end.

Her fingerless gloves were thick across the knuckles. Their style matched the new boots, angular and blocky for someone of her tiny frame, yet somehow appropriate for her powers.

A mask of a similar sharp-angled design covered her face, like a larger and more stylized version of a domino mask. The unusual shape subtly altered the curves of Natalie's face underneath, obscuring her identity for anyone who didn't already know her. It slightly curled up at the ends, suggesting that even her eyes were smiling, which fit her perfectly. If the FabriKater had included standard Spectrum tech, the white eye lenses could shift between thermal and night vision, and act as an augmented reality HUD.

While the design matched her abilities, the color scheme matched the person herself. The mask, gloves, and boots were a soft pink with black piping along the edges. The bodysuit began with a base color of creamy white, but rippled with striations of pale pink, light grayish blue, even sparkly gold, as if the suit was made of marble quarried from the earth. Although the veins appeared random like natural stone, they culminated in a shape across her chest—an upswept mountain peak.

Zoe smiled. "Now you look like the hero you always were."

Natalie returned a grateful smile. "Thanks."

"Right on, friend." Kelvin held up his hand. "Functional fashion five."

They slapped five, sharing genuine if muted laughter. This was a good moment. But the hard moments weren't over.

Jim only noticed all this peripherally, lost in his own thoughts. He sat cross-legged where his sister had spent ten years imprisoned, staring at the fractured floor with his head in his hands, lost in his own thoughts.

Summer had gone Apex. She had become Framework, fought the Spectrum, and ended up here. Then she had slowly overthrown the Lighthouse systems and the heroes' minds, putting events into motion that would bring Jim here to set her free. His sister lived, and he believed the hero was still inside her.

Or, at least, he wanted to believe it. But if Lock was in there, right now Framework was stronger, and her idea of saving the world was global extinction. Because you couldn't feel pain if you were dead—which made perfect sense to a psychopath.

He still had so many questions. What had pushed Summer hard enough to trigger an Apex event? What did the Spike have to do with any of it? Why had the Spectrum kept it all a secret? How did Framework plan to accomplish 'saving the world,' and how long would it take her to do it? When he found her again—

and he *would* find her—would Jim be able to bring Summer back before Framework succeeded? If he failed, would he have it in him to do what was necessary?

The others were still talking, and they had questions of their own. Did Framework really vaporize Lord Neon? Had they just seen a Spectrum hero die? Why had Eli and Skypuncher both collapsed when Zoe destroyed Framework's comm? They were also clearly trying to give him space—he noticed them covertly glancing in his direction but not moving toward him.

They would probably learn the truth about Eli and Lord Neon at some point. He himself only had part of the picture—Eli's claim to actually be Lord Neon, the Spectrum hero being some part of him externally manifested. But even that limited knowledge wasn't his to give away. True, the hero had used Jim's secrets to manipulate him into coming here. In fact, if they survived, he and Eli would be having a tense conversation about that. But Jim considered it a moral victory to make the harder choice and keep the man's secret. He mentally gave himself a weak high-five.

Take that, heroes.

Distantly, he knew his thoughts were bouncing too quickly to settle on anything. Probably to avoid truly processing what had just happened—how a decade of hopes and dreams had been blasted away the moment they collided with reality.

Summer. If he found some way to bring her back, would his next fight be against the Spectrum, to keep them from shoving her in a cage again?

Was that the kind of question that led to becoming a villain?

He broke from his reverie as Zoe and Kelvin and Natalie sat down with him. Each faced him with their own brand of . . . was it sympathy or suspicion?

"So," Zoe said. "I saw what you did back there, letting Framework get away."

Jim tensed.

Kelvin put a hand on his shoulder. "We get it. Whoever she is, family comes first." He considered. "Well, unless family really does turn out to be a world-destroying villain. Then I think it's okay to put humanity first, or at least–"

"The point is," Zoe interrupted. "Framework has to be stopped. But after that—when it comes to protecting the Spectrum from your sister, or protecting her from the Spectrum—we're with you."

Jim stared at them, incredulous. "Really?"

"We're family now, Jim," Natalie said. "Your problems are our problems."

His eyes burned. A lump appeared in his throat. He swallowed down the overwhelming surge of emotion. "I don't deserve you guys."

Zoe smirked. "That's true."

"Sooo, now that we're a family," Kelvin said, glancing between them. "What exactly are we supposed to do next?"

EIGHTEEN

AS the team traveled back up through the Lighthouse, they weighed their options. If Skypuncher went down because his connection to Summer was severed, maybe the other heroes did the same, which meant the Dare contestants were safe now. It was only a theory, but reinforced by the silence they encountered as they progressed through the levels.

They also didn't stumble onto any Dare contestants, which suggested the survivors were staying hidden in case the Spectrum was still out there hunting. Someone needed to tell them what happened, help them regroup and recover.

Then there was Framework, who after a decade of captivity was in the wind. She could be anywhere on the planet, and they had to find her before she "saved" everyone.

"Seems like we have two choices," Kelvin said as they stepped onto a lift. "One, leave the station right now and find a way to track Framework down, then foil her plot. After we figure out what the plot even is. Or two, help here first."

"I like the second one," Natalie said. "Tell everyone the fight's over. Get them together, help the injured."

"Mourn the dead," Zoe muttered.

"Um . . . yeah," Natalie said. "And collect the unconscious heroes. They're victims, too. Someone made them do this."

Someone. Jim noted that she kindly avoided saying who.

You never asked why.

Because I didn't want to know, genius.

"As much as I want to help everyone, and knowing this is a jerk thing to say," Kelvin said. "Can we really spare the time? We're talking about a global threat. Doesn't every moment count?"

"Oh," Natalie said. "I guess that makes sense."

"We can't deal with Framework alone," Zoe said. "We need help to search the planet, and if she won't be reasoned with, we'll need as much power as possible on our side. Anyone who saw the battle in Sydney will understand that. So, there's a reason to start here first. Once they catch their breath, we'll ask them to do what they came here to do."

"Be heroes," Natalie said.

Kelvin mulled it over. "That's a good point."

He still didn't seem completely convinced. The others must have heard the doubt in his voice, because they all turned to Jim, apparently looking for some kind of tie-breaker.

He raised his eyebrows. "Sorry, you're asking *me*? The least objective person on this station?"

He wanted—*needed*—to go for Summer this very instant. But he had just enough presence of mind to know he couldn't make a fair decision.

He blew out a breath. "I will say—and this is only a guess— that after being suppressed for so long, she may need time to recover. But that's a dangerous wager."

"Sure could use Eli right now," Kelvin said ruefully. "Who knew a janitor for heroes could be so wise?"

Jim chose again to stay quiet. Another moral victory. Yay.

"But I see your point," Kelvin continued, looking to Zoe and Natalie. "And I trust you both. So, let's do your thing."

Natalie touched his arm. They shared a look, and Kelvin nodded to some unspoken thing that passed between them.

"So, we're regrouping," Zoe said.

"Right!" Natalie gave an enthusiastic fist pump. "And, um, then what? What kind of mission are we preparing for?"

In the awkward pause that followed, they looked to Jim again. He understood the unspoken question. Was this a mission of mercy, or a march to war? For him, whatever Summer had become, his answer was the same. He just hoped the others would back him up.

Huh. Somewhere along the way, he'd stopped thinking of this as a solo mission. How about that?

"Find my sister," he said. "Bring her home."

"And . . ." Zoe hesitated. "What if we can't? What if Framework won't stop?"

"I mean my real sister," Jim clarified. "Framework may have control, but Summer is still in there. I saw her. I just need to reach her."

They gave a collective nod.

"Okay," Zoe said. "So, we have a plan. Or, the beginnings of one."

His friends shared a private look. Just an instant, but he saw the veiled doubt behind their eyes. They didn't believe it would go the way he wanted, but they were being true to their word and sticking with him. He felt a surge of gratitude. Their doubt was understandable—they didn't really know Summer.

Do you really know her anymore?

Pipe down or I'll make you listen to the entire Michael Bolton discography.

He shoved the dissenting voice away. For Jim, this was not about heroes versus villains. It was not about defeating evil and saving the day.

It was a rescue mission.

"What a dump," Jim said. "Oh, right, we did this."

He had forgotten how intense their battle in the Spark had been, and how much of the Spectrum's command center they'd decimated. That fight felt like it happened a month ago. Had it really only been a day?

They divided duties and got to work. Natalie began clearing an area for the three unconscious heroes, as well as for the others, when they were gathered. Kelvin found a functioning terminal and scanned through news and social feeds across the global meshwork, focusing on anything related to heroes and villains. Zoe approached the Spectrum's round table at the center. Activating the hologram system floating above it, she searched for a way to reach out to everyone on the Lighthouse and sound the all-clear.

Jim found a terminal in a quiet corner and sat down. His job was to think about his sister and come up with some theory about where she might go and how she might begin. She had talked about going back to where it all started, but never explained what that meant. So he would have to bring all his knowledge and insight to bear. It was a bitter twist of fate, being the person who knew a villain better than anyone in the world.

For a while, they worked in relative silence, everyone going about their tasks with grim determination. Jim fiddled with the terminal, performing random searches while the real work happened in his mind. Any other day, this would feel like a peaceful break in the tension. For him, it felt like they'd spent all this time inching up to the edge of a shadowy chasm, and now they were planning how to leap into the darkness.

"Found it," Zoe announced. "I can broadcast through the Lighthouse PA and the Gauge network at once. Everyone ready?"

Receiving no objections, she keyed the system on.

"To everyone still standing, the Dare . . . the Dare is over. But there are no winners. This is not what any of us were told. For years, the Spectrum has kept a villain secretly imprisoned on this station, and everything that happened here was part of their attempt to break free. They succeeded, and have escaped back to Earth." She paused and looked aside, as if gathering her next thoughts. "We'll worry about that soon. Right now, it's likely that all Spectrum and Prism heroes on the station have fallen unconscious. They were controlled by this villain all along through their comm network—manipulated into hunting us. Now it seems that connection is severed. If we're right, then the danger has passed. Eventually, we'll mourn the fallen. For now, we need to regroup and heal who can be healed, then see to the threat that was just unleashed on the world."

Calling up a virtual keyboard, she tapped out a series of commands.

"I'm sending directions and access codes to your Gauges. Those who can, we urge you to join us here in the central command center. Any Bio Controllers with healing powers, you're about to be very popular. If you choose to leave instead, please at least check in so we know you're okay. Those too injured to get here, reach out with your Gauge or phone and help will find you. I'm also sending directions to the infirmary level for those who need to go straight there. When we're back on our feet, we'll talk about what to do next. Right now, the heroes on this station are down, and we're the only ones who know what's going on, which means it's up to us to pick up their slack. We all came here wanting to be like them. Well, now we get our chance, and the stakes are all too real, and–"

She cut off, swallowing hard. Her eyes glistened.

"I know you don't know who to trust. This probably sounds like a trick to flush you into the open so the heroes can hunt you down. All I can do is promise you I'm telling the truth and beg you to listen. *Please*. We need each other, and then everyone's going to need us."

Pushing her shoulders back, she made herself stand straighter.

"I'm Zoe Blake. Some of you know me—you know what I used to be. I'm trying to be something better now. But I can't do it alone. The world needs heroes more than ever, and right now, we're all it's got."

She stopped to consider, and then with a small shrug, she keyed the comm off.

"Wow," Natalie said. "That was, like, bonkers inspiring!"

"You said it, Nat," Kelvin said. "If I could fight, I'd totally be ready for battle now."

Zoe blew out a breath. "I just hope it works."

Jim's terminal pinged. His aimless wanderings through the network had returned a result. He sat bolt upright. "Well, that's not good."

"I tried my best," Zoe said defensively.

"No, not that." Standing, he gestured at the machine. "A bunch of banks just had their electronic funds vanish. It happened all around the world—every country with a major banking system." He set his jaw, looking grim. "It's her. She made her first move."

"But she was never a thief, right?" Natalie said. "Why would she want all that money?"

Kelvin snapped his fingers. "She needs to buy something!" Receiving flat stares in return, he looked down. "You, uh, probably assumed that."

"We'll just have to see what she does with it," Jim said. "Hopefully, we'll have enough time to react."

He hadn't meant it to sound ominous, it just came out that way. The threat wasn't hypothetical anymore. A villain was making moves, and the good guys hadn't even put their pieces on the board yet.

Reluctantly, Kelvin raised his hand. "Hate to pile on, but I just got something, too. I'll send it to the main terminal."

He tapped out commands, transferring his discovery to Zoe at the Spectrum's table, where the team now gathered. As the text and images scrolled through the air, he narrated to give context to what they were seeing.

"Skypuncher blacked out when the comms broke, and we assumed it would be the same with all heroes on the station, right? Well, it wasn't just them." He pointed up at the images. "It seems every Prism hero across the world dropped at the same time. Some were in the middle of missions when it happened. Guys, *all* of the world's most trusted heroes are unconscious and vulnerable, and every bad guy on the planet is hearing about it. We've *got* to rescue them."

He pointed at one particular feed—a cell phone video posted to social media, showing a Prism hero fighting in the middle of a street and then just falling over.

Natalie's voice trembled. "We need to move faster."

"Local heroes and law enforcement will step in, but they're going to need help," Zoe said. "If anyone up here joins us, we'll organize teams and send rescue. If not . . . I guess we'll just do our best."

There was a quiet moment where each privately soaked it in, feeling their own versions of hopelessly overwhelmed. This had already been so much bigger than the four of them. Now the game had multiple boards and they had only a handful of pieces. How could they save the heroes *and* do the heroes' job at the same time?

A ping broke the silence. Zoe received a message. She opened it, scanned the contents, then closed her eyes and pressed a palm to her chest.

"Thank God," she breathed.

Seconds later, she got another ping. Then two more followed, and then the floodgates opened. One after another, they reached out, checking in, organizing help and giving notice that they were on their way.

Zoe had asked for heroes, and they were coming.

She received another ping, a different sound, and it drew her attention. Brightening, she tapped the keys and splashed the system info across the holographic display.

"Full scan results," she said. "Now we know everyone on the station and their current location." Then her brow furrowed and she tapped more keys. "Wait. That can't be right."

But the system confirmed it, and that ominous feeling returned. The Lighthouse had recorded Framework's pod launching, which they had witnessed themselves. It also showed a second pod launching twenty minutes later, but the system couldn't see who was inside it.

The scan also revealed that all heroes and visitors were still on the station, except two. Astro-Ninja, whom they'd barely avoided fighting outside the Reliquary, when he and Heatsink had stopped to interrogate Eli. And Red Plasma.

At that moment, the main doors to the Spark whooshed open. A costumed woman walked in, unconscious bodies slung over each shoulder.

"Heatsink!" Natalie gasped.

Astro-Ninja's partner, a Prism hero, and conspicuously *not* unconscious. There was a scorch mark on the side of her face where a Spectrum comm unit would sit. Which begged a question.

Why was she still awake?

Jim knew he was way too distracted, and this was proof. By the time he thought it, his friends were already springing into action. They formed a line between the hero and the command center and prepared to fight.

NINETEEN

"STOP right there!" Zoe commanded, drawing Dark Sympathy. "Friend or foe?"

"Wait–" Heatsink began.

"I think it's pretty obvious." Natalie's fists became boulders. "Taste rock, hag!"

"Whoa whoa whoa!" The hero raised both hands, then clutched at the bodies trying to slide off her shoulders like potato sacks. She shifted awkwardly to keep a grip on Solstice and Royal Justice. "Friend. I'm a friend."

"That's exactly what an enemy would say!" Kelvin cried.

Natalie was right—this *was* Heatsink. Jim remembered her from nine years ago, when she'd filled a Prism position to replace a fallen hero. That hero had died in Sydney.

Tall, with a sturdy frame, thick black hair and light brown skin, Heatsink wore basically the same costume she'd worn on the day of her induction. The thick, stretchy jumpsuit started out orange on top and faded to white at her boots. Now, standing there with a harried and half-dazed look in her eyes, she seemed far less imposing than when she'd tried to interrogate Eli. She breathed hard, like she'd just finished running a race.

"I won't hurt you," she panted. "I would never, I promise. This . . . this all feels like a bad dream. I remember doing everything, b-but it's all through a fog. It wasn't *me*."

"How are you still awake?" Zoe demanded.

"Can I put them down, please?" Heatsink indicated her passengers.

"Slowly," Jim said.

Heatsink nodded and complied, moving predictably and with no sudden moves. Her eyes never left them as she set her fellow heroes down. "I'm a Thermal Controller. I can move heat around at will. But there's a secondary augment that I don't advertise—a resistance to acute mental attacks. Probably why I didn't go down when the comms blew."

Zoe narrowed her eyes. "You resisted that, but still got controlled?"

"If a psionic attack is quick and sharp, I can usually repel it. Slower, more subtle mental stuff, though? I'm as vulnerable as anyone. I . . . I'm still struggling with what you told us. A villain, here on the Lighthouse for a decade, and the Spectrum kept it secret?" The hero pursed her lips as if knowing how implausible her explanation sounded. She appeared to make a decision, then removed her mask to reveal prominent cheekbones and large brown eyes. "I'm Chinook Siku from Homer, Alaska, a Prism hero for nine years. *I am not your enemy*. And I don't take kindly to having my mind altered. Let me help and I'll take your villain down myself, I don't care who they are."

Jim and Company exchanged looks, gauging how each was feeling. Everyone seemed to relax, which was a strong sign that they believed the hero. Her vibe was solid and her explanations were credible enough. Jim shrugged—if believing her turned out to be a mistake, it would be far from the worst mistake he'd made today.

"Tell us what happened," he said.

Heatsink looked relieved. "When my comm blew, I almost went down, but I managed to shake off the effect. Then I saw three more of us drop, out like a light. But . . . my wingman was there, too, and he seemed unaffected. That puzzled me."

"You mean Astro-Ninja," Kelvin said.

"Yes. It didn't make sense—he has no psionic powers. I asked how he'd resisted, and he attacked out of nowhere. Hit hard, knocked me down and ran. Could this villain still be controlling him?"

The team exchanged another look, this one of dread.

"He's not on the station anymore," Jim said, heavy with implication.

"The sympathetic hero," Zoe said. "The one Framework said gave her that comm unit. Could it have been him?"

Heatsink flinched. "Wait, did you say Frame–?"

"It's no crazier than anything else today," Kelvin said to Zoe. "He helps her escape and then follows in a pod, aimed for wherever she's going. Red Plasma, too."

"Or Red Plasma dropped and Astro-Ninja scooped him up," Zoe said. "We don't know either way."

"Good point," Kelvin said. "So, Framework has at least one friend backing her up, maybe two."

Natalie cracked her stone fists together. "Either way, let me at 'em!" Then she winced, glancing at Jim. "Um, but I'll try to be gentle."

Jim chuckled. "If anyone could punch someone gently, Nat, it's you."

"Hey!" Heatsink broke in. "You're saying my partner might be a traitor working for FRAMEWORK? That's who they've had locked away? FRAMEWORK?!"

Her eyes filled with a frenzied despair, like everything inside her wanted to reject it. Like it couldn't be real. Jim could relate.

"This is impossible." She covered her mouth with both hands as if to hold in a scream. Her chest heaved with heavy, labored breaths. Ironically, she looked like she might pass out.

Natalie's stone fists dissipated as she stepped forward and pulled Heatsink into a hug. She was half the hero's size, yet she got her arms all the way around and held tight.

"Everything sucks right now. I know." She said. "But we're here with you, and we're not going anywhere."

Heatsink hugged back now, clinging hard as tears fell.

"That's it, just let it out." Natalie patted her back, speaking gently. "You're going to need so much therapy after this."

"I hate therapy!" Heatsink cried through the tears.

"I know, I know you do, but that's what big girls do when they need it, right?" Natalie cooed like she was putting a toddler to sleep, rocking gently while rubbing her back. "Sooooo much therapy, biiiiig strong hero tears, it's aaaaaaall okay."

Kelvin stepped up, arms wide, and Natalie folded him into the hug. He gave a contented sigh. "Like mashed potatoes and gravy."

Before they could puzzle out what that meant, more news scrolled across the displays, drawing Jim and Zoe's attention. People everywhere were noticing Prism heroes dropping like flies, and a distinct lack of the Spectrum showing up to save them. They were starting to ask questions. Wasn't the Dare happening on the Lighthouse right now? What was going on up there? Everyone from street toughs to major villains were mobilizing, with local hero teams and special law enforcement divisions gearing up to meet them head-on. Still, the questions would keep coming until the world's most super special heroes made an appearance.

They couldn't worry about that. Publicity and image were a problem for the real heroes when they woke up. As far as Jim was concerned, the Spectrum had earned itself a black eye, whether or not the public knew it yet. And those left standing had real work to do.

"We need to form temporary Prisms *fast*," he said. "Before the power vacuum gets out of control."

"Agreed. Once everyone gathers, we can–" Zoe cut off, pointing at the corner of one display. She lowered her voice so only Jim could hear. "Hey, look at that."

He leaned closer. "More scan results?"

"I told the system to keep running them, make sure we didn't miss anything out there," Zoe explained. "And I expanded the scanning perimeter. Which is how it found *that*."

Jim followed her subtle gesture. When he spotted the new results, his back went ramrod straight. They shared a look, a covert nod, as understanding passed between them. Then Zoe swiped the data to clear it away.

"Deal with it later?" Jim proposed.

She nodded. "I want to see how it plays out first, but I'll make sure we're ready."

When they turned back to the team, Heatsink had mostly recovered and untangled herself from Natalie and Kelvin. Wearily squaring her shoulders, she stood tall with visible effort.

Zoe aimed a look at Kelvin. "Mashed potatoes and gravy?"

"Oh. Heh. I said that out loud." He rubbed the back of his neck, cheeks going red. "Comfort food. That's how the hug felt. It was, uh, nice."

Jim hovered on the edge of teasing the large man. Then he just . . . stayed quiet instead. Was it sympathy for his friend, or did he not have the will to keep the jokes going?

His thoughts drifted back to Summer, as they seemed to every few minutes. Where was she right now? Was she in pain?

"Okay," Heatsink said, wiping her eyes. "How can I help?"

Zoe's eyebrows raised. "You're not taking command?"

Heatsink gave a wan half-smile. "Honey, I just came out of a very long mental occupation by the world's most danger-ous villain. Until I can trust my own thoughts again, I'm letting someone else make the decisions. I know how to contact gov-ernment agencies and law enforcement, and I'll give just enough information to get them mobilized. Apart from that, you tell me what to do." She held up a finger. "One condition—I want to be there when you confront Framework. You guys seem to be running the show, so I assume you'll take that job for yourselves, which means I'm sticking by you until this is over. Agreed?"

Natalie shivered with glee. "Work with a Prism hero? Of course we agree! Right, guys?"

They did agree. Who were they to turn down free help? Then, just as they began to make plans, the main doors whooshed open again.

The Dare contestants had arrived.

Twenty-three. That's how many answered Zoe's summons, each with varying levels of shock and relief. Kelvin and Natalie were corralling them now, dividing them into makeshift Prisms, while Jim and Zoe worked on the big picture. True to her word, Heatsink was reaching out to let authorities know help wouldn't be coming for a while. At least, not the help they expected.

Of those that hadn't come to the Spark, some were dead—more than Jim wanted to think about—several more were recovering in the infirmary, and two had chosen to go home. If only that were an option for all of them. What wouldn't he give to be in Versus right now, prepping for the next service, lining up another disappointing slap fight, polishing the old bar that was his and couldn't be taken away by heroes or villains. At that thought, his gaze shifted to the corner where all the unconscious heroes lay. Sleeping through this felt like a good option, too.

If he ever saw his bar again, would it still feel like the refuge he'd tried to make it? Could anything ever be the same?

"It's not enough," Zoe muttered. She glanced up at Jim, then at the small crowd. "We need more people."

"I'll post an ad on Chadslist," Jim said.

She turned, facing him fully. "Stop that."

"Stop what?"

"Stop pretending you're okay. Not with me, or Nat, or Kelvin. Not after what we've been through together."

Jim wasn't often rendered speechless, but it happened now. He worked to recover. "Um, I'm s–"

"And don't apologize. You're allowed to be screwed up right now. Just be real about it—with us, at least." She held his gaze for a moment. Before he could formulate a response, she resumed working as if the moment hadn't just happened. "What do you think of New Beijinsk?"

"Not bad for a fun weekend, but I'm not sure I'd want to live there," Jim replied. Zoe shot him a look, and he held up his hands in surrender. "Habit. Sorry. Are you asking if my sis–um, if Framework would go there?"

"It *is* the tech Mecca of the world."

She made a good point. Thirty years ago, New Beijinsk had been an unremarkable bay city on the West Coast. Now it was the nineteenth largest metro area in the world. Tech giants had transformed it into the global center for "personal augmentation," a gentile term for cybernetic bio-enhancements. Artificial limbs, synthetic muscle fibers, eyes with multiple enhanced viewing modes, cortical data storage, color-shifting fiber optic hair, even implanted data ports. And that was just the vanilla stuff. Jim suspected it was where Kelvin's Chaos Merchant-sponsored implants had been installed.

Everything even remotely tech-related—including a booming black market for biotech—had grown up around that cybernetic industry, transforming New Beijinsk from a declining port town into a towering neon-lit megalopolis. It was even the home turf of a notable villain, Badland, who leveraged that same tech to create his pet monstrosities, the Turbo-Lizards. Not the worst place in the world for a code-based parahuman to hide.

Except . . .

"If it was anyone but Summer, I'd agree, but she couldn't stand that place. Said being there filled her head with static." As his thoughts turned to the past, Jim gave a wistful smile. "And even if it hadn't, she hated what they did. *Tech should be elegant, Jimmy, like a symphony. What they do is like screaming while banging rocks with other rocks.*"

The memory of his sister—of the bright hope in her eyes even while she rejected the very foundations of that glowing cybernetic city—brought back the feelings of that day like Jim was experiencing them for the first time. Gazing at Summer as she shared her philosophies on what technology should do for humanity, how it should serve and uplift everyone, he had known the world was not ready for her. That one day she would become undeniable.

He could never have predicted how right, and how wrong, he would be.

Zoe brushed his arm. Jim realized then that he'd fallen silent, staring into the distance. He looked down, working to pack those memories and feelings back into the locked box where he normally kept them, more grateful than he could express that Zoe said nothing. She just gave him the moment he needed.

"Hey, sorry to interrupt," Kelvin said, appearing behind them. "But you guys should hear this."

Everyone had gathered around the fallen heroes and a Dare contestant who knelt among them. Eyes closed, she rested one hand on Skypuncher's forehead, the other on Turbula's.

As the crowd pressed together, Jim made the mistake of breathing in deeply. Catching a distinct aroma, he made a face and whispered to Kelvin. "With everyone so close, it's apparent that none of us have showered in a while."

"Whew, you said it, buddy. Let's hope evil doesn't smell us coming."

Jim inclined his chin at the kneeling woman, whose costume and aesthetic practically screamed *I Love Tim Burton Movies*. "Who is that? The spokes-hero for Hot Topic?"

Two Dare contestants standing nearby overheard and laughed. One angled toward Jim.

"That's Grimvision, a psionic," she said. "Her brother's a Prism hero. Darkman or Sadboy or something."

"Gloom?" Kelvin said.

She snapped her fingers. "That's it, yeah."

Jim chuckled. "Apparently, their family has a brand."

"I see it," Grimvision announced, her voice surprisingly high-pitched and elf-like. "A construct made of thought patterns, built to collapse if the comm network failed. A trap for their minds. I can't begin to guess how Framework did this, or how long it took."

So, word had spread, and they all knew that Framework was behind everything. Jim wasn't sure how to feel about that. Right now, he just felt sad.

"I can break them free. I think. But it will take time, and I'll need a quiet place to work." Grimvision opened her eyes. "Leave me here. I'll take care of them."

With that settled, Zoe summoned everyone to join her at the Spectrum's table while Grimvision went about her work. As they gathered, she called up various screens with team rosters and assignments.

"This may not look like much, but it's the best we can do with so few of us," she said. "By dividing–"

"Uh, why is the *villain* in command?" A tall woman demanded in a booming voice. She looked around to gather support. "Who wants to take orders from her?"

Another woman, short and blocky, whirled on her. "*I do.* The heroes are down, and we're facing real villains. I'll take all the help I can get. So you can either shut your soup hole or go home."

Agape, the tall woman made an offended sound and crossed her arms, but didn't move or speak further.

Zoe faltered, hesitant now.

Jim spoke under his breath. "Just take the win, Moxie. You've got a new fan."

She stifled a chuckle, and it seemed to break the spell. Shooting Jim a grateful look, she stood taller as she faced the crowd again.

"Twenty-three of you volunteered. Grimvision is helping the heroes, and Widget has volunteered to act as overwatch, coordinating team actions from here." Zoe nodded to a slim, angular and very pale man, who nodded back. "That leaves twenty-one. We've divided you into teams of three, balancing your powers as much as possible, to create seven Prisms. While there are various mission types, the most critical will be finding and rescuing all the real Prism heroes who've gone down around the globe. Once they're safe, there will be plenty of other fires for us to put out. So I hope you weren't planning on going home anytime soon." She paused. "We may not be sleeping for a while, either. Let's do the big stuff first, then see if we can run in shifts."

Jim cleared his throat and spoke mid-cough. "Ahem-showersfirst-cough."

Zoe considered. "If you need to clean up before heading out, just make it quick. Keep in contact with Widget, ask for backup if you need it, and stay safe out there. We can't afford to lose anyone else."

"What's your team doing?" Zoe's blocky new fan asked.

"We're going after Framework. We'll be following Interruptor's lead to track her down, obviously, but if you need us, you can—"

A man wearing chunky gladiator-type armor made of ice and bone perked up. Vapor wafted from his armor as he raised a hand. "Wait, why *obviously*?"

"Yeah, how is that guy hunting Framework?" another asked. "Who even is he?"

"He's nobody, like the rest of us," someone responded. "He must know Framework!"

Then it all spun out of control, one person's guesses leading to another's deductions, all piling on top of each other until they somehow arrived at the group consensus that they weren't getting the whole story and Jim must be familiar with Framework in some way that made him uniquely qualified to track her down. Which was frighteningly close to the truth. And the questions kept coming.

"How do you know Framework?"

"Why didn't you stop her the first time?"

"Who is she really?"

"Did you know she was still alive? Did you know she was here?"

Zoe grimaced, looking sick to her stomach as she caught Jim's eye. "Sorry. Dumb slip of the tongue."

Jim shrugged. This moment actually ranked pretty low on his list of Things That Suck Today. He couldn't care less what these wannabes thought of him.

Kelvin held up both hands, speaking above the din. "Whoa whoa, hey everyone, just because he's Framework's brother doesn't mean—"

"You're Framework's BROTHER?!"

It felt like eight people shouted that at the same time. Jim just stood there, letting the tide of confusion and outrage wash over him.

"Sorry, buddy," Kelvin muttered. "I'll stop trying to help."

"Don't worry about it," Jim said. "They were going to find out eventually. Heroes are as gossipy as old ladies in a bridge club."

"Hey, leave Ji—I mean, leave Interruptor alone!" Natalie cried. "Yes, Framework may want to destroy the world, but Interruptor's not the same as—"

"She wants to *DESTROY THE WORLD*?!"

At least a dozen people shouted that one simultaneously, followed by another dozen variations of *IS THAT TRUE?* all aimed at Jim. At least they wanted the same answer now, which meant they quieted down after demanding it.

And it was the worst question to end on, because it wasn't about him—it was about Summer. He felt his hackles raise, his defenses going up.

"No, it's *not* true. She doesn't want to destroy the world," he snapped. Then he looked down, knowing what came next and powerless to stop himself from saying it. "Just, um, all the people on it."

There was a pause, a stunned silence. Then twenty-three voices shouted at once.

TWENTY

"**WE** could've handled that better." Natalie cringed. "Sorry, Jim."

Thirty seconds after the accidental revelations, Jim had just turned and walked out of the command center while voices raised behind him. He'd waited in a pod bay, where the team joined him now. They'd calmed the crowd enough to get them back on task, aided by a stern talking-to from Heatsink. Everyone still wanted answers, but had been convinced to put that on hold. There was a crisis to deal with, after all. Heroes, even aspiring ones, were so predictable.

He could hear the sounds of other pods launching now—wannabes racing to save actual heroes while Widget coordinated their efforts.

Jim made a flippant gesture. "Well, it's not like I'm trying to get a job here. You're the ones who have to face your new coworkers on Monday. If we survive."

"I think the whole recruitment thing may be over," Zoe said. "Considering it wasn't the Spectrum's idea in the first place."

"Oh," Natalie said, crestfallen. "Right. I hadn't thought about that."

Kelvin put a hand on her shoulder. "After everything you've done here, they'd be crazy not to recruit you anyway. Just wait, I'll tell them the whole story. Um, after convincing them not to arrest me for working for the Chaos Merchant. And planting unfriendly code in their computer system. And—you know, I'll stop talking now. Come on, Nat, let's get the pod ready."

The two of them moved to the craft, leaving Jim and Zoe alone. They simmered in a moment of quiet tension before she met his eye.

"I really am sorry," she said. "I don't suppose you'd let me blame it on stress and fatigue?"

Jim touched her right shoulder and then her left, as if he were granting a knighthood. "As the king of saying the wrong thing at the wrong time, I dub thee Zoe the Forgiven. May the land prosper under your rule."

Though she didn't smile, her gaze grew warmer. "All this would have gone a lot worse without you here, you know."

Jim began to protest. She didn't let him.

"It doesn't matter why you came here. You stayed. You helped people you don't know, and even people you spent a decade hating. We . . . I . . . won't forget it."

The warmth in her eyes hit Jim square in the chest and spread until it filled him. He felt himself ever so slightly leaning toward her, as if she generated gravity that he couldn't resist. Was it his imagination, or did she lean in, too?

"So, I was thinking." Kelvin approached, blissfully unaware of the moment he'd just killed. "This will be a sensitive subject, but someone's gotta ask. Isn't your sister powerful enough to have a Price? If we could find her off switch, that would be a game changer."

Jim wasn't sure how to respond. Then Heatsink arrived, removing the need.

"True, she probably does," she said. "But finding a high-level para's fatal flaw is hardly an exact science. We don't know how random a Price is, or if it's even random at all. If nothing else works and we have to rely on figuring that out, we're in serious trouble."

The idea weighed heavily on Jim. What if they did stumble onto some inexplicable weakness? Would he be able to use it? Could he watch Summer fall like she was any random bad guy? He shook the thoughts away, once again donning nonchalance like a mask.

"Start with strawberries—they always made her itchy," he said lightly. "Or you could bring her to the movies and make a phone call during the show."

"If anyone does that, I'll take you down myself," Zoe said. "No mercy."

"It's ready!" Natalie called from the transport pod. The silver orb had bloomed open, and she had already strapped in.

The others piled in after her. Nestling into the plush seats, they click-clacked harnesses to lock themselves down for high-speed flight.

Jim was the last. He paused before he climbed in, turning to cast one last gaze over the Lighthouse bay. A feeling swept over him, identical to what he'd felt in Meltzer Park before getting into one of these for the first time. A heavy understanding that once he got in the pod and closed the door, nothing would ever be the same.

"You okay, buddy?" Kelvin called.

Jim stifled an amused grin. At least this time he was going with friends, ragtag as they may be. He'd forgotten what that felt like.

Ooh, tender moment, his inner voice teased. *Would you like warm milk and a blankie before your friends tuck you in?*

Keep it up. I'm this close to signing you up for CatFacts.

You wouldn't dare.

Come on, idiot, give the people what they want.

Jim chuckled to himself. *Fine, idiot.*

"Yeah, all good," he said. Joining them in the pod, he clapped his hands together. "Okay, who's ready to show the world the worst team-up they've ever seen?"

The team gave halfhearted cheers, limp fists in the air.

"Personally, I'm looking forward to marching to our doom," Kelvin said.

"Yeah!" Natalie said. "I hope doom's ready for a black eye."

The orb closed and they shot into space.

As their bodies caught up and their brains stopped rattling around in their skulls, the wraparound screen of the orb's inner surface switched on to reveal the expanse of space and the blue planet beneath them.

Heatsink touched the display, bringing up a navigational interface. "So. If you wanted to find your sister, where would you start?"

The stars filled Jim's vision, a million pinpoints of light, as a memory surfaced.

Eleven Years and Seven Months Ago

Sweat coated Jimmy's face and poured down his back. He'd never fought this hard for this long. His muscles trembled as power raged through him. He would not quit now.

Summer panted. Standing beside him but not seeing him, she was throwing everything she had at this.

Games of Gotcha always ended in seconds, and Summer never lost. Today, though, was different. At the end of their last game, an instant before her actuators closed the trap around Jimmy's electrical pulse, he realized something. They had only ever stated two rules for the game—Jimmy runs, and Summer tries to catch him. They had never said the runner couldn't use every part of the chaser's game board to his advantage.

So now, as he guided his little pinpoint of light through the maze of wires covering the inner surface of the old warehouse, Jimmy didn't just run. He closed Summer's switches behind him, spun them to create new connections, and flicked them open again when they tried to trap his signal.

Summer's code may control the game board, but it was nothing without his electricity. If she wanted to catch him this time, she'd have to get more creative.

"You're getting tired," she said through gritted teeth. "I've almost got you."

"Keep dreaming, Lock," he retorted, knowing full well that she was right. It took everything he had just to keep standing, much less manipulate the game board.

"Give up now and I'll buy you a donut with sprinkles."

"Sprinkles are for winners. I'll buy it myself."

Summer gained ground. He growled, frustrated with himself. She was ramping up the pressure now, changing how and when she flipped her switches, and distracting him with witty banter while she did it. That was the toughest part about dueling with family—she didn't just know his power, she knew everything. Especially his weak spots.

And it was working. They both saw it now—she almost had him. Still, Jimmy ran on, digging deep, hoping to find a new gear.

"Here it comes . . ." Summer whispered.

He whipped around a corner, narrowly avoiding the trap she'd tried to spring, and doubled back. He almost smiled in triumph. Then he realized Summer was holding her breath, which she only did in the moment before doing something big, and his heart lurched.

In getting away, Jimmy had chosen one of the "highway" paths, a long and straight stretch of wires with no detours, which sacrificed maneuverability for pure speed. He'd wanted to put some distance between himself and his pursuer, which would give him more time to make interesting choices at the next junction.

Only, Summer had seen it coming and set a trap. Now, directly in his path, two actuators sparked and buzzed as they snapped closed, effectively destroying a section of the highway and cutting off his only escape. He flipped the pulse around, driving it back the way he'd come, hoping to burst through the next junction before Summer could box him in.

He filled with dread. "No, no, no . . ."

A heartbeat before her trap closed around him, the batteries powering the Gotcha board popped and sparked. The Raspberry Pi computers melted. The whole system died, plunging the warehouse into darkness. A moment later, the emergency light they'd installed flickered on.

"Huh," Jimmy said, trying to hide his elation. "I guess it's a draw?"

Summer chuckled, shaking her head. "You live to fight another day, Lode."

Stumbling over to the ratty couch they'd found, he collapsed onto the threadbare cover and tried to ignore the squeaky springs that poked him. These past few months, they'd scavenged a bunch of random stuff from forgotten alleys or Chadslist ads—like the air popper Jimmy had nailed to a wooden pedestal as their mascot, which Summer had pretended to be annoyed by, but he'd caught her secretly grinning about it. Slowly, they'd made this place into something that felt like a second home. No matter how broken or smelly it was.

He gulped deep breaths, unsure if he should feel relieved or disappointed about his performance. His sister sat beside him, more controlled in her movements, clearly not as spent as he was.

"How . . . how long was that?" he asked.

Summer checked her phone, and her eyebrows shot sky high. "Nine minutes, twenty-two seconds!"

His jaw fell open. "Whoa. No wonder I'm dead."

"Totally."

Despite the fatigue, he swelled with pride. He was learning, growing, getting better and stronger and smarter. Someday, he'd be ready to face a real villain with powers of their own, and he'd make them think twice.

He hoped.

"Although," Summer began, and based on her tone, he knew what was coming. "This went different for a reason. Remember, it's important *how* we play the game. If we don't fight with honor, why should anyone else?"

"But I didn't break any rules," he protested.

She pursed her lips. "Not technically. But if you had won today, could you have been proud of the victory?"

"You bet I would."

Summer's brow furrowed.

"When we're out there facing real bad guys, if I have a chance to win, I'm taking it. If cheating means the villains go away and everyone else goes home safe, I'll take that deal every time. It's like Velocity—they don't give points for who followed the rules best. All that matters is who won."

Wow. He had no idea where that came from. But the more Jimmy said, the more he realized it was what he believed.

"Hmm," Summer said, looking thoughtful. "Well . . . I don't agree. Being a hero isn't just about fighting the villain. We're supposed to set an example, hold ourselves to a higher standard. We can't be beacons of hope if people don't trust us."

"I guess. But what if you could only save a life by breaking the rules?"

"Heroes find a way, Jimmy. That's why so few can do it."

"Highreach," Jim said, feeling a surge of wistful melancholy. He reached for the display. "Old warehouse in the Pendulum district."

As he punched in the details, Zoe slid a small cylinder from the pocket of her sleek encounter suit, no bigger than a lipstick. With a flick of her thumb, she flipped the lid open and began peeling off little circles of what looked like clear tape embedded with circuitry. She offered one to each of them.

"Here, stick this behind your ear."

"Oh, thanks, but I don't typically wear jewelry," Kelvin said.

"In high school, I wore a pinky ring for a week," Jim said as he worked. "Those were dark times."

"They're communicators," Zoe said. "It'll vibrate our speech through your skull bones, and do the same for us when you speak. Even if it's a whisper. Almost silent, untraceable communication."

She offered one to Heatsink, who leaned away, staring at the device like it was a venomous snake.

"It's a closed network, and there's no telepathic element," Zoe explained. "Just normal covert tech. No one's hacking your brain with this."

After a moment's hesitation, the hero accepted the patch and affixed it to the skin behind her left ear. Jim finished directing their ship, then slapped a patch behind his right ear.

"Groovy," he said. "Now if anyone crosses me, I can sing *Black Betty* right into your heads, and there's nothing you can do to stop me."

"Please don't," Heatsink said. "It'll be in my head for a week."

"Don't worry, I'd never be that cruel. I don't even know the real words."

The silver orb reoriented and dropped through the atmosphere. Beneath their feet, a series of gigantic steppes in the southwestern desert raced up to meet them.

As Jim watched them come into focus, he muttered to himself just loud enough to be heard. "Whoa-oh, Black Betty, panda lamp . . . whoa-oh, Black Betty, bramble jam . . ."

Heatsink cringed. "You're the devil."

"Ham or lamb."

Natalie and Kelvin burst into laughter as Heatsink gripped her head in both hands like she was trying to squeeze the ear worm out of her mind. Zoe stared quietly between their feet, her gaze going sharp as the glittering steel of Cloudreach and the dark stone of Highreach came into focus. Twin cities rising from an arid expanse—if your idea of twins came with a healthy dose of irony. Jim figured Zoe was putting on her game face, mentally preparing for whatever they were about to face.

The seven million people in the Reaches were still too small to see. Jim couldn't help feeling that was symbolic—the world's greatest heroes placing themselves so high, they couldn't even see the people they'd sworn to protect. He thought back to Thunderous, the very definition of a street-level hero. Highreach had loved him because they knew he loved Highreach. Little Jimmy Riven had wanted to be him so badly.

What a difference a decade made.

Heatsink fixed Jim with a doubtful look. "You really think Framework is hiding somewhere you'd so easily guess? Wouldn't she expect you to check there?"

"Maybe. Or maybe not. Summer always preferred her popcorn microwaved." Jim chuckled to himself, choosing to ignore the confused looks he got in return. "It was our old hideout, a long time ago. The odds of her being there are low, but not zero, and we have to start somewhere." He tapped the display again. "It's in that corner of–"

The entire screen flashed red. An alert blared.

Jim rocked back, hands up. "Okay, I'm nineteen percent sure I didn't do that."

"Come in, Pod Six," Widget's voice called through speakers hidden in the orb's inner workings. "Do you read me?"

"Got you." Heatsink opened a video window. "We're en route to Highreach."

"Ah. Yes. Well." Widget cleared his throat and pulled anxiously at his collar. "About that . . ."

"Speak your mind, Widget. Time's wasting," Heatsink said.

"Ah. I, um, have need of your team elsewhere, actually. Not far, mind you—just a little hop over into Cloudreach, in the Tenacity district. There's a situation and the other Prisms are too far away to respond."

"We're hunting Framework," Zoe said pointedly.

"I am aware, yes. However, one might describe this situation as, ahem, critical. These particular villains have two Prism heroes and are threatening to, um, you might say they're threatening to kill both if their demands aren't met. Because, well, they *are* threatening to do that. In those words. Nasty business. So distasteful and, might I say, rude."

He seemed genuinely offended. Jim wondered how he'd expected villains to act.

Then he let the words really hit him, and his heart sank. Of course it wouldn't be as simple as shutting out the world while he tried to save Summer. Of course there would be fires to put out and lives to save, and of course there wouldn't be nearly enough help for him to pretend it wasn't happening. Or who was the cause. How had he ever let himself think otherwise? How, after stepping out from behind his bar, had he still believed he could hide? Out of nowhere, a tide of despair rose to smother him.

Hands wrapped around his. Jim looked up.

Natalie. She held onto him with a look of sad understanding. Then Kelvin reached out and wrapped his big hand around hers. Zoe followed, completing their pile-on of comfort.

"We'll find her, Jim," Natalie said. "Summer's our family, too. We just have to make sure there's a world to bring her back to."

"You said it, Nat," Kelvin said. "But talk about a tough choice! Do we save two lives now, or try to save them all? It's the Dare all over again."

"I'd vote for saving all lives," Zoe said, though her tone was soft. "But it's your call Jim. What can you live with?"

Jim grimaced. "I can live happily the rest of my life without another grand moral dilemma, that's for sure."

His frustration was only the emotion simmering on top of a deeper cauldron of disquiet. Not because he didn't know what to do, but because he'd already chosen. He'd chosen the moment Widget reached out, and it made him want to toss himself out of the pod at thirty thousand feet.

Saving heroes before his sister, and going to Cloudreach to do it? *Cloudreach*? Ugh. Talk about a double insult. Yet, just like the rescue on the Lighthouse, it seemed Jim could not stop coming back to Summer's words from all those years ago.

"We can't afford to lose good people from this world. Not even one."

He gave a deep, resigned sigh. "Don't tell anyone I did this, okay? It's bad for my brand."

"Of course," Kelvin said, grinning. "You're not a hero, you're just riding with them."

"Like a carpool," Natalie agreed. "But for saving the world."

Zoe just nodded, projecting quiet support.

Heatsink eyed them all. "You guys are weird."

"Hey," Natalie said. "We're *quirky*. It's why we're so lovable."

TWENTY ONE

"EAT LEAD, PIGS!"

Officer Ramos ducked behind a portable barrier as machine gunfire slammed into the concrete. And the pavement around him. And the building behind him. He leaned around the barrier to return fire with his laughably inadequate handgun.

"WHO WANTS TO DIE TODAY?"

More bullets poured from the second-floor windows of the office building across the intersection. The barrier rocked and juddered under the assault. He thought he heard something crack inside it. Those machine guns packed a punch—he got the feeling his protection wouldn't hold out much longer.

Ramos looked side to side. His fellow officers were pinned down, the enemy showed no signs of slowing, and SWAT was still eight minutes out. If they didn't get heavier backup, or the ransom these villains demanded, he feared for the Prism heroes they held hostage. And who knew what they would do to everyone trapped in that building?

A missile flew by overhead with a loud *whoosh*. Half a block away, his squad car exploded. A second missile decimated the car beside it, then a third took out the police transport van.

This intersection was becoming a war zone, and all Ramos could think was, "My lunch was in that car."

A new voice screamed from the second-floor windows. "FIVE MORE MINUTES AND LITTLE FRACTAL IS DEAD!"

Ramos shook himself, forcing his thoughts back on task. They couldn't just hold here and buy time. Someone had to do something. Gripping his pistol in both hands, he took a series of quick breaths, psyching himself up to dive into the line of fire. Maybe he'd make it across the intersection. Maybe he could–

A sonic boom shook the air. From high above, a Spectrum pod shot from the sky like a bullet and stopped inches above the ground. Wind blasted from it in all directions. Ramos held up an arm to shield his face from dust and debris. When he lowered it, he could see his reflection in the orb's surface. It was so close, he could almost touch it.

A small orb popped out of the larger one and bounced into the intersection. The sphere unfolded, and a translucent energy shield bloomed across the road. Bullets rebounded off its glow with muffled pops and pings.

Ramos sighed in relief. Finally, the heroes had arrived. Everything would be okay.

The orb opened to reveal a hero he'd never seen before—a man with brown hair and a dark blue jacket. He waved at Officer Ramos.

"Hello, sir," the hero said. "We've been trying to reach you about your car's extended warranty."

"What did you say?!" a woman's voice barked from inside the orb. "Ugh, just move aside. Idiot."

The man lurched and disappeared, replaced by a familiar hero.

"Fill us in," Heatsink said. "We'll do what we can."

"Laughter relieves stress!" the man in the blue jacket called defensively.

"Right," Ramos said, collecting himself. "Right. So, that building is owned by Surefire, the armored truck company. Bottom floor's a garage, the next three are offices. From what we've gathered, a team of offenders decided to avoid banks and rob the truck depot itself."

A brunette in a red-eyed mask appeared. "Is there any money in the trucks while they're here?"

Ramos smirked. "Nope."

A large man in a domino mask crowded the opening. "Ah, so these aren't the smart kind of villains."

"I'm guessing not," Ramos said. "But they're packing serious heat."

"Don't worry, so are we!" a small Asian girl said, brandishing tiny fists. "We've got this."

"They're holding two Prism heroes. Fractal and Anvil, I think." Ramos pointed at the second story of the building. "When there was no cash in the trucks, they started ripping through everything, eventually went up to the Surefire offices. That's when the heroes got here. But then they dropped cold, and now these guys want ransom as their new payday."

"Civilians?" Heatsink asked.

"Word is they all moved to the top floor and stayed hidden. But if these guys don't get what they want . . ."

"Who's in there?" the red-eyed brunette said.

"Man in a powered suit. Two bodybuilder-looking women we're just calling Lady Rambos. They're the screamers with the big guns."

As if to punctuate the statement, missiles exploded across the energy shield.

"CASH OR BLOOD, PIGS!"

"Well, they seem fun," the man in the blue jacket said.

"They have a leader," Ramos continued. "Little man, calls himself Grizzly. Not sure if he's a para or just wants a tough moniker."

"What about ULTRA?" Heatsink said.

The Ultimate Threat Response Alliance—a joint task force built specifically to deal with parahumans and street villains.

Ramos shook his head. "Got their hands full. SWAT's coming, but slowly."

"Got it," Heatsink said with a curt nod, like this was just another day at the office. "Thanks, we'll take it from here."

"Great. How do you plan to–?"

The pod closed. Then it shot back into the sky.

"Hey!" Ramos called after it. "Where are you . . . ?"

"You've gotta admire their determination to make that acronym work," Jim said. "I mean, someone *really* wanted to name a team ULTRA."

Heatsink glared at him. "Extended warranty? Really?"

"Hey, we all saw them blow up the guy's car. Now he has to take the bus home after a firefight. Sue me for offering a little hope."

Shaking her head, Heatsink turned to Zoe. "You're plotting an approach?"

Zoe nodded, tapping the screen. "From a direction they shouldn't see us coming. Hopefully. Beyond that, I don't really have a plan yet. Don't know these villains, and we won't know the situation until we're inside."

"About that . . ." Kelvin said.

"Smash 'em all!" Natalie cut in. "That's my plan."

"And that's why Smashers don't make the plans," Heatsink snapped.

"Guys!" Kelvin broke in. "Um, I have an idea."

"Keep going, slow and easy," Zoe said under her breath. "Looks like it's working."

Jim heard her clearly, thanks to the comm patch. Peering over her right shoulder, with Natalie doing the same on her left, he watched the screen on Zoe's forearm. She had sent thumb-sized drones through the ducts, and now they watched the enemy through vent grates from multiple angles. While the three of them waited for the right time to move, Heatsink crouched nearby with her palms pressed against the floor and a tight look of concentration on her face.

After vertically dropping their pod to the Surefire rooftop, they had quietly made their way down to the third floor. Now the villains were beneath them, showing no signs of awareness that they had company. The energy shield on the street was still active, so they likely assumed the team was out there. Clearly, these weren't the brainy type of bad guys. But that didn't mean they weren't dangerous.

The villains were slowing down now, eyelids drooping as if they'd all grown sleepy. In the front office with the blown-out windows, Yasi and Yandi—the Cuban "Lady Rambos" whom Zoe had recognized as enforcers for hire—had stopped shoot-ing at the street and now swayed like they were ready to col-lapse.The stocky Indian man in the powered exoskeleton, whom Jim had dubbed Mecha-Guy, stood as if the armor was the only thing holding him upright.

The only one who seemed unaffected was Grizzly, a slim man with rust-colored hair and freckles. His wardrobe—tan chinos and a striped button-up shirt—suggested *file clerk* more than *murderous villain*. As if he'd been working in an office yesterday, and today had decided to make a drastic career change.

Grizzly was the only parahuman. Yasi and Yandi and Mecha-Guy had no green orb inside them. They were normals, powered only by what modern science could provide. Probably synthetic implants and tremendous quantities of steroids for the ladies, and several degrees in engineering for the gentleman.

None had any idea that Heatsink was above them, extracting the heat from their bodies. It was slow going, but that had been necessary to keep them from noticing the effects, and to give Kelvin time to work.

"Ready for a distraction," Kelvin whispered into their heads.

"Coming up," Jim said.

Phone in hand, he opened the remote interface tethered to the transport pod and sent instructions. The orb moved to hover in front of the building, in full view of the villains.

"Smile, jackass," Jim muttered.

Its surface plates undulated, emitting a bright flash and a loud vibrating pulse that rattled the building. Two more followed in quick succession.

"Stay alert!" Grizzly shouted. "I think they're scanning us."

"I'm ready," Kelvin whispered. "Go anytime."

Sharp, angular stone grew over Natalie's arms up to the shoulders, where it formed thick pauldrons. Her eyes flashed with anticipation. Jim focused on the video feed for Mecha-Guy, whom he'd be challenging soon.

Zoe glanced at their babysitter. "Heatsink, say when."

"Almost," the hero said. "I've almost got them. Just a little more . . ."

On the screen, Mecha-Guy's head lolled back and his mouth hung open. Only his eyes were moving, and they were growing glassy and lazy. Then the display on his augmented reality visor changed, and his gaze sharpened.

Jim tensed. Mecha-Guy's armor was responding to whatever that visor had seen. Its power flowed differently now, glowing brighter in his senses.

"Something's wrong," Jim said. "Go now."

"No, wait," Heatsink said.

"Now!" Jim insisted.

"You don't give orders, you ridic–"

Below them, Mecha-Guy spun and aimed a cannon at the ceiling. With a loud *fizzzzzz-choooooo* he fired a sizzling energy beam that pierced through and struck Heatsink full-force in the chest. With a guttural cry, she flew up to crash into the ceiling, then dropped in a heap amid falling debris.

"Heroes above!" Mecha-Guy shouted.

With Heatsink down and her thermal-leech effect dissipating, the villains woke up. And they were not happy about it.

TWENTY TWO

THEY made sure that Heatsink was still breathing. Then Natalie smashed a hole through the floor. Half the plan was already in shambles, so they went with the standard hero Plan B.

Punch the problem until it went away.

Natalie dropped through the hole. Zoe deployed her mask and goggles and followed. Jim went last. One by one, they scattered as they hit the floor below, aimed at their chosen quarries.

Dashing left, Jim reached a mid-sized private office just as Mecha-Guy filled the doorway. The villain's visor flashed red, targeting Jim, and he took aim with his beam cannon. Jim dove forward, somersaulted, and slid through the enemy's augmented legs. He scraped fingertips across the exoskeleton as he moved past it, and visions of the machinery's internal workings began to assemble in his head.

While sliding into the office behind Mecha-Guy's back, Jim expanded his senses. Gripping every cable, conduit, and electrical wire within his radius, he flexed and *pulled*. They burst through the walls and ceiling to wrap around the villain's arms and legs and yank him back into the office, away from the other fights.

"Ah-ah-ah, why leave when we're just getting to know each other?" Standing, Jim beckoned to the villain. "Let's have a chat."

With a nerdy, semi-intimidating growl, Mecha-Guy ripped his suit free of the bindings and smacked his fists together.

Zoe had barely hit the floor when she started running. The corner office facing the intersection had gone quiet, nothing explosive flying at the cops, which meant the sisters had likely heard the armored guy's warning and were preparing to respond. Zoe wouldn't give them the chance.

Reaching the doorway, she placed a foot on the doorjamb and kicked off. Instead of entering the office at normal height, she absorbed a rush of Aethyr and leapt.

"KILL IT KILL IT KILL IT!" Yasi cried.

The twins swept massive assault rifles back and forth in a frenzy, filling the air with red hot lead tipped with burning magnesium.

"DIIIIIEEEE!" Yandi screeched.

Zoe flew up with blinding speed, almost phasing from one point to the next, then pushed diagonally off the ceiling and bounced off the nearest wall. Her feet touched down just long enough to flip forward. As she passed mid-leap between the twins, she flicked her wrists. Thumbnail-sized devices attached magnetically to the assault rifles and emitted a high-pitched whine, red lights blinking.

"What the–" Yandi began.

As Zoe hit the ground and rolled up to her feet while spinning to face the enemy, she triggered the devices. With a *whine-thunk-POP*, they emitted a focused arc of energy and sliced the rifles in half.

"That was my favorite gun!" Yasi said, angrily throwing the two halves away.

"*Our* favorite gun," Yandi added.

The twins stood side by side and glared at Zoe, forming a wall of augmented flesh between her and the door. They towered over her on tree-trunk legs, veiny tattoo-covered arms so muscled they could barely fit through the armholes of their tactical vests. They drew identical weapons—wicked serrated knife in one hand, oversized .50 caliber handgun in the other.

Yandi spat on the floor at Zoe's feet. "We'll taste your blood for that."

Grinning, Zoe cracked her neck.

"If you stop now, we could be friends," Natalie said. "Why don't you just surrender? I really don't want to hurt you."

Grizzly smirked. "You must be new here."

He cracked his knuckles slowly, ominously, one by one. Coming from him, the move was not intimidating. At all.

They stood in the open center of the office space, demolished desk and cubicle debris shoved to the side in piles. Sounds of fighting echoed from the smaller perimeter offices around them. Natalie's friends had engaged their targets.

But this fight was hers. She would do it her way. "I kind of think you're already losing. Won't that damage your street cred? But if you *choose* to stop . . ."

"Not stopping until I've got my money." The villain jabbed a thumb over his shoulder, indicating something behind him. "Or until these Prism fools are dead. It's one or the other, honey, your choice."

Now Natalie's look of sympathy became a sly grin. "What Prism fools?"

Grizzly gave a derisive chuckle, as if she were an idiot and he knew something she didn't. Then he glanced over his shoulder and his arrogance turned to alarm.

"No!" he cried.

Anvil and Fractal, the unconscious heroes he'd kept bound and gagged in a corner that he alone guarded, were gone.

"*NOOOO* where are they?!"

Natalie giggled. "Oops!"

The villain loosed a wordless bellow, high-pitched and weak at first. Then it deepened, becoming a resonant growl of destructive hunger. Natalie's laughter turned to horror as the small man multiplied in size while sprouting razor-sharp teeth and thick, smelly fur.

The moniker suddenly made sense as Grizzly completed his transformation into a twelve-foot-tall, eight thousand pound dire bear with six-inch steel claws. With a roar that chilled Natalie to the bone, he charged.

Jim leapt, then dodged, then leapt again. The movements weren't driven by his powers, but being a parahuman did boost him physically beyond normal people, and the enemy inside that battle suit was normal. And, for someone smart enough to build that contraption, not so clever.

Mecha-Guy blew holes in what had probably been a nice office, trying to put at least one of those holes in Jim. Though he struggled against the constant waves of building parts that burst through the walls and flew up to impede him.

Jim kept moving to buy himself time. Faced with a unique piece of unfamiliar one-off tech, he needed to watch and feel how it worked, give his senses a chance to map the power flows. Then he would make his move.

"Stand still!" Mecha-Guy shouted, blasting wildly.

"No, thank you!" Jim slipped past an energy beam, which shattered the last remaining window and flew into the sky.

That's it, almost there. Just keep coming at–

The villain's chest plate popped open to reveal four small missiles. Jim's eyes widened—he had missed those. The first missile fired at his face.

As he fell back, the world seemed to move in slow motion. His parahuman senses concentrated into a tight beam of awareness and met the projectile in mid-air, enveloping it. The explosives inside had armed the instant it launched. He could feel power racing between targeting and guidance and propulsion, the system locked onto him like a bloodhound.

With all his focus trained on it, in a blink Jim knew the missile as if he'd built it himself. So he knew if power surged through the starboard thruster, and the onboard computer shut down for an instant and had to reacquire a target, the arc of its new flight path combined with rebooting systems would result in something like *this*.

Halfway to Jim, the missile veered back the way it had come, acquired the nearest hot target, and impacted Mecha-Guy's chest plate. All four missiles detonated. With a cry, he blasted backward and through the wall into the next office, burying halfway into the floor.

He refused to stay down, pulling himself out of the floor crater and stumbling to his feet. Jim felt a grudging respect for the tech nerd's grit, and the build quality of his machine. Not every battle suit could take that kind of hit and keep going. It sparked and lurched and some plates fell away, but still.

Jim stepped through the hole in the wall, adding a bit of theatrics by pointing ominously at his foe.

Mecha-Guy seethed. "You . . ."

He raised the beam cannon and fired. Jim made his mechanical knee joint buckle. The suit lurched and the shot went wide.

"You have . . . grr, you have no idea . . ." The villain yanked at his knee, but the machinery locked and wouldn't straighten. ". . . no idea who you're dealing with! I am . . . I am . . ." Making a fist, he punched the knee joint until it pounded back in place, just in time for his gauntlet to fall to pieces. "I am the Machine King!"

Stopping short, Jim adopted a reverent gaze full of fake wonder. "Oh, your highness! Please forgive your humble subject. I beg for mercy and offer a gift."

Holding out an open palm, Jim wrapped his power around the armor. Then he made a fist.

Mecha-Guy's battle suit peeled off his body like an onion. Suddenly under his own power, the villain dropped to his knees. He rattled his head as if to clear away stars. Then he surprised Jim again by screaming in rage and standing with his fists up.

Jim stepped back and his opponent's swing went wide. "You're determined, I'll give you that." He moved aside and a poorly telegraphed kick hit only air. Mecha-Guy kept coming, an odd combination of furious and awkward.

"I do have somewhere else to be, though," Jim said, breezing past blow after attempted blow. "So we need to finish this. Sorry for what's about to happen."

Mecha-Guy threw yet another punch. Instead of dodging, Jim commanded broken plates of armor to wrap around the villain's arm and lock it down. He tried swinging with the other arm and Jim did the same again, effectively placing both of the enemy's arms under his control.

With a gesture, Jim commanded Mecha-Guy's right hand to smack himself in the face. Then he did the left hand, then the right again, knocking the villain's head side to side.

"Hey, stop hitting yourself," Jim said, delivering smack after smack. "You did a half-okay job here. It just wasn't your day. Please, as a favor to me, stop hitting yourself."

Mecha-Guy stared in wide-eyed confusion between his hands and Jim and then his hands again. The smacks continued until he dropped to the floor, toppled over, and didn't move. Under Jim's command, the remaining shards of armor locked around the villain's body and dangled him outside for the police to recover.

"You know," Jim said with a parting glance back at his foe, who swayed helplessly in the breeze. "Now that I think about it, I'm not actually that sorry."

Zoe flowed like water between flashing blades and flying bullets. Battle joy glimmered in her veins as she became impossible to touch, her enemy snarling in frustration as they racked up miss after miss. She wielded no weapon, fighting instead with speed and precision and batting blade thrusts aside with the lightly armored gauntlets of her slim encounter suit.

The Lady Rambos were tough and experienced and augmented about as much as a normal person could be. But they had never fought Moxie.

"Kill her!" Yandi barked.

"Shut up, I'm trying!" Yasi retorted.

They struck simultaneously.

Zoe grabbed Yasi's knife hand and Yandi's gun hand and pulled them together. The point of Yasi's blade jammed into Yandi's gun barrel just as she pulled the trigger. The twins yelped as Yasi's knife tore from her grip and Yandi's gun warped and cracked.

Leaping up, Zoe came eye-to-eye with the monstrous twins and executed a 360 split kick, whirling like a helicopter. Her boots smashed into their faces and their heads rocked like speed bags. They stumbled back from her, dazed.

In mid-air, Zoe produced two glass spheres the size of golf balls, transparent except for a mottled purple liquid in the center. It was time to end this, and as juiced as the enemy was, tranquilizer darts would likely do nothing. So she sent a small electrical pulse through her gloves and into the spheres, and the liquid center began to swirl.

"Catch!"

She flung the spheres like her arms were slingshots. The glass shattered across the twins' torsos and the purple liquid expanded, enveloping them and becoming thicker and denser by the second. By the time Zoe's feet hit the floor, the liquid had turned solid, encasing the Lady Rambos up to the neck in blueberry-colored tactical foam.

For anyone but a parahuman, the Violet Beauregarde Bomb was unbreakable. The twins would not be going anywhere, anytime soon.

Yasi bared her teeth as if they were fangs. "Aaaarrrrrggggh, I'll bite your face off!"

Zoe turned, about to leave them for the authorities, when all that movement from Yasi made something glint in the light. Whirling, Zoe climbed up the foam like a spider until she was face to face with the villain.

"That's right, come get some, you-*hurk*!" Yasi cut off as Zoe gripped her chin and twisted her head to the side.

Zoe loomed closer until she could smell the enemy's awful breath. Her goggles flared a brighter, angry red. She adjusted her mask's voice modulator and spoke with a menacing growl, like a serrated blade cutting through bone.

"I like your earrings," she said, using her free hand to relieve the woman of the little diamond starbursts dangling from her lobes. "Now they're my earrings."

The giant woman screamed in her face. Chuckling derisively, Zoe leapt to the floor and pocketed her prize. She left her vanquished foes behind without looking back.

Natalie fell back, overcome by primal fear as Grizzly smashed the floor at her feet and the ceiling overhead, swinging massive arms and claws wildly to pulverize everything in his path. Wide-eyed, the young girl forgot for a moment who she was and what she could do.

"Please stop!" she cried.

"WHERE ARE THEY?!" the dire bear roared, rattling her teeth and chilling her blood.

He struck toward her. Natalie reacted too slowly and caught the full blow on her left flank. The force spun and flipped her like a rag doll. A half-standing cubicle ripped to pieces as she flew through it and hit the floor with a resounding crack.

Clutching her side, Natalie worked to catch her breath. It was clear now why Grizzly didn't need other parahumans on his crew. Not when he could do this.

A shadow fell over her. She cringed away, feeling a rush of shame along with the panic she couldn't shake. The villain brandished his claws, rumbling guttural threats.

Then Natalie glanced down at herself and noticed something. Where Grizzly had delivered that massive blow, there was now a hairline scratch in her brand new costume.

Her jaw clenched. The world flashed red.

Grizzly drew back and delivered what he must have thought would be the final blow. But as Natalie remembered who she was, Marble reached up and caught the villain's hairy fist.

She squeezed. He cried out in shocked agony.

Regaining her feet, she sprouted a thick layer of armor— black stone veined with red that almost seemed to flash with internal light. She took that sizzling red fury inside her and pushed it outward. The armor grew, layer after layer of parahuman-powered battlestone enveloping her until her size matched her enemy's. Then it was Grizzly's turn to fall back with fear in his eyes.

She still clutched his fist. Twisting his giant arm until he cried out, Natalie raised her other fist, sprouted thick studs across the knuckles, and struck like a thunderclap.

"YOU! DON'T! SCARE! ME"! She hit him again, then again, and again, punctuating every word with a follow-up blow. "AND! YOU! SMELL! REALLY! BAD!"

She let go and Grizzly stumbled away, stunned and swaying like he might collapse at any moment. Drawing back as far as her arm would go, Natalie gave a final earsplitting shout. With all that mass and power concentrated at the end of her fist, she hit like a falling mountain.

Every window on the second and third floors shattered. Grizzly flew back to crash through a wall, then another, and dropped to the street below with an echoing thud. He lay unconscious at the feet of the SWAT team that had just arrived.

Jim had ended his own fight in time to see how Natalie ended hers. Now, as he approached cautiously, her armor receded until only the young girl remained. She was breathing hard, fists clenching and unclenching. There may as well have been cartoon steam rising from her.

She noticed Jim and fixed him with an intense stare. "He scratched my costume."

He nodded, quietly filing that away in his *Things to Never Do* box. "I get it. One time, a guy on the train stepped on my favorite shoe, and I glared at the back of his head for the entire ride. He probably never got over that."

For a moment, she just stared at him. Then she giggled and her eyes calmed.

"Wow, Nat," Zoe called through the series of holes in the wall. Standing at the ledge that Grizzly had flown over, she peered down at the street. "I bet his mother felt that hit."

"Whew," Natalie said. "I've never fought a giant bear before. What a day, right, guys?"

"Tell me about it," Kelvin said.

In the far corner of the office, where the prone forms of Fractal and Anvil had disappeared from, Kelvin reappeared. As did the two Prism heroes. They had never moved at all. The team gathered around them now, collectively recovering while Jim used the remote interface to call the transport pod to pick them up.

"Great work, buddy," Natalie said, playfully slapping Kelvin's shoulder.

"Heh. Thanks, Nat. Who knew avoiding fights at all costs would come in handy?"

Zoe's mask folded back to reveal a wry grin. "If this were the old days, Kelvin, I would've hired you by now. We could have retrieved some fun–"

Heatsink burst into the room and moved toward Zoe as if preparing to strike. Zoe whirled toward her, hands up. The hero reached for her, then at the last moment turned and gripped something unseen.

Someone gasped, but it seemed to come from nowhere, in a voice Jim didn't recognize. Then Heatsink's body tensed and the unfamiliar gasp became a cry.

The air between the hero and Zoe shimmered. A woman appeared, wrapped head to toe in iridescent material. She held a long black stiletto in her hand, poised inches from Zoe's neck, stopped only by Heatsink's grip on her arm.

A stealth assassin. Dread crept up Jim's veins. They had let their guard down and nearly paid the price.

"Not today, villain," Heatsink said. "Not any day ever again."

The assassin's arm went stiff, coating with frost from the elbow to the tip of her stiletto. Heatsink gritted her teeth and tightened her grip and the assassin screamed. Then her weapon shattered. Then her arm shattered up to the elbow. They dropped to the floor in icy chunks, so deeply frozen that they crumbled to powder on impact.

Heatsink's free hand was glowing now, as if she'd shunted the absorbed heat into it. Twisting, she thrust her open palm at the assassin's chest and fired all that heat and radiance in a concentrated burst. The assassin tumbled away and lay face down, unconscious.

The hero slapped her hands together, casually brushing off icy dust while four sets of bewildered eyes stared at her.

"I . . . I didn't know heroes would do that," Zoe said, slightly breathless.

"How *did* you do it?" Natalie said, wide-eyed.

"Thermal vision," Heatsink said. "I saw her heat signature through the cloaking field."

"Hmm," Kelvin said, tapping his chin in thought. "But you didn't see us on the Lighthouse, when you and Astro-Ninja questioned Eli. Interesting."

"What do you mean? How do you know about that?"

"We were there. Like, within arm's reach. I just made us invisible and prayed it would hide us enough."

Heatsink gave him a reappraising look, tinged with respect. "Your power must block infrared light, too. Impressive. Most can't do that."

"I . . . um, thank you," Zoe said. "I think you just saved my life."

"You'd make a killer bartender," Jim said. "If the hero thing doesn't work out, I'll hire you. *Come to Versus for the coldest drinks in town.*"

"I'll keep that in mind," Heatsink said.

"I promise mediocre pay and all the chicken fingers you can . . ."

Jim trailed off. Something was approaching. A wrongness that he'd felt faintly in the distance without having realized it, a growing itch in the back of his mind. But now, whatever it was, it was here.

The world lurched, turning on its side. Jim felt his knees hit the floor. Someone asked if he was okay, but the voice was too muffled to identify. Jim realized then that the world around him hadn't moved—only he had. But something about the world had changed. A slow-moving wave had come from over the horizon and enveloped them. And with sinking dread, he knew the source. The signature was as familiar as his own hand.

"Summer . . ." he breathed.

"What's wrong, Jim?" someone said.

As the moment passed and Jim's senses recovered their equilibrium, he blinked hard and lifted his head. His friends came into clear view again, their eyes radiating concern. He wished he could reassure them. But that might not be possible anymore.

"Window," he said. "I need a window."

They helped him up, then followed as he stumbled into one of the broken perimeter offices. The floor-to-ceiling windows had blown out, giving an unimpeded view of the street below and the next few city blocks. Beyond that, the buildings rose higher and blocked further view. But this was all Jim needed to pair sight and sound with what he'd felt inside.

He pointed up. "The drones."

Police drones—a routine sight over the Reaches—were all gathered in formation and flying away in the same direction.

He pointed east, two blocks away. "The crane."

A large, unmanned construction crane had pulled away from a half-built office building, and was now rolling down the street while workers dotting the exposed steel frame called after it in confusion. The crane moved in the same direction as the drones.

In the intersection below, SWAT radios were going haywire, squealing and skipping across channels until they just turned the devices off. Then they switched themselves back on.

"What's happening?" Natalie said.

"I have a feeling Framework is happening," Kelvin said.

"So, she *is* here, somewhere close," Heatsink said.

"No. This is happening everywhere." Jim glanced at Zoe. "Can you call Widget?"

She nodded, then tethered her forearm screen to the transport pod and bounced a signal up to the Lighthouse. Widget appeared, looking strained and harried, and began to fill them in.

"The effect is sweeping across the planet like a wave," he said. "All sorts of devices are just sort of *waking up* on their own and doing stuff. Picking up materials and then gathering. Some are building things—we have no clue what yet—while others are occupied with tasks we haven't figured out. Many of these machines aren't designed to be autonomous, yet they appear to be making their own decisions."

"She's building something," Zoe muttered, heavy with dread.

"So much for needing recovery time," Jim said.

"When it comes to Apex paras," Heatsink said. "Forget everything you know."

Jim worked to manage his own dread. There was something he needed to ask, though he wasn't sure he wanted the answer. "Widget, where did the wave originate?"

"Near as I can tell, central Sydney."

You don't have to ask anything else. It doesn't have to be you.

He asked anyway. "What's happening there?"

"Basically, all the heavy construction equipment for miles is gathering at Hyde Park. They knocked down that big, ugly wall, and they're building something new."

"You mean they're building around the Spike."

Widget hesitated, seeming reluctant. "Well, um, essentially, yes. Sorry."

So, this is what Summer had meant by going back to where it all started. Jim felt more than one hand on him—his friends offering comfort.

"There's more," Widget said.

Jim's shoulders fell. "Of course there is."

"Local heroes and ULTRA squads are on scene, and it seems there is a growing crew of . . . let's say *unsavory types* surrounding Hyde Park. From low-level street toughs to known villains, they're forming a perimeter to keep everyone away. We'd need a considerable force to even think about punching through."

"All the money that disappeared," Natalie said. "It wasn't for what she's building. It was to hire protection for it."

"How could you know that?" Heatsink challenged.

Natalie looked down. "It's what my family would do."

Heatsink looked on the verge of making her explain further. Jim broke in. "I think you're right, Nat. The Summer I knew wouldn't leave anything to chance. She saw everything like a game board in four dimensions."

"So, what are the machines building *here*?" Kelvin asked.

Jim shrugged. "There are hot spots of electrical activity out there. Mostly, I can feel them gathering in Meltzer Park. But I have no clue what she's building. We didn't exactly talk about this stuff at family dinner."

"And we don't know why she made the Spike in the first place, so we have no clue how she's going to use it now," Zoe said.

Jim shook his head. "She didn't make it. Summer told me that on the Lighthouse, right after . . ." Right after he set her free, though he couldn't bring himself to say it. "It was already there when her Prism went to Sydney."

"Wait, is that true?" Kelvin turned to Heatsink. "Then who did make it? What for?"

Heatsink just looked at him, her face a blank mask.

"She won't tell you," Jim said, looking sidelong at the hero. "Summer wouldn't even tell me."

"You've been lying to the world all these years?" Natalie said, sounding hurt.

"We didn't tell the world anything," Heatsink countered. "We just let you all believe what you wanted, and everyone chose to believe Framework created it."

"If she didn't put the Spike there, why go back to it?" Zoe asked. "What is it to her?"

Doubt crept into Heatsink's impassive mask. "I don't know."

"Too bad we can't study it, figure out why it matters to her," Kelvin said. "Too late for that now, obviously."

At that, Heatsink's determination seemed to crack. Sighing, she looked down, then nodded to herself as if she'd just made a decision.

"We can do the next best thing," she said. "Who knows, maybe it'll give us something we can actually use."

Jim's brow furrowed. "What are you talking about?"

"The Spike. Or the Spikes, I should say," Heatsink said. "There's more than one."

TWENTY THREE

"**SHUT** the front door," Kelvin said. "No, shut every door! Are you serious?"

Heatsink returned a flat look. "Do I seem like someone who jokes around?"

Jim rolled his eyes. "Obligatory confusion and outrage. I, for one, am shocked that the world's favorite heroes would let them believe something untrue."

The hero bristled. "You know, not everyone finds ironic detachment a desirable quality."

Jim prepared a devastating retort. Then his thoughts flashed back to moments before, when Heatsink had saved Zoe's life. He swallowed the epic burn, telling himself he could use it on someone else later.

"Where are we going?" he said instead.

"The biggest, shiniest building in Highreach."

"You mean the Atherton building."

Heatsink nodded. "It's built right on top of a Spike. I'll make some calls on the way, try to find someone willing to take us to it."

Zoe perked up. "Actually, I have a friend who can help with that."

"So, how many are there?" Kelvin asked.

"How many what?" Heatsink deflected.

"I think he was pretty clear," Jim said. "How many taco shops are there in the metro area? It's important."

The hero ignored him and responded to Kelvin. "Is there really a reason for you to know how many Spikes there are?"

Kelvin shrugged. "Might help save the world."

"Well, if it comes to that, we can talk then."

Sheepishly, Natalie reached out and knocked on the massive steel door in front of them. "H-hello?"

"I, uh, don't think anyone lives in there," Jim said. "They'll probably come from that way."

He thumbed over his shoulder, back down the darkly lit concrete hallway they'd used to get here. Like any multinational corporation, Atherton Industries kept its share of secrets. They were standing in one now.

Amused, Zoe bumped Natalie's shoulder. "That was very polite, though. She'll appreciate it."

She did not explain who she was referring to. After making a single hushed phone call from the Spectrum pod, Zoe had guided them to a utility entrance well out of public view, where the captain of the on-site security team had admitted them. Without a word, he'd led them down several levels, through increasingly stringent security checkpoints, all the while passing fewer and fewer people, until they reached one very long, very empty underground corridor that ended where they stood now. Jim had a feeling this door could repel most conventional weaponry, and probably a healthy percentage of parahumans.

"Hey," Kelvin half-whispered, as if afraid the door would overhear him. "Should I go invisible? You know, just in case of . . . well, just in case."

"You're safe here, don't worry," Zoe said. "And it wouldn't help, anyway."

She didn't elaborate.

Heatsink shot her a wary look. "And when do you plan to tell us who we're meeting?"

The sound of a closing door echoed in the distance, followed by two pairs of footsteps. Jim thought he heard one pair of hard-soled boots, another of high heels. He was trying to deduce what that meant when their mysterious host stepped around the corner.

Natalie gasped and then covered her mouth, embarrassed. Kelvin and Heatsink hid their astonishment with moderate levels of success. Jim settled on raising his eyebrows.

Tess Atherton, CEO of Atherton Industries, was walking toward them in shiny heels and a form-fitting white dress that could have blended in at a board meeting or a cocktail party. Her long auburn hair was swept over one shoulder, and as she came closer, Jim could see the faintest smattering of freckles across her nose and cheekbones. Though in her early thirties—young for such a high-profile job—she looked even younger in person. But as she approached, her walk, her posture, her eyes and perfectly symmetrical face all projected laser-like focus.

"Uh, Zoe," Jim said quietly. "When you said *I have a friend who can help with that*, I thought you meant like a janitor you bribed."

Zoe gave an amused glanced over her shoulder before breaking from the group. Then, even more astounding than Tess Atherton's presence here, was her reaction to Zoe as they collided in an enthusiastic hug, effusively greeting each other and giggling like teenagers. The might-as-well-be-sisters vibe around them was palpable as they reunited, their friendship as unmistakable as it was unexpected.

"Yowza," Kelvin said under his breath. He leaned toward Jim. "I think I'm in love."

"You know we're still wearing the comm patches, right?" Jim asked.

Kelvin grimaced. "Aw, nuts. Sorry, everyone."

"I don't blame you," Natalie said.

"Neither do I," Heatsink agreed.

Neither could Jim. Tess Atherton made a striking impression. It wasn't just the wealth and power she wore like armor. Although, they didn't hurt—confidence was sexy, after all. It was the eyes that promised *you'll never guess what I'm really thinking*, the physique that challenged *try to keep up with me*.

The biggest surprise of all, though, was one that only Jim could see. Tess Atherton had a glowing green orb inside her. She was a parahuman. He'd heard her name in the media enough to realize this was not common knowledge.

"No ring on her finger," Jim said to Kelvin. "Shoot your shot. You could do worse than a pretty billionaire."

"What?" Kelvin shook his head. "No, not her. I meant the fox with her."

The woman behind Tess Atherton—statuesque, lithe, radiating strength and potential motion, fire red hair pulled back in a severe bun. Her outfit was a cross between a classic black Armani suit and the sleek, stealthy getup that Zoe wore under her Moxie costume. While she wore no visible weapons, the green orb inside her suggested they may not be necessary. She stood with hands behind her back, stoic and unmoving except for piercing green eyes that constantly threat-assessed everything and everyone. In contrast to Tess, this woman's eyes promised *I will cause you pain*.

Personally, Jim only had eyes for the petite brunette with the smoky eyes. But far be it from him to judge someone's taste. He shrugged. "No ring on her, either. Close that deal and she'll probably teach you how to kill a man with your thumb."

Until now, Zoe and Tess had been caught up in their reunion. But when Jim said that, Tess aimed a sharp gaze at him.

"With her pinky," she said, her posh Londoner accent carried on a voice that sounded like fingernails dragging over velvet. How had she overheard their conversation? Arm in arm with Zoe, she approached. "Hello. I'm Tess Atherton, and this is my assistant, Sliver. I am well aware of your time constraints, so further pleasantries will have to wait. What you seek is here."

Moving past them, she pressed her palm to the giant door. An interface glowed to life from inside the steel. As she went about bypassing the security, Jim noted Sliver had stopped only a couple paces away from him. He shifted closer.

"Hey. What do you assist with?"

She didn't look at him. "Anything."

"Hm, really." He cocked his head as if pondering this. "Pizza delivery? Hair appointments? Quiet assassinations?"

Sliver skewered him with a gaze that could slice through stone. "I take care of what needs taking care of, in whatever manner is required."

A deep metal *clank* cut off Jim's reply, followed by the *pop-hiss* of a seal being released. The door swung inward a few inches, but stopped before fully opening. Tess faced them with the door at her back, like a tour guide.

"What lies beyond is as mysterious as it is dangerous," she said.

"Ah, the secret recipe for Blaster Cola," Jim said. "I had a feeling."

Tess glanced at him dismissively and turned her head. But after a tiny pause and a subtle narrowing of eyes, she turned back and fixed him with a more direct stare. Head tilted, she appeared to study him as if he were a jigsaw puzzle and she couldn't find the corner pieces. Then, as quickly as it had appeared, the look evaporated, and she resumed as if nothing had happened.

"It is difficult to describe, being in its presence. The closer you get, the more you feel it, the more you will understand. Observe to your satisfaction, but do not *under any circumstances* touch the Spike. Direct contact may disrupt your powers, deliver a mild concussive shock, do nothing at all, kill you on the spot, or you may disappear altogether. Are there any questions?"

Natalie raised her hand.

Tess nodded to her. "Yes?"

"Hi. Will there be snacks? I'm starving after all the fighting."

Heatsink cast an incredulous glare at her. "Are you a literal child?"

Tess hid an amused grin behind her hand as she leaned to whisper in Sliver's ear. The scary redhead nodded and slipped back down the hallway, already speaking to someone unseen.

"Refreshments can be arranged," Tess said, a twinkle in her eye. Then, as she leaned against the door and pushed, her amusement dissipated. "For now . . . brace yourselves."

The CEO had a flair for the dramatic. Jim could appreciate that. Though he couldn't help wondering—if the Spikes were really so dangerous, why had they spent the last decade doing nothing but stick out of the ground?

When the door opened and they stepped inside the chamber, any remarks he may have been preparing for the occasion died on his lips.

The chamber was bowl-shaped and roughly the size of an average sports arena. Observation decks dotted the perimeter, some open-air, others protected behind invisalloy. A network of support beams and scaffolding covered the walls and the ceiling, with countless varieties of scanning device hanging from them, all aimed toward a single point in the center of the floor.

In a space this big, the Spike should have seemed insignificant. Yet it filled Jim's vision and his thoughts, pushing everything else to the periphery.

In person, its actual shape was more like a rhinoceros horn—thick and strong at the base, curving up to a sharp point high above. It seemed much larger than the Spike in Sydney until Jim remembered how far underground they were now. Atherton Industries must have excavated, revealing more of the Spike, while in Sydney they only saw what was above ground.

How it looked was barely worth mentioning, though, when compared to how it felt—as if Jim had been walking under the warm sun on a bright summer day, then between one step and the next, slipped into a deep forest on a dark winter night. The chamber had a ring of spotlights among the scanners, yet all of them were dark. The Spike exuded a glow of its own, silvery and ethereal, casting the chamber into ghostly light and shadow.

Its surface was dark gray stone, uneven and roughly hewn, as if chiseled by ancient tools. Veins of shiny silver crisscrossed the surface, flowing languidly like rivers of thick, viscous liquid. Those veins were the source of the light bathing the chamber. Periodically, they flared brighter, sending out a wave of cold and billowing fog. The entire chamber seemed to flare along with it, as if every atom vibrated in sympathy.

The door had opened onto floor level with a straight path to the Spike. Jim didn't notice his legs moving, so it almost felt like he was floating toward it. He only registered his team's presence around him distantly. Something about this *thing* beckoned him to come closer while shrieking at him to run for his life. What was it, really? What secret did it hold, and how was it connected to Summer's true fate?

Someone was speaking to him, but the voice was muffled and trivial, meaning nothing.

A hand gripped his forearm and held like a vise. Jim blinked hard, coming back to himself and realizing what he was doing. His arm was outstretched, his palm inches from the Spike.

"Gah!" He recoiled and fell back a step.

Tess Atherton released her grip on his arm, though her eyes stayed locked onto his, as if waiting for something. In his memory, he could hear the voices now that had felt so unimportant—his friends trying to call him away from the Spike.

"Sorry," he said, embarrassed.

He expected a rebuke from Tess, but she looked at him with understanding. "You hear its call. A vibration in your mind, resonating with the deepest, darkest parts of you. It is why none are allowed in here alone—so that we are not overcome."

Feeling awkward and exposed, Jim nodded thanks. "I think I know what popcorn feels like in the microwave now."

"Ooh, popcorn, that sounds good," Natalie said.

Once again, Tess studied Jim as if she were trying to disassemble him. Then it disappeared as if it had never been there, and she addressed the whole team.

"I am required elsewhere. Do what you need to, stay as long as you like, and keep a close eye on each other. Knowing what the Spike can do is not the same as resisting it."

Nodding to the team, exchanging another warm hug with Zoe, she bid them farewell and left them alone with the strangest, most deeply unsettling thing Jim had ever encountered. And that was saying something.

"So," Zoe said. "Anyone else feel really weird around this thing?"

"Glad it's not just me," Heatsink said.

"I feel like it's looking at me," Kelvin said.

"Hm," Natalie said. "I still just feel hungry."

"I thought I'd know what to do when we got here," Jim confessed. "That somehow I'd just figure out how these things connect to Summer. Now I'm questioning why we did this."

He faced the Spike and let it fill his vision, taking comfort from having friends at his back. Even the electricity in the chamber flowed oddly, and it was different now than it had been when they arrived. As if physical laws did not know exactly how to behave around this thing.

"Any ideas?" he said over his shoulder. "Maybe I'm missing something. I don't think I'm exactly objective right now."

No one responded. By the sound, or lack thereof, no one was even moving. Jim felt a surge of fear—maybe the Spike was taking them over now, as it had him. He whipped around, intent on playing goalie to keep them from touching it.

On seeing his friends, he tensed. So, that's why the electricity in here was flowing differently. He saw that for what it really was now—fingers of power slithering up through the team's electrical devices and into their minds. Just like back on the Lighthouse, when . . .

"They're not in danger," Summer said from behind him.

Turning once again, Jim faced the thing that was now hovering between him and the Spike—a conglomeration of scanners and computers and other bits of random tech, melded together into the grotesque approximation of an upper torso and a head. It hung from the rafters on thick cables like a twisted marionette.

Even the suggestion of Summer pierced Jim through the heart. He tried to focus past that. Something told him the world depended on it.

"I don't like when you do that to my friends," he said.

"We need to talk," her machine face said. "I'm not ready for us to meet in person. Not yet. So this will have to do."

Jim braced himself. Others would say this was futile, but he couldn't believe that. He had to try. "Whatever you're building, you don't have to finish it. You can stop right now. You can . . . come back and be my sister again."

The machine seemed to hesitate—if that was possible for a mechanical puppet. "You would welcome Summer back, even now? Even after such brutal vengeance?"

"I know you don't see it as vengeance," he said, trying to empathize. "You see it as mercy."

"Oh, no," Framework corrected. "What we do now is mercy. What we did before, on the Lighthouse? That was vengeance. To show the Spectrum there are consequences to their actions."

And there it was—the answer to the question Jim had kept choosing not to ask, because he knew it would make him sick to his stomach. In summoning Jim to free her, why had Framework needed to cause all that chaos and death in the

Dare? The answer was she hadn't. She'd done it to punish the Spectrum for imprisoning her.

It was Framework, not Summer, he repeated to himself over and over, working to mask his revulsion. *Remember who you're trying to save.*

"I've been thinking about that first night, taking down the Twisted Pair gang," she said, seeming unaware of his inner struggle. "You remember?"

Jim eyed her warily. "Yeah."

"Everything felt so simple back then. Sometimes, I wish Detective Stills had been right. I wish . . ." The machine shook itself. "I need you to know something. If you come for me, and if you truly want to stop what's coming, I will make you kill me. You'll have to do it yourself."

Jim's insides twisted. That . . . he couldn't let himself think about that, either.

"But I'd rather avoid a confrontation altogether," Summer continued. "It's a needless complication, and it would interrupt my purpose. Whatever happens, though, I promise I will not kill you, nor will I allow anyone else to. That would hurt Summer, and I need her with me until the end. Your friends, however, will be fair game. In fighting me, you risk all their lives."

Jim saw now, more clearly than ever, the two halves of his sister's fractured mind. Intertwined, opposed yet symbiotic, flowing from one identity to the other. He wondered how much she even understood herself.

He shook his head. "You've made a huge tactical error. I already know your endgame."

"The fact that you're standing here now proves otherwise."

"Oh, I don't know your plan yet, but you already revealed how you want it to end, which means we have no reason to hold back. If you win, we're all dead anyway. So, why wouldn't we choose to die stopping you?" He stepped closer, trying his hardest to project confidence. "And the more you build, the more power you use, the more inevitable you make it that I'll find you.

Surely, you know Sydney is my next stop. Why build there if the Spike isn't your doing?"

The machine considered a long moment before answering.

"When the heroes captured me, I remained dormant for some time. I still wanted to save the world, but didn't know how to do it anymore. How was I supposed to take away all this suffering without causing more in the process?" Framework looked away, staring at the darkness around them as if staring into the past. "And then the Spectrum handed me the answer. After I killed Anchor, they brought in a young man to replace him. I knew about him already, of course, because I knew basically all the information in the world. But when you know everything, sometimes it's hard for the right thing to stand out. Then the Spectrum plucked Red Plasma out of obscurity and lifted him up to their level. With his power and my limitless knowledge, I *had* it. I knew how, with one masterstroke, I could save everyone from their pain without causing any more ever again. That's what put me back on the path to this moment."

Jim worked to focus, pushing through the cascade of revelations. He might not get this chance again.

She's not Summer, she's Framework. Treat her like it.

"You didn't answer the question. Come on, Framework. If you're going to play this game, then really play it."

Machine parts whirred and clicked, approximating a sharp look from Framework's puppet. A warning from a godlike being to a mere mortal. But then, as if goaded by the challenge, she continued.

"That day in Sydney, I was desperate. People were begging for help and then dying, and we didn't even know what we were fighting yet. I had to do something. When I got close to the Spike . . . when I touched it . . . that's the last moment I felt like Summer Riven. I saw one hero touch it and get vaporized. But for me . . . in an instant, I connected with every computerized device on the planet. Absorbed the entirety of human knowledge and experience, every single bit of information that's ever been digitized. In a flash, I knew I could bend, not just code to my will, but anything *connected* to something powered by code. Between one heartbeat and the next, they were all mine. They were all *me*. And it didn't stop there. My powers kept expanding until they reached through the Spike and touched what was on the other side."

A spark shot up Jim's spine. "The other side? What does that mean?"

She continued unabated. "For a moment, I wasn't even human anymore. I was just pure information. It . . . it makes sense, I suppose, the Spectrum using Framework to cover up what happened. What we were really fighting. If people knew . . ."

"What was it?"

The machine shook its head.

Jim gave her a flat look. "People got used to cyborgs and superpowers. Whatever it is, they can handle it."

Framework scoffed. "As someone who knows the entirety of human history, I have less faith."

"Okay, so whatever you were fighting, the Spike came with it, right? And touching it changed you?"

Framework nodded.

"If I knew what you were fighting, maybe I could undo what happened. At least, enough for you to be Summer again."

"You're assuming I *can* go back. Or that I want to."

Jim was drawing close to a key truth. He could feel it. Unconsciously, he leaned forward. "Summer. What was it?"

The machine's voice turned ominous. "Something worse than me."

That gave him pause. He pushed through it, pleading. "If there's something worse than you, we should be fighting it together. Please, Summer."

The puppet gave a kind of digital groan. Jim thought it was trying to approximate a sigh.

"I had really hoped to avoid this," Framework said. The puppet lifted higher until she looked down on Jim. "But to be honest, I'm not sure Summer's will is strong enough to face you in person again. So I have to try something drastic. Just remember, Jim, you made me do this. It's why I led you here."

He raised an eyebrow. "Why *you* led me here? I beg to–"

Hands gripped him from behind. With ironlike strength, one hand clutched the back of his neck, the other his left wrist. He felt himself shoved forward.

Toward the Spike.

"Framework invites you to join her," Heatsink hissed into his ear. "If you survive."

TWENTY FOUR

HEATSINK wrenched at Jim's wrist, forcing his hand up to reach for the Spike as they careened toward it. Jim dug in his heels, fighting the forward momentum. But she had caught him at the exact right moment, vulnerable and distracted, and now he was losing ground.

"You're the spy!" he said.

"Duh," she replied.

This whole time, she had stood there pretending, never really frozen by Framework at all. Now the Spike loomed closer, filling Jim's vision. He cast a glance over his shoulder. His friends were still frozen in place. He could see the blue-white energy racing through a device on each one's person—Framework's gateway into their minds.

He made Heatsink fight for every inch of ground, but she had better leverage and was still gaining. His hand hovered dangerously close to the Spike.

"The thing is," he said through gritted teeth. "We kind of already knew that."

Heatsink faltered. "What?"

With his free right hand, Jim reached behind his ear and tapped the comm patch in a distinct pattern. He felt the power in Heatsink's patch reroute and then surge. She cried out as her body jolted and shivered and her grip went slack.

He brought his elbow back and felt it crunch against her nose. The hero stumbled away.

Whirling, Jim moved to strike again, but Heatsink recovered too quickly and leapt at him. With one hand, she released a disorienting burst of light and heat. With the other, she formed a truncheon of ice and swung at his midsection, no doubt hoping to knock him back into the Spike. Doubt and panic flashed through Jim. His opponent was faster and surprisingly strong, and this might just–

A deep black shadow whipped between them, knocking the club from Heatsink's hand and shoving her back a step. Then it was gone. For a split second, they stared at each other, wondering what that had been and where it had come from.

Jim recovered just a hair faster—enough to tap the pattern on the comm patch again and deliver another disrupting shock to the hero. She cried out and dropped to one knee, ripping the patch from her skin.

Jim aimed parahuman senses at his friends' devices and Framework's freakish mechanical golem. Then he gave their internals a twist. At once, they sparked and died and the puppet ripped to shreds from the inside, releasing the team from Framework's control. They lurched as their minds resumed working.

Still down on one knee, Heatsink made a swirling motion with her hand. Jim and his team found themselves frozen to the ground, ice covering them up to the knees. Jim heard the team calling out as they worked to get free, but his attention narrowed to Heatsink as she recovered and stalked toward him, her face contorted with rage.

She rocked to the side as a swarm of Zoe's darts slammed into her. With a frustrated huff, she made a grabbing and throwing motion. The air behind her crystallized as she sucked up heat and threw it like a burning wave at Zoe.

Stone spikes burst through the ice at Natalie's feet to cut her free. She slid in front of Zoe, arm up, and sprouted a shield to block the heat. As the wave parted around her, some of it washed over Kelvin enough to scorch his costume and melt the ice pinning him to the ground.

Heatsink didn't waste the wall of ice she'd just created. Whirling toward Jim, she closed her hand into a fist and the wall burst into spiky shards. As she prepared to fling them at Jim like missiles, her head disappeared.

While the fight intensified, they had all sort of forgotten about Kelvin. Their friend always found ways to be useful, but from the edges of a battle. Until now, when he must have seen his friends reeling from the assault of a powerful and experienced hero—a fight that, if they lost, could have dire consequences for the world—and leapt into the fray.

As Heatsink's head disappeared, effectively rendering her blind, as Jim braced for an icy assault, as Zoe and Natalie weathered the heat wave and prepared a response, Kelvin snatched a stun baton from Zoe's belt and rushed in. Leveraging his long arms and lanky frame, he wrapped the corrupt hero in a bearhug and jammed the baton into the small of her back. Shivering, screeching with agony-fueled rage, Heatsink returned the bearhug with one of her own.

Then she lifted Kelvin off the ground and flung him into the Spike. In a burst of light, he was gone.

Three voices cried out in horror. It couldn't be. It couldn't. Kelvin had just disappeared to hide from danger. He couldn't be dead. He couldn't.

Natalie loosed a sound Jim had never heard—a wail of desperate agony that crested into white hot rage. As the bubble of invisibility faded from Heatsink's head, she recovered her vision just in time to see a stone fist flying at her.

Natalie hit so hard, Jim's teeth rattled. Heatsink smashed into the ground and bounced like a stone skipping across a lake. She tumbled to a stop face down and didn't move.

A sharp pain in her side snapped Heatsink back to consciousness. The tip of a boot had jabbed into her flank. She awakened to find herself trussed like a turkey with steel wire, lying on the cold ground of the chamber, peering up at three figures backlit by the glow of the Spike.

Jim saw no sorrow in her eyes. No regret. Kelvin was dead, and she was not sorry. It took every ounce of self-control not to palm one of Zoe's knives and slip it between the hero's ribs.

He stood arm-in-arm with the friends he had left. On either side of him, Zoe and Natalie fought to keep control as silent tears fell, as their bodies trembled with agony and outrage. His own eyes were burning, a dam threatening to break loose if he didn't keep it locked down. There would be a time to mourn his friend—he knew eventually it would sweep over him whether he wanted it to or not. Just not now. Not yet.

"Summer wanted me to go Apex," Jim said. "That's why you told us about this place—to get me close to a Spike. Am I right?"

Heatsink returned a hard stare, keeping quiet.

"You gave her that comm, years ago," Jim continued. "And you were never under her control. Why would you be? You'd already devoted yourself to her. Maybe she thought I'd come around, too, if I went through what she did."

"Why would you do this?" Natalie half-sobbed, as if pleading to understand. "She's a madwoman."

Heatsink's gaze sharpened. "You'd have to be mad not to see she's right. Look at us—look at what we do. We fight waves of evil that will never end, in a war that we'll never win. If that's not meaningless, I don't know what is. Between eternal pain and oblivion, I choose oblivion."

"And you're choosing it for everyone," Zoe said tightly, barely controlled. "I should have thrown you into space like you did to Astro-Ninja."

Surprise crept onto the hero's face. "How did . . . ?"

"We kept scanning the station during the rescue," Jim said. "Even the surrounding space. That's how we found his body floating out there. So when you told your story about his betrayal, we knew it didn't add up."

"We prepared, then waited for you to reveal yourself. We just underestimated how far you've fallen." Zoe shook her head. "You killed him for a cover story."

Heatsink sniffed dismissively. "He would have died soon anyway. Just like your friend."

Natalie burst forward with a cry, jagged spikes bursting from her hands.

Then Zoe was there, clutching her in a tight, unyielding hug. "Not like this," she said, soft but firm. "She's not worth the cost. And you know Kelvin wouldn't want it."

Natalie screamed through the tears.

Jim crouched next to Heatsink, putting his face right above hers. "If you were a hero, I'd say something like *our friend is the only reason you get to keep breathing*. But that doesn't mean much to you, does it?"

Heatsink responded with a look of defiance.

"So, I'll just do this."

Jim gripped the patch on her shoulder and ripped it free, leaving a ragged tear in her costume and a blank space where the Spectrum insignia used to be. With a careless flick of the wrist, he let it flutter to the ground. Heatsink's eyes followed it all the way down. Though she tried to hide it, he caught a glimmer of uncertainty and the briefest flash of regret.

He turned his back on her and joined his friends, folding into their shared embrace, letting it comfort him. If only for a moment.

Jim recoiled from the bright sun. Down in that chamber, he'd almost forgotten what warmth and daylight felt like.

Behind him, the door to the Atherton building clicked shut. Tess had arrived shortly after their confrontation and volunteered to take charge of Heatsink, freeing Jim and Zoe and Natalie to continue on. She would keep the former hero locked down until they could send someone to retrieve her. That would be a problem for a day when the world wasn't about to end. Unless it actually did end today.

As they had returned to the surface, Jim had filled them in on his conversation with Framework. They moved now as if the knowledge hung heavily around their necks.

Natalie hugged herself despite the warmth. She gazed around them with weary, half-focused eyes. "What . . . what do we do now?"

Zoe's left arm buzzed. She held it up and accessed the screen.

"Oh, thank heavens," Widget breathed, clutching his chest. "I've been calling and calling and I feared the worst."

"We were deep underground," Zoe explained. "My comm must have just synced back up with the pod."

Jim leaned over her shoulder. "What's happening?"

"Bit of a good-news-bad-news situation. We have had some successful rescues, Prism heroes reclaimed and brought back here. We have also had failures that required reinforcements and a second attempt. Those are, shall we say, in progress. Also, the more Framework builds her global network of, er, whatever it is, the more she's commandeering data resources. So, the more she overtakes, the more the world's ability to see what she's doing and respond diminishes. Fortunately, the Spectrum networks have not yet fallen. If that were to happen, I . . ." Widget looked at something offscreen and stopped cold, his eyes going wide. "Oh. Oh, no."

For a moment he only gaped, looking shellshocked, slowly shaking his head.

"Widget," Jim prompted.

The man blinked, tried to speak, then had to stop and clear his throat. "Um, something just happened in Sydney. And, um, in several dozen other places around the world. I . . . you should just see it."

His fingers flew over the keyboard, and the video of his face switched over to display multiple camera feeds. From the look of it, these were coming from across the planet. As the images played, Widget explained what they were seeing.

"Everything Framework was building—we thought it was all brand new, that she was just starting now. Well, it seems that was only partially true. She must have been hiding *these* behind cloaking fields until now. It seems they've been here all along, and now all she has to build is the network between them."

True to his description, the video feed from Sydney showed a metal ring-shaped skeleton around what used to be Hyde Park, a network of pylons and support braces. Then, all at once, the empty center of the ring shimmered and a massive industrial structure appeared there fully formed.

It was shaped like a giant hockey puck, multiple stories tall and hundreds of meters across. The surface was a mottled pattern of grays, like a mosaic of metal pieces scavenged randomly and welded together. Across the world, smaller versions of that same structure appeared, all guarded by a swarm of hired villains.

It appeared to be solid all around, with no doors or openings. Until the camera drone ascended to bring the roof into view, revealing a round opening at the center, perhaps fifty meters across. With the inner workings cast in shadow, Jim couldn't see any details. But as he watched, a light appeared from a within—a red glow like one he had seen before.

"So, she does have Red Plasma," Zoe said. "That's not good."

Jim's heart plummeted through the ground. They were even closer to losing everything than he'd suspected. And *she* was at the center of it all.

He felt something inside him shatter.

Oh, Summer, what have you done?

"If I'm right, she's been doing this for years," Widget continued. "Quietly redirecting resources, building under cover, preparing while covering her tracks. And our timetable just got a lot shorter. Framework may be almost ready to . . . well, to use whatever this is."

Gently grasping Zoe's arm, Natalie turned it to get a full view of what may very well be the end of the world. After taking in every frame, she peered desperately up at her friends.

"We need to go to Sydney."

"You're right," Zoe said, activating the call for the Spectrum orb. "Can't fight on the fringes anymore. We need to strike at the heart. Widget?"

"As we speak, I am aborting all other operations and redirecting everyone left standing to Australia for a . . . a final defense. It will take a little time, but they'll get there."

Jim couldn't move. His chest felt like a boulder was pressing down on it. Every ounce of the past days chose this moment to crash down on him.

Now that the time had come, the questions he'd been asking himself loomed large. *Can I save the world if it means letting Summer go? If I face her, will I be able to do whatever is necessary?*

And now, from deep inside him, the answer rang out like a bell.

No.

Jim had just watched a new friend die, and he was barely coping. What would happen when it's the person he loved more than anything in this world? He knew now that he would only be able to stand there while she scoured all life from existence, starting with him. Which meant he was a liability.

"You . . . you should go without me," he said, avoiding his friends' eyes as he spoke. He had to do this. The shame he felt now would be nothing next to what he'd feel if he got in the way at the wrong moment. "There's, uh, still investigating to do here. Old haunts to visit, make sure she's not hiding there."

"But we need everyone," Natalie protested. "Jim, we need y–"

Zoe put a hand on her arm, stopping her short. But her eyes remained on Jim. "If they told me I had to fight my sister, I'd tell them to suck it. I would never. Not even to save the world." She gave him a look full of understanding. "Go do what you need to, Jim."

A wave of the most intense gratitude he'd ever felt washed over Jim. He must have looked relieved, because Natalie gave him a shockingly strong hug.

"I still don't deserve any of you," Jim said.

Zoe smirked. "You're still right."

"But you've got us anyway." Natalie said. "And there's nothing you can do about it."

The silver orb appeared above them, blooming open as it lowered. Once again, whether or not Jim got inside, nothing would ever be the same after this.

"Gotta go now," Zoe said. "Take care of yourself, Jim."

All he could do was nod. Anything he'd try to say would only break him open and spill him onto the pavement. He stood as tall as he could while his friends strapped in and lifted into the sky, flying to defend the world from perhaps the most dangerous villain that ever lived.

His sister.

Then they were gone, and once again, he was alone. As he'd been for years before these impossible days. It seemed poetic that everything would end the way they had begun.

Well. If the world was about to breathe its last breath, Jim could only think of one place to go. He started walking.

TWENTY FIVE

JIM lost track of how long he wandered. By the time he arrived at Versus, the early prep staff were already bustling around the place, getting ready for tonight's service. They were quieter than usual, as if focusing extra hard on their jobs would keep the world outside at bay. He could relate. He'd been trying that every day for ten years.

But not today. Stepping behind the bar, he grabbed the ring announcer's mic and pressed the button.

"Hey, everyone. Change of plans."

Front of house staff paused to look his way. Kitchen staff stayed in the back, but he could hear the activity quiet down. They were listening.

"We're closed tonight." He considered. "Actually, the next three nights. You'll still get paid, don't worry. But, um . . . just go home and be with your families."

He wondered if he should say more. But as he started to try, he realized that was all he had in him.

He shrugged. "See ya."

Replacing the mic on its hook, he retreated to the back office and settled into his desk chair while the staff switched gears from prepping to shutting everything down. Before long, Versus was dark and silent and empty except for the same ghost that always haunted it, walking half in the world and half in shadow. It seemed fitting to Jim that if it all ended today, for him it would end here.

I tried, he thought. *I really tried this time. It didn't matter.*

If there was a silver lining, at least Summer would no longer feel her own pain. At least–

"So," Eli said. "You've decided to feel sorry for yourself until everyone's dead."

"Whoa!"

Jim nearly fell backward out of the chair. He righted himself, shot to his feet, picked up a Versus-brand paperweight and flung it at the man suddenly standing on the other side of his desk. The little red boxing glove flew through Eli and hit the floor behind him.

"Good guess. I'm not really here," the Custodian said.

"I didn't guess. I was really trying to hit you," Jim replied. "Though, given your *other* identity, I'm betting you're tougher than you look."

"Lord Neon isn't another identity. He's a different aspect of me. I didn't mislead you at the beginning—I *am* an Enviro Sensor. But I'm also an Empath, a Mediapath, and much more. The hero you know, though, is a result of my most unusual power, which I do not advertise."

He stopped, and for a moment, they just stared at each other.

Jim narrowed his eyes. "Are you pausing dramatically, or waiting for me to ask?"

"There is a layer of existence where information meets reality. Where it goes from theoretical to actual."

"Did you notice how I didn't ask for–?"

"That layer is where my true power operates." Eli grasped at the air as if reaching for the right words. Jim gave up and let him talk. "I can wield that information, making it real. Move it from the realm of thought and theory into physical existence.

So, in a way, Lord Neon is a projection of parts of me. He is the inner idea of me made real."

"Very interesting," Jim said flatly. "Thank you for forcing me to learn about you. I assume this means you broke out of that mental thing Framework did to you?"

"With Grimvision's help. She is quite skilled."

"And a fashion icon. What a double threat. Is there something I can help you with?"

Eli's tone softened. "First, I'm sorry about Kelvin. Despite how he got to the Lighthouse, he seemed a good man."

Jim looked down. The sympathy in Eli's voice pierced him right through the heart. He wasn't ready for it.

"Second, as I speak to you, we're moments from our arrival in Sydney. If we don't take the fight to Framework now, I fear we will never get the chance. Much as the Spectrum would like time to recover, that is a luxury none of us have." Eli glanced around the office as if trying to appear casual. "When will you be joining us?"

Jim pursed his lips. "You don't need me there. You don't *want* me there. Just beat her the same way you did the first time."

"The thing is . . ." Eli looked down now, awkwardly clearing his throat. "Last time, we didn't beat her. Framework pushed herself too hard, burned too brightly, and then collapsed into a coma. We thought her power was permanently broken, and so we brought her back to the Lighthouse to be put into stasis. Then, at a moment we were distracted and vulnerable, she woke up and lashed out. In her weakened state, she did not prevail. However, before we could subdue her, she used her powers to take control of Geometron and deal one final blow, which landed on Anchor. That is how he died."

"Wow." Jim blew out a slow breath, taking a moment to process that. "She used Geometron to kill her own husband. No wonder she's angry."

"Correct. We managed to contain Framework, then called a hero out of retirement to help us keep her that way."

"You mean Arbiter."

Eli nodded. "And for ten years, she spent every waking moment keeping the world safe."

"Then I showed up and ruined the party."

"That sounds suspiciously like self-pity. That's not who you are, so I'll ignore it. And we both know that she was already winning by the time you arrived. She would have gotten out eventually, with or without your help." Eli cocked his head. "But if you feel the need to atone, you can stop hiding here and join the fight. As you and I speak, we have engaged Framework's perimeter guard, but they are numerous and strong and well-prepared, and we are not at our full strength. Meanwhile, something inside her structure is spinning up. Its power is growing. This will not be an easy fight, and we have limited time to finish it. We need everyone."

"Eli, Lord Neon, any other personalities lurking in there, you've all got to understand—I cannot be your savior. Put me face to face with Summer and I will fail, trust me."

"I do trust you, Jim. I have faith in who you are, who you can be, even more than you realize," Eli said. "And we're not fighting Summer. We're fighting Framework."

"Even she doesn't know when she's one or the other. How am I supposed to . . . ?"

Jim trailed off as two memories surfaced—one from the distant past, the other from earlier today. Two moments in time that he hadn't realized were connected until just now. He watched them in his head, letting them play back side by side. The more clearly he remembered, the more he couldn't stop seeing the truth he had missed. Like a hammer striking a bell, the realization vibrated through every cell in his body.

He dropped heavily into his chair. "Holy . . ."

The memories were clear as day now, every detail rendered perfectly as they played on a mental loop, showing Jim over and over what he now couldn't deny.

"I've been thinking about that first night, taking down the Twisted Pair gang. You remember? Sometimes, I wish Detective Stills had been right. I wish . . ."

She had said that mere hours ago. And many years ago, Stills had said . . .

"There are others, too–the ones who still have something good inside. Deep down, they want us to stop 'em. They want good to win."

"She reached out to me," Jim said. "While Framework made her threats, Summer found a way to ask for help. I . . . I think . . ."

"What is it, Jim?"

Jim met his eye. "I think Summer wants me to stop Framework."

Eli leaned in. "So, what are you going to do about it?"

Jim burst from his chair. Moving to the closet door, he threw them open and dove inside. It must still be there. Some piece of it, at least.

"Exactly what she asked for," he said over his shoulder as he ripped through stacks of old boxes. "Stop Framework for Summer. Defeat who she is to save who she was. Help her find some kind of peace."

"I'm sorry, but this must be said," Eli said. "You do know what that may require?"

"I know I can't hold back. I have to give this–give *her*–everything I have." He stepped out of the closet, holding an old box with the lid folded shut. "If she could, Summer would wager her life to save the world. But I'm not Summer. So if this goes badly, you should know that I would choose her over the world. Every time." Opening the box, he dug inside. "Though, that's not exactly Plan A."

Eli gave a nod of understanding. For the briefest moment, he wore a knowing little grin before it disappeared.

"Fair enough," he said, and gestured at the box. "What's that?"

Jim gave a frustrated huff. "The one time I try to do something poetic . . ."

He upturned the box, spilling its contents onto the floor. Out poured a pile of random, forgotten junk.

And one child-sized domino mask.

"Part of my old Lode costume—the one part I didn't burn. I'd hoped to wear it again, to get Summer's attention. But apparently I've outgrown it."

"Ah," Eli said, a strange glint in his eye. "And . . . what if you arrived in something better?"

"You going to conjure a new costume for me?"

Eli reached for one of the closet doors and pulled it fully open. "When you first wore that Interruptor costume, I told you the blue jacket was more than just a disguise. Moments ago, I said that I have more faith in you than you realize. Now, I believe it's time to show you what I meant." As he moved the door, the floor-length mirror bolted to the inside swung until it reflected Jim head to toe. "Picture the jacket in your mind, as it is now."

Jim shot the hero a doubtful look, but followed instructions.

"Now imagine it as something different. Pick whatever you like, and then impress that mental image onto the jacket, along with your will for it to be so."

Now Jim really hit him with a look. "Are you filming this for some of kind prank show?"

"Trust me."

Once more, Jim complied. With a gentle, silent whoosh like wind rushing over his body, his blue Interruptor jacket transformed into the world's ugliest brown-and-orange plaid sport coat.

"Wow," he said, really meaning it. "A shapeshifting jacket. That's actually kinda cool."

"It's not a jacket." Eli tugged on the hideous lapel. "Try again. Only, this time, don't think of a specific garment. Think of switching back to a default setting and impress that desire upon it."

Again, Jim complied. The garment transformed completely, from the color to the material to the style and cut and flow, growing to cover more of his body than a jacket. All the while, Jim watched himself in the mirror. When he realized what he now wore, he recoiled, feeling the sudden urge to rip it off and throw it in the corner.

"Relax." Eli held up a calming hand. "Slow down and really look."

Jim stopped on the verge of disrobing. Stepping back to the mirror, he let himself drink in the sight.

A cape. A *black* cape.

It wrapped around his neck, fastened tight yet perfectly comfortable. Then it flowed over his shoulders and cascaded down his body as if every thread had been woven specifically for him, gently swaying in the nonexistent breeze.

Jim shook his head, grinning. "Well, your timing sucks, but the fact that you chose me for your first practical joke is pretty flattering. Nice try, but if I wear this on the street, even villains will want to beat me down."

Eli shook his head right back. "Jim, this is anything but a joke. Do you remember crawling through the Shran tubes, where you so flippantly proposed that the Spectrum should have two other capes?"

"Yeah, black and white."

"You were right. They have existed for many years, offered in secret and worn only in the shadows, each bearer chosen by the Spectrum for a very specific purpose. And now we offer the black cape to you."

That stunned Jim into silence. He stared at himself, and at the impossible thing wrapped around him.

"The white cape is given to someone more visible, in the public eye for something other than typical hero work," Eli continued. "A helper and a beacon for good in different ways than battling villains. I will not reveal the current White Cape, but suffice to say they are very good at what they do. As for this black cape, its previous bearer . . . moved on some time ago, and we have been searching for a replacement ever since."

"Is that why you came to my bar? To look into me?"

"Truthfully, no. I came because of Framework. Though, in a strange twist, I find myself grateful to Summer, because observing you convinced me that you are the one for the job. By the time I gave you that jacket, I had little doubt. Now, after all that has transpired, I am even more sure than before. You *are* the Black Cape, Jim. You need only to accept it."

Jim gave a gentle scoff. "I'm not exactly the philanthropist type you described."

"That is for the bearer of the white cape, not the black," Eli countered. "The differences are key. While the white is more altruistic do-gooder, the black is more . . . covert investigator, operating from the shadows to neutralize threats that the Spectrum cannot deal with openly."

"So, like a one-man CIA."

"Without the assassinations. But that is only half the job." His tone took on extra weight. "The other half is to be a reality check for the Spectrum. To call them on the things they need to be called on. Stand up to them and speak for the little guy. And if the worst should happen and a hero *turns*, to stand between them and the innocent. To put them down quickly and quietly and without hesitation, so that the world does not lose faith in us. A failsafe."

"You mean a last resort," Jim said. "Against the world's most revered heroes."

Eli nodded. "Isn't that what you've been doing from the moment you put the jacket on? You just didn't realize it."

"I also didn't do that alone."

"Nor would you be alone going forward. If and when you want help, ask and you will have it."

Jim couldn't stop staring at himself in the mirror. He'd spent a decade hating heroes—the Spectrum in particular. Now he was wearing one of their capes?

"Having the guts to stand up to us is half the battle. You've already proven you can do that. I suspect you'll enjoy it," Eli said as if he'd heard Jim's thoughts. "As for the other half, well, perhaps if you stop suppressing your talents and start developing them, you might discover there's more inside you than you realize."

"Okay, seriously, stop making good points," Jim said. "Do you have any idea how hard it is to debate someone who already knows everything?"

Smiling, Eli held up his hands in surrender. He took a step back and fell quiet, as if giving Jim the space he needed to process.

With a handful of the cape in his grip, Jim ran his thumb over the material. It felt silky and fabric-y and soft and strong and smooth and tough all at once. There was a subtle glisten to the microscopically fine weave, like a hint of diamond dust that caught the light from different angles. The feel of the material brought back a recent memory, which called to mind another question.

"It's a layer of protection, too, isn't it?"

"Correct. Because it interfaces with your thoughts, the cape may also respond to threats, working with you as an active shield."

That explained what happened in the Spike chamber, when Jim was fighting Heatsink. Some kind of shadowy interference had prevented her from landing a particular attack. Even before he'd been aware of it, the cape had kept him safe.

What else could this thing do?

He envisioned something new and willed his desire into the cape. It became like mist as it transitioned from one form to the next. This time, the change was head to toe, all-encompassing.

He wore a sleek, updated version of Jimmy Riven's old Lode costume. The knee-length jacket was all black except for the sleeves. Before, the sleeves had faded from dark blue to white in the suggestion of electricity. Now glowing lines continuously arced from wrist to shoulder, as if lightning were coursing up his arms. The old store-brand black pants and blue sneakers were gone, replaced by gear akin to the Interruptor costume. As a final touch, instead of a basic domino mask, he wore something more stylized and angular that covered much more of his face. His hair was darker now and streaked with blue-to-white highlights, as if electricity was coming out through his follicles.

So, this thing can do more than just fabric. Interesting. Jim couldn't stifle a grin. *Summer would love this.* The thought came unbidden and nearly brought him to tears, as painful as it was true.

It was then that Jim knew. He had felt it happening back on the Lighthouse, but now it was real. Somehow, this old life was pulling him back in. All he'd wanted was to run his crumbling old bar and be left alone. Then all he'd wanted was to find the truth about Summer and be left alone. Now, as the world faced what could be its final moments, he could feel the life he'd carefully constructed around himself cracking and falling away.

Mere days ago, he would have raged against it. Now, he could no longer deny how those few days had changed him. Or maybe they had just reminded him who he was before losing faith in . . . well, in everything. Either way, the Jim Riven who returned from the Lighthouse would never be able to simply return to his forgotten corner and resume letting the world pass by. He just couldn't admit it to himself until this moment.

Yet, he wasn't the old Jimmy Riven, either. That naïve kid, with a two-dimensional, primary-colored view of the world, had been too innocent for his own good. He would have adhered to the mantras and principles of heroes even when the heroes were dead wrong.

He had lived two lives as two different people, each clinging to the extreme ends of opposing viewpoints. Maybe now he could start a third life somewhere in the middle, as someone better. As the best of both.

He blew out a breath, clinging to this last moment before everything changed. "I'll never be a hero, you know. Not like you want. I'm just not that guy anymore."

"Jim, I know who I'm recruiting. I would never ask you to stop being you. We *need* you. I believe we have for some time."

With that, they both knew he had accepted, and the world just got a lot stranger.

He was the Black Cape.

"Before this becomes official," Jim said. "I have one last thing to do as Lode."

TWENTY SIX

SKYPUNCHER plowed through the burnt-out shell of a car and hit the ground face-first, his jaw carving a furrow in the concrete. He flipped up to his feet, shaking it off as Boneblack charged in. The villain's hulking frame burst into napalm-like liquid fire. That stuff could burn through solid iron.

"You're gonna regret coming here!" Boneblack raged.

He delivered a face-melting blow, only to have it slam into the ground where the hero had stood an instant before. Behind Boneblack now, Skypuncher gripped the sides of his head.

"You first."

Heaving backward, Skypuncher flipped Boneblack upside down to pile-drive him into the ground. Then he spun them both in the air and did it again, and again, gouging craters into the ground with his enemy's face. On the fourth spin, he released the villain while kicking him full-force between his shoulder blades. With a reverberating *boom*, Boneblack shot into the sky like a missile and disappeared among the clouds.

A news helicopter veered out of the way just in time to avoid a collision. Half a dozen of them hovered over the battlefield, far too close despite Skypuncher's warnings. He'd have to keep a better eye out for them. They may be foolish, but they were innocent, and right now they were the eyes and ears of the world.

Reorienting himself, he assessed the battlefield, taking in every detail with parahuman speed. Hundreds of villains of every class and level formed a seemingly impenetrable cloud between the heroes and Framework's giant . . . whatever it was. She must have paid them extremely well, because only a few had fled when the Spectrum arrived. Clearly, their employer hadn't told them that, if she won, they wouldn't live to spend it.

Prism heroes were arriving in waves, flown in from all over the planet, and local Australian heroes were giving everything they had. Then there were the contestants from the Dare, who fought like they had something to prove. Skypuncher felt a surge of shame whenever he saw them. The things he remembered doing to them . . .

He made himself put that away. If he didn't focus on this moment, there would be no one left to apologize to. By his count, they were still waiting for a third of the Prism heroes to arrive, which should happen soon.

He had the feeling it wouldn't be soon enough. Not even close.

Millennia skidded to a halt by his side, shield up to cover them both. She whirled her sword to flick some kind of glowing orange goo off the blade.

"This isn't working," she said. "We need to stop fighting like heroes and start fighting like warriors. The sight of their own entrails will make them scatter."

From nowhere, Lord Neon appeared to stand on his other side. "Ferocity will not win the day. Precision will. We are trying to punch through from multiple directions when we should focus all our power in *one*."

Who should Skypuncher listen to—the ancient princess with thousands of years of experience, or the man who knew everything? The Spectrum was built to protect the world from evil, not to fight a war.

A stream of morphing mechanical shapes snaked through the roiling crowd. They came near and coalesced, resolving into Geometron.

"Something's happening in there." She motioned at the structure. "I feel a change in–"

The metal plates on the surface began to move, shifting and rearranging into a new pattern. The motion gave Skypuncher brief glimpses of the inner workings of what now appeared to be a single, giant machine. A red glow inside it flashed brighter, lighting up every seam between the plates as they locked into their new form. Then a cage-like shape ascended through the circular hole in the roof, like the steepled fingers of a steel skeleton. Inside the cage, red energy swirled like a second sun.

All around them, the fighting stopped, hero and villain alike transfixed by the sight.

"Red Plasma." Road Rash arrived at the head of a rushing wind. "She's using his power."

A persistent energetic hum vibrated through everything and everyone. Intensifying by the second, it grew into a roar that filled the air for miles.

Skypuncher's heart sank. They were too late. Framework's moment had arrived.

The power sizzled inside him now, building to a crescendo and . . .

The roar stuttered. The red energy faltered.

There was a moment of quiet, as if the world hovered on a precipice. Then the red glow dimmed, and with a groan of mechanical protest, the steepled cage receded into the structure.

For a moment, the line dividing the two sides blurred as everyone in the crowd asked the same questions. Had they all just been about to die? What stopped it?

Skypuncher caught motion over his shoulder. Booted feet landed behind him.

Road Rash pointed. "Who is *that*?!"

Skypuncher turned to see a masked man, grinning as he stood on the roof of a smashed SUV. He clutched massive bundles of power cables in both hands, gathered from all across this decimated area of the city. Waves of electricity flowed over his body, yet he seemed unconcerned. In fact, he looked quite at home.

The costume was updated, but Skypuncher recognized it, and he smiled.

Drinking in the scene while raw power coursed through his veins, Jim breathed a theatrical sigh of relief.

"My oh my, it's good to be back." He caught sight of a familiar old villain and pointed. "Lowdown! Still ugly, I see. How's your mother?"

Lowdown made a rude gesture, then sucker punched the hero he'd been fighting. With that, the crowd of heroes and villains descended into pandemonium again.

Jim stepped down to the ground, dropping the cables he'd been clutching. They had served their purpose, allowing him to siphon enough power to interrupt whatever effect Framework's machine had been building up to, while also boosting his own Faraday level. It was a temporary stopgap, but it had bought them time.

While the battle raged around them, Jim strolled up to the Spectrum. "I'm sure you're all wondering why I called this meeting."

Geometron cut off his approach, shaking with fury. "You'll be in chains, like her!"

She reached for him, only for Skypuncher and Lord Neon to both grab her arm.

"Be calm," Lord Neon said. "We need him."

"And you know what he is to us now," Skypuncher said.

Geometron fumed, but relented. Jim buried the urge to say something snarky. Right now, he was on the clock.

"You have an Apex villain problem," he said. "I've got you covered. Make a path for me?"

Lord Neon nodded, gesturing to include the whole team. "All our power together, like a focused beam. Enough to deliver one person to the machine."

"Except for Clarion." Skypuncher scanned the crowd. "Where is–"

A sound like distorted electric guitar cut through the chaos. Jim recognized the opening riffs of Scorpions' decades-old anthem "Rock You Like a Hurricane."

"Here I am!" an amplified voice half-shouted, half-sang. "Rock you *like a me-icane!*"

The sound took shape, becoming two giant hands that split the crowd enough for the Sonic Controller to arrive with his own fanfare. On seeing Jim, he pointed and then made devil horns with his fingers.

"Sweet costume, bro, I dig it. Very metal."

"All right, everyone, form up," Skypuncher ordered. "We'll start with Shiny Keys, then launch into Spartan Ray with a Surround Sound kicker. Toad in the Hole next, then we end on Alpha Spitfire with a twist. All good?"

The Spectrum heroes nodded as if that combination of words made sense.

"Was that a list of moves, or your breakfast order?" Jim said.

Looking like a battle commander out of a history book, Skypuncher stood tall and pointed forward. "Go!"

Lord Neon spread his hands out to either side. A hundred meters to the right and the left, giant versions of him appeared from nothing and waded into battle. The behemoths drew momentary attention, splitting the crowd's focus and pulling it away from the Spectrum.

Clarion spun his staff dramatically, as if trying to spin the air into a tornado around him. For an instant, the entire battlefield went silent. The space around Clarion's staff vibrated and hummed, a dense cloud of collected sound that he shaped into a wall of wavy distortion, like ripples of heat on a summer day.

"Taste my sound!" he growled.

He thrust his staff forward. The wall extended, becoming a tunnel that shoved through the crowd, casting hero and villain alike out of its path.

Stepping up to the tunnel, Geometron morphed from humanoid to a series of interlocking hexagons wrapped around the tunnel like a layer of mechanized armor. Bursts of energy arced between the shapes—an additional layer of shielding. Jim knew people wondered how she was able to do stuff like that with only half of her body being cybernetic. After what he sensed during their fight on the Lighthouse, he knew the answer.

He felt a hand on his arm. Then everything became a blur except for Jim and Road Rash, who clutched him while dashing down the tunnel.

"This is fun isn't this fun I'm having so much fun Lode that's your name for now isn't it but I remember trying to kill you when you were Interruptor hahaha isn't that weird anyway off you go!"

Jim blinked and they were two-thirds of the way down the tunnel. He caught up with all those words just as she let go of him, and then she was gone. Stronger hands clutched him now.

"Trust me," Skypuncher said.

"You know, anytime someone says that–"

Jim yelped as Skypuncher hurled him at the wall of the giant machine. He had just enough time to wonder how many of his bones were about to shatter.

An instant before smashing into a metal plate like a bug on a windshield, Jim watched with relief as Millennia's shield flew in. Glinting like burnished copper, it bashed into the wall with a reverberating *clang* and punched a hole right through it.

Diving through the hole, Jim tucked and rolled past layers of armor and pinballed between a network of support beams until he tumbled down to ground level. He somersaulted to his feet and sprinted deeper into the machine.

The structure constantly moved and reshaped itself. As he ran, he dragged his fingers along the undulating walls. His senses spread through the inner workings, showing him its form and function. This thing was incredibly complex. He could perceive it all now, but couldn't yet understand it.

He found a tunnel that angled toward the heart of the machine and swerved into it, hoping this wasn't some kind of trap that would collapse like a trash compactor. Limited time meant he had to take a risk.

"Jim."

And there she was. He had expected this, so it didn't make him break stride. He kept running and tracing his hand along the right wall to maintain a connection. A face appeared in the wall to his left and traveled with him as he moved, a continuous distortion in the metal.

"Don't waste your time," he told the strange machine face.

"I'm only doing what's best for the world. Look at them outside my walls. Look how they fight each other, and for what? None of them have the answer. No solution is permanent except *this* one. I hoped you, of all people, would understand that. Please, Jim, help me save them."

"Heh. Well, I guess I've heard worse sales pitches." Jim looked at her now. "But it doesn't change why I'm here. I'm gonna shut you down, Framework."

The machine face scowled. Jim responded with a grin.

"It's okay," he said. "Summer asked me to."

The face disappeared, and the tunnel warped sharply. Jim felt the machine shifting around him and changed his approach. He flowed along with the new configuration, his path unbroken.

There—he saw red light ahead and dove for it. The way closed behind him, just barely too slow to block him. He rolled and skidded to a stop on his feet.

Staring up at the massive central chamber, he tried to soak in as much detail as possible before this got real. The machinery constantly rearranged itself. After contact with the device, he understood now that it was working to manage and manipulate unfathomable amounts of destructive energy.

To his right, Jim spotted a small, enclosed chamber within this large one. The chunky thing looked as if it could have been milled from a single truck-sized block of steel. Giant industrial cabling snaked from its back and sides to plug into the greater machine around it. An invisalloy panel was set into the front, revealing the unconscious form of Red Plasma. The entire thing wreathed in a red haze as it extracted his power—rumored to be a unique combination of light and nuclear radiation—and pumped it into Framework's machine.

In the center, the Spike dominated the space like the one under Atherton had. The same waves of cold and fog billowed from it, and the same silvery veins pulsed with internal light. For this one, though, there was a key difference. Whereas Atherton had studied their Spike from a distance, Framework had attached cables and twisted mechanical structures directly to hers.

No, wait. The closer Jim looked, the more they appeared to phase *into* the Spike, somehow disappearing inside the stone. His thoughts flashed back to Summer's words about something on the other side.

"Something worse than me."

"It's almost poetic, isn't it?"

Framework stepped around the Spike wearing giant battle armor, sharp and angular, as if she'd cobbled it together on the fly from whatever tech was near at hand. Just like she had ten years ago. Jim shivered at the unwanted memory.

"Disparate technologies brought together, a symphony of form and function with a single, grand purpose. With it, I will erase pain from the world." She paused. "Worlds, actually. You stole the power I needed out there, Jim. You interrupted my process. But I have progressed too far now and that trick will not work again. The Cascade is inevitable."

The Cascade. Hearing the term brought everything together in Jim's thoughts. All that he'd sensed about this machine clicked together in its final form. He now had a working scale model in his mind's eye. And for the first time, he saw clearly what Summer was doing.

"The Cascade," he repeated, thick with dread. He peered up at the cage of swirling red energy above them. "Red Plasma's energy. You're super-concentrating it until there's a chain reaction."

"Which my substations across the world will channel and amplify. The effect will be like dropping shards of the sun onto the planet. Everyone gone in a flash. They won't have time to feel any pain. They'll just cease to exist."

Staring at the doomsday machine, at the grotesquery of Framework's armor, at the hero being slowly drained, Jim felt gutted to his core. Summer—his Summer—would rather have died than become *this*.

He spun the image of the machine in his mind, looking for weak points. But it was so complex and unlike anything he'd ever seen, he'd need hours to find a kill-switch. There just wasn't enough time.

Framework stepped closer. "I'm glad you're here, Jim. It feels right for you and Summer to share this *final moment*."

On the last words, her voice intensified. Jim had been distracted by thoughts of the machine, and Framework must have noticed. He heard a noise, felt the machinery shift in his senses, and turned just in time to see a razor-sharp lance of steel fly at him.

While it moved as if in slow motion, filling his vision, Jim recalled their conversation at the Spike. Framework had promised not to kill him, for Summer's sake.

She lied to me. Hmph. Villains these days.

The air beside him shimmered. Then something crashed into Jim and knocked him to the floor. Steel sliced through the space where he'd been a split second before. He rolled away as more lances chewed into the spot where he'd fallen.

Regaining his feet, Jim reached toward Framework's armor and wrenched at the first thing his senses touched. She grunted and went down on one knee, and the assault ceased.

Then Jim caught sight of his savior and gasped. Grinning, Kelvin gave a silent salute, then shimmered and disappeared.

"You cannot stop it!" Framework bellowed.

Jim watched her yank on the armor's collapsed knee and struggle to stand, riding high on the knowledge that his friend was alive. That despite years of plotting, Framework's disciple had failed when it counted.

No plan was perfect. No machine was unstoppable. No villain could account for every possible move. At their core, even the smartest and most powerful of them were still only human. They only knew what they knew.

Then Jim knew why he, and no one else, had to be here at this moment. Because Framework may know everything in the world, but Summer knew what Summer knew, and that was in her machine, too.

He turned a full circle, studying the monstrous thing with fresh eyes, letting every moving part fill his thoughts. And he saw it there, as clear as the memory it awakened.

They had transformed the inner shell into a sort of life-sized game board. At key points and junctions, those wires intersected with makeshift levers attached to actuators and a few other components Jimmy didn't quite understand, but Summer seemed perfectly comfortable with. Together they created Gotcha's three-dimensional maze—true paths and false paths and collapsible paths and movable paths, along with switchable traps built from those levers and actuators.

His goal? Send an electrical pulse from the batteries, guide it through the maze, and return it home to the batteries once again. Summer's goal? Block or trap that pulse in the maze, preventing it from returning home. They had played at least three dozen times now.

And Summer had never lost.

There wasn't one single kill-switch built into the machine. There were a thousand tiny ones, and if he could flip enough of them, turn the machine back on itself . . .

Gazing up at it, Jim smirked. "Gotcha."

TWENTY SEVEN

JIM had never actually won their game. But this time was different.

This time, he had a reason to.

All the energy he'd absorbed roared to life inside him, expanding the sphere of his power to encompass the entire structure. Eyes closed, arms wide, he let Framework's machine fill his mind and went to work.

With a mental gesture, a small piece of the machine switched and began channeling Red Plasma's power in a different direction. Then Jim switched another piece, then another, and another, sending the power this way and that, sometimes in a new direction and sometimes doubling back on itself. The changes began to interrupt the carefully planned pattern that Framework needed to create the Cascade.

"Wait," Framework said. "Wait, stop. What are you doing?"

Jim reached deeper into the machine. He grabbed larger pieces scattered throughout the machine, some related to his strategy and others chosen at random. He slammed some forcefully into new positions while gently suggesting a change to others.

He heard clanking footsteps, watched in his mind's eye as Framework's armor approached. He kept working.

"Jim," she said regretfully. "You know I can't let you do this. Not even for Summer's sake. I'm sorry."

He opened his eyes to see her towering over him. The battle suit's left arm rearranged into a massive hammer. She raised it high and took aim. He kept working on the machine, determined to keep this up until the very last moment before he had to retreat.

Then Framework lurched and cried out as if struggling with herself. Jim tensed, on the verge of running.

A black blur streaked into view. With a metallic screech, the hammer sliced away from the battle suit and clanked to the ground. Stone fingers burst up through the ground and then spread into a complex latticework around Framework, pinning her in place. The villain struggled against her bonds, but the stone kept growing over her in overlapping layers, not giving an inch.

Zoe appeared at Jim's side, wielding Dark Sympathy and a devastatingly cute little grin. "Are you really trying to save the world without us?"

Jim grinned back. "I was thinking about it, yeah. My bad."

"That's a no-no, Jim!" Natalie called as she moved to the Spike and began smashing the machinery attached to it. "Family saves the world together."

"I knew you had this in you." Zoe kissed his cheek. "Now, what are you waiting for? Bring this thing down."

"Red Plasma," Jim said. "When it happens, get him out."

"You got it."

Zoe sheathed herself in Aethyr and zoomed away.

"You think I don't know every inch of my machine?" Framework spat. "This is anything but over."

Her presence dove into the device. Jim could feel it chasing after him, setting right what he had made wrong, even creating new pathways for the power that hadn't been there before. It was like trying to solve a Rubik's cube as an opponent came behind and changed every move, while trying to stab him. Jim raced forward, his mind working faster than he'd thought possible, leaving his body behind to become streams of pure thought and electrical control racing through the inner workings of the Cascade device.

The battle for the world did not come down to muscle. No punches thrown, no energy beams fired. It was a chess match between two people who knew each other better than anyone. They stood unmoving, face to face, will against will, with the great machine in each of their grips. It writhed around them like a living thing.

Jim tossed up traps and blocks and trips and false paths, shielding his changes from being easily reverted, all while shifting larger and larger swathes of the machine with single commands. Piece by piece, Framework slowly fell behind. She growled in frustration and redoubled her efforts. The machine shuddered, threatening to collapse in the iron grip of two opposing masters.

Jim almost had it, but Framework kept hanging on, nipping at his heels. She had rigged the game from the start and all she needed was time. If she ran out the clock before Jim could finish, it wouldn't matter what he'd done or how close he'd come.

All these moves and countermoves, and it came down to one missing piece. He only needed one piece in a place where there was no piece now—a bridge to a new connection—but she blocked him time after time.

He had to do something Framework couldn't anticipate.

"Summer," he said. "Summer, look!"

He sent the mental *revert to default* command, and the shiny new Lode costume transformed. Stepping closer to Framework in her imprisoned armor, he turned for her to take in the full sight of what he wore.

For a moment, nothing happened. Then the battle suit stopped struggling against the stone, and he knew he had her attention.

"They . . . they gave you the black cape," she said, sounding truly shocked. And in this moment, truly like his sister. "Jim. I'm so proud of you."

Though Jim had created this moment, he couldn't have predicted how deeply it would hit him. Tears burned behind his eyes.

"More than anyone, I needed you to see this," he said. "To know that what you always wanted to happen actually did. It happened because of you, Summer."

"This is a gift, Jim. Thank you." She gave a long, weary sigh. "I suppose we should keep going now."

"Wait." Jim held up a staying hand. "What if we didn't? What if we both stopped right now? We can choose to end this here, if we choose together."

"We can't. I have to complete my mission, and you have to complete yours, and neither of us will stop until one succeeds and the other falls. That's the way of things with heroes and villains."

Jim shook his head. "I'm not a hero."

"Of course not. They don't give the black cape to heroes, Jim. They give it to those who aren't bound by their code, who can do what needs to be done."

Jim pondered, taken aback. He had bet on Summer knowing what the black cape was, but hadn't thought beyond showing it to her. Then he realized the implication of what she'd just said, and his eyebrows shot up.

"Wait," he said. "You think you're the hero and I'm the villain?"

The armor affected a shrug. "If it helps, I still love you."

Jim blew out a breath. "Wow. Never trust a nice moment, Jim. You know that."

Summer laughed. He hadn't heard that in a decade, and it pierced him through.

"Okay, Jim," she said with melancholy affection. "Back to our game, then?"

He hated this. He hated everything about it and always would. But it was what he'd come here to do. Eventually, every game had to end, and there had to be a winner.

"*Back* to it?" he said. "I never stopped playing."

Framework gasped, and Jim knew she saw what he had done. While Summer was distracted by their exchange, a last moment between long-lost siblings, Jim had quietly maneuvered the game board into his ultimate gambit. He only needed one piece to complete his redesign of Framework's machine, and until now, she'd blocked him from finding one.

So he made Framework herself the last piece.

Jim slapped his hands together, and the machine responded. Mirroring his motion, it deployed two mechanical appendages that reached through the stone restraints and latched onto Framework's armor. The pathway he needed was now complete.

"Jim!" she cried, struggling against her bonds.

She's an Apex parahuman, he told himself desperately. *She can survive this. She will. SHE WILL.*

"Jim, please don't!"

Jim gave the command. His new pathway activated. Now there were two opposing flows of Red Plasma's energy—the one he'd let Framework fix, and the secret one he'd snuck in underneath it. Instead of working together to concentrate all that power, now they turned against each other, competing for dominance.

The machine shuddered and groaned. Deep inside it, something important snapped.

"No!" Framework screamed. "*NOOOO!*"

Jim knew he'd hear that scream for the rest of his days. If there were going to be any days past this one. He peered up as it all fractured around him, machinery breaking down and raw energy bursting free. This place didn't have long.

She'll survive, he promised yet again. *They'll keep her safe, locked away somewhere.*

And Jim had kept his promise to himself that one day Summer's loss would be answered for. Though it hadn't happened like he'd imagined all these years. Still, it was done. Now the only thing to do was wait. He closed his eyes, feeling something like satisfaction.

For you, Summer. And for Highreach. Always.

From out of nowhere, a hand gripped his shoulder. Jim's eyes sprang open, then widened in shock. Kelvin stood there, shaking his head.

"No way, pal," Kelvin said. "It's not even close to your time yet."

His grip tightened. The world around them became a rushing blur. Then they were standing outside, a half mile away. Jim watched from a distance as hero and villain alike fled in all directions, while Framework's machine destroyed itself.

It began as surges of red light and rending metal. The ground trembled. Booms like thunder filled the sky. Then matter gave way to energy. In a single instantaneous burst of light, like a red sun had descended to Earth, the great device turned to ash. Then it was gone, leaving silence in its wake.

Jim stared, not knowing how to feel. They had won. But there had been a cost.

Eventually, three pairs of arms wrapped around him.

"Red Plasma's safe," Natalie said. "We got him out."

"Thanks, Nat." Jim looked to Kelvin, a thousand questions in his eyes.

His friend gave a shrug and a sheepish little smile. "Guess what they said about the Spike is true. I'll explain later."

"Do you want to go back?" Zoe asked. "To . . . to see if . . ."

Jim nodded. "I need to. Kelvin?"

"You got it, friend."

Another rushing blur took the four of them back to ground zero. Though from a distance it appeared that everything had vaporized, there were still piles of debris left behind, most of them warped and scorched beyond recognition.

With two exceptions. The Spike, which was unmarked, as if nothing at all had happened around it. And the one Jim knelt before now. Framework's battle suit had blackened to a crisp, but it was still there.

She survived. She's still here.

Jim repeated it to himself as he approached the burnt husk and pulled at the remaining plates of armor. His friends kept back, letting him do this alone without having to ask. Yet another thing he'd feel gratitude for later.

The pieces crumbled until only the innermost layer remained. Jim grabbed with both hands and yanked with all his might. It peeled away, revealing the cockpit buried deep inside the torso of the giant battle suit. It was still intact—not even burned.

And it was empty.

Jim blinked. Had the explosion reduced Summer to atoms? That couldn't have happened without burning anything else. So, what happened to her? Where was she?

"As I suspected," Skypuncher said.

Jim turned to see Skypuncher, Lord Neon, Millennia, and Geometron had joined them. Probably to see what he'd come to see, though for different reasons.

"As did I," Geometron said. "For someone with Framework's abilities, there would be no reason to pilot the armor from the inside. She could be anywhere in the world and we would never know it."

"Then she's still out there," Millennia said, gripping her sword tighter. "Still a global threat."

"A threat, yes, but not a global one," Lord Neon said. "Not yet. It took Framework years to get to this moment, and her network is being dismantled as we speak. She may no longer be captive, but even an Apex villain will need time to rebuild. Possibly years."

"Maybe she'll have help." Geometron cast a hateful look in Jim's direction. "How convenient that our greatest enemy still has family. When she returns, we'll be ready to take down *any-one* under her influence."

She wanted so badly to run him through with something sharp. Jim could see it in her eyes—the rage, barely contained, fueled by grief. She must have loved Anchor very much.

"I know what you really are," he said. "I saw the truth back on the Lighthouse, when I stopped you from killing those kids. When I took control."

Geometron's red eye flared and her fists clenched. Her anger was just a mask, though. Behind it, there was fear.

"And I promise you . . ." Jim stepped closer, facing her fully and refusing to back down. "No matter what happens, I will *never* tell anyone. I know what it's like to carry a secret, and yours is safe with me."

The hero blinked, taken aback. Her rage faded, chased away by surprise and confusion and barely concealed relief. It occurred to Jim then that, in revealing his knowledge of Geometron's true origin, he may have given her even greater reason to get rid of him. Oh, well. He'd just have to chance it.

He glanced over her shoulder. Then, with a curt nod to the stunned Geometron, he stepped around her and approached who he really needed to speak to. This conversation had been a long time coming.

"I think it's time I stopped blaming you for everything that happened. You may not have handled it perfectly, or the way I would've wanted you to, but you did your best in what I see now were impossible circumstances. And you kept my sister alive." He offered his hand to Skypuncher. "Thank you for that."

The hero accepted his hand. He gave a tentative smile, as if a heavy weight had fallen from his shoulders. "I look forward to working with you . . . Lode? Interruptor? Black Cape?"

"Let's start with Jim." He gave a lopsided grin. "I look forward to pointing out when you're all being idiots."

Skypuncher chuckled. "We'll be in touch soon. The Black Cape is always needed." His eyes twinkled. "Your world is about to get a whole lot bigger."

TWENTY EIGHT

JIM saw Highreach in greater focus. Before leaving to search for Summer on the Lighthouse, he had walked these same streets, only seeing the city through the haze of memories that haunted him. Now, having made peace with at least some of his past, he could love the city anew.

Two days ago, he saved the world with the help of his friends. Now people were rebuilding what Framework had destroyed, and life would continue. They would never know how close they came to the end. It was probably better that way.

After his conversation with Skypuncher, the Spectrum had taken full command of the scene and the surrounding area, helping Sydney get back on its feet. Though a handful of villains had been captured, most escaped in the chaos. Still a successful mission, given that life on the planet continued.

Jim had only gotten a brief moment to say goodbye to his friends and promise to see them soon. Prism teams had separated them and whisked them off in four directions, each to be debriefed. The Spectrum wanted a full account of everything that happened, from the moment they set foot on the Lighthouse to the last moment in Framework's machine. They had taken pity on Jim and the interview had been mercifully brief—maybe a product of his relationship with the villain, or maybe a perk of his new standing with the Spectrum. If the black cape could get him out of boring conversations with heroes, he considered that worth the trade.

He suspected, though, that Skypuncher had told them to go easy and give him time. For that, he was grateful, and he was using it as best he could. Versus would be closed until tomorrow, which gave him a day to just wander the streets, reacquainting himself with his home and remembering why he loved it, sharing that with the memory of who Summer had been.

"So, that's how I knew you'd see the green line," Eli said. "With all my Sensor abilities, I see parahuman power, and I found in you the potential to see it, too."

He floated beside Jim, a translucent vision that only the two of them could see, projected directly into Jim's thoughts. Lord Neon had his hands full—putting the world right again, rebuilding trust in the Spectrum—but Eli had wanted to check in on Jim himself.

"Makes sense. You know, in a this-life-is-crazy kind of way," Jim said. "You haven't answered my question, though."

Eli cleared his throat, looking down at the sidewalk. "Understand, Jim, I have never spoken this out loud to anyone but the Spectrum and a handful of others who know the truth."

Jim gave a lopsided grin. "Good thing it's only us capes here."

Eli chuckled, then grew serious. "Summer was right about Prism heroes being sent to the Spike in Sydney. We hadn't even learned about the other Spikes yet. It had just appeared there in Hyde Park, coming from nowhere without warning, and we had to investigate. By the time her Prism arrived, the fighting had already started, and it was intense. They were losing badly until she touched the Spike and went Apex. Single-handedly, she defeated the threat and shoved it back through the Spike. Then she herself *became* the threat, and we had to deal with her. You know the rest of the story. Despite all that happened after, I believe your sister's instincts were right. If that same threat rises again, it will be much worse than the first time. So, since that day, we have quietly built contingencies. However, at best, they are a guess. We don't really know what would happen, or if we could protect the world from it."

"Hmm, interesting. Especially since you're still not actually saying anything," Jim said, poking at the phantom beside him. Then he took his biggest swing. "Whatever this secret is, Summer paid the price for it."

Eli sighed. "They call themselves the Vir. The Spikes, near as we can tell, function as inter-dimensional claws that hook into our world and then act as bridges so they can cross the barrier between realities. One power they wield—which we believe is the key to the Spikes—is something called Silvyr, their reality's version of our Aethyr. You've seen it before. Those veins flowing over the Spike."

Jim nodded. "So, they were some kind of invading force."

"Tip of the spear, we believe, sent to secure a beachhead on our world. A staging ground for a larger incursion. But then Framework happened, and she repelled them with such staggering ferocity, we believe it's why we have not seen them again." Eli gave Jim a heavy, ominous look. "We also believe it's only a matter of time. Eventually, they will try again, and when they do, it will be with overwhelming force. And they won't take no for an answer."

For a moment, Jim stared at the hero. Then he chuckled. "You're really serious. So, the Spike was a first contact situation? Little green men from some other world?"

"Not little, and not green. And not just some other world—another plane of existence. One we still know frighteningly little about."

Now the weight and magnitude of the secret hit Jim. They were one isolated little planet in a quiet universe—as far as they knew. That had been Jim's idea of reality for his entire life. To believe this for twenty-eight years, and then learn that somewhere out there was a whole other universe that might be preparing to strike, and it could happen tomorrow for all they knew . . .

Eli eyed him. "Now you understand why we kept it quiet."

"I do." Jim gave a mirthless laugh. "Summer was right."

He fell silent then, and Eli caught the look in his eyes. "We'll find her, Jim. This time we'll bring her in peacefully. She'll be kept safe, and so will the world."

Jim nodded, wanting to believe it. "I know you'll try. *We'll* try. I just hope . . ." He trailed off. What did he hope? He wasn't sure. Then he glanced over Eli's ghostly shoulder and chuckled. "Well, that figures."

"What does?" Eli turned. "Ah, I see."

Apparently, Jim's random wanderings through Highreach weren't so random after all. He was standing across the street from Washburne Avenue. From here, he could see house 116. His old home, and the first hideout of Lock and Lode, before life had happened to his family.

"I'll leave you now. This feels like a private moment," Eli said. "Until next time, Jim."

"Right."

Jim gave a distracted wave as Eli's specter faded away. He couldn't take his eyes off the old house. Whoever lived there now, they were taking good care of it. The paint looked fresh, and the tiny front yard had little pops of color within a neatly arranged cactus garden.

Jim's feet moved on their own, depositing him on the sidewalk in front of the narrow little two-story home. He gazed up at it, filled with a sudden ache and longing. Was this how it felt when people said they needed closure?

Whatever it was, he found himself knocking on the door.

"Hi," he said when it opened. "I'm not here to sell you anything. But I have kind of an odd request."

Jacob and Maya, the young couple living there, listened as Jim explained who he was and what this house meant to him. Arms around each other, they projected heavy trepidation as he spoke in circles and then finally got to the point—a request to come inside for five minutes and just . . . look. Just be in this place, see the rooms where his happiest memories were made.

"We, um," Maya said, glancing back inside the house. "We're not really prepared for company."

"Maybe another day," Jacob suggested. "Just not now."

It had been a silly idea. Of course they wouldn't let a stranger in based on some unverified history with their house. They were being smart. Looking down, Jim nodded while a wave of crippling sadness crashed over him.

"Sure, I understand. No problem, " he said to the welcome mat at his feet. Then he looked up. "Hey, one thing. Is the lemon tree still there, out back? We planted it when . . ."

He trailed off. In the blink of an eye, electricity had just surged through the house, then switched off entirely, then returned to normal. It had been so fast—inhumanly fast. If he hadn't been standing this close, even he would have missed it.

". . . um, when my sister graduated high school," he continued, feigning nonchalance as he cast a sharper gaze over the house. "Just, uh, a lot of good memories under that tree."

The young couple must have noticed the shift in his demeanor. They pressed closer to each other, holding tighter.

"It's there," Maya said. There was a tremor in her voice now. "We . . . we love it."

"We do," Jacob said. "When you come back, we'll make you some lemonade."

"Another day," Maya said.

"Yes, another day," Jacob repeated.

Jim saw it now—the fear behind their eyes. But they weren't afraid of him being inside their house.

They were afraid of something already there.

"I'd like that," Jim said.

He stepped backward and off the porch to create distance between them. On the walkway, he could see the entire house now. He'd have to move quickly, get this done in one fell swoop, or it could spin out of control.

"I'll try again next week, or–" The house suddenly glowed brighter in his perception, not a surge but a sustained swell of power. He pointed at the couple and waved toward the street. "Get out! Now!"

They just stared back, wide-eyed and frozen.

"Now!" Jim cried. "Summer, wait–"

The top floor windows shattered outward, raining glass. The roof imploded. The couple screamed and fled toward the street.

"Keep running!" Jim called after them. Then he faced the house, stepping further back as he spoke. "Summer, don't do this. Just hear my voice."

His childhood home collapsed. But the shattered remains didn't fall down. They pulled together and rearranged themselves.

Memories resurfaced, unbidden and unwanted. News feeds of buildings in downtown Sydney coming to life on their own, transforming, adding to layer upon layer of armor around Framework. Before it ended, she had turned skyscrapers and city blocks into a living extension of herself. In the modern age, nearly every standing structure had some kind of computer running its internal systems, from Wi-Fi to air conditioning. Anything even touched by a device running on computer code was hers to command.

He stood next to a light pole now. Slapping his palm against it, Jim *pulled*. A rush of electricity surged from the city power grid and down into his veins.

"Please don't make me do this," he said.

Atop the jumbled remains of the house, a seam formed and then split open, revealing Summer there inside it.

"I can't go back in their cage, Jim!" she cried. "I won't!"

The house slammed shut and then *stood up*. Summer had transformed it into a mobile suit, which now stepped over

Jim and moved away. If she kept going in the same direction, it would take her further into the city, where the buildings got much bigger and stronger. And more populated.

Summer squeezed her makeshift battle suit between two houses, leaving them cracked and leaning, then leapt over the next street and punched a hole through the roof of a small corrugated steel warehouse. The building shivered with a loud clatter, then flew to pieces and absorbed into the suit, giving it thicker plates of armor.

As Jim watched her go, this time he felt no hesitation. Only certainty. Today would not be a repeat of all those years ago. Today, he would end it for real, and for good. The black cape material rippled around him, transforming from street clothes to the modern, updated Lode costume he'd worn in Sydney.

With no time to plan, he could only think of one way to do this, and even that was a gamble. He gestured at a row of a dozen cars parked along the street. Riding high on all the power he'd absorbed, he *pulled* at them, too, sending commands through their electrical systems and into their frames. Tires squealed as they surged toward him and their shapes began to change.

TWENTY NINE

IT wasn't supposed to happen this way. She should have had more time! But Jim just had to get sentimental.

Now Framework had no choice. Instead of receding into the shadows to recover and plan, she had to do this the hard way, like she had in Sydney so long ago. This time she would do it faster, better. This time, she knew how to build herself into something that couldn't be stopped. And this time she had two cities at her fingertips. Saving the world would begin here.

As she absorbed the little warehouse—a nice way to warm up—Framework cast her awareness across the Reaches. Code blanketed everything everywhere, streams of digitized purple flowing like the lifeblood of the world. She sent out a burst of code in all directions, a wave of disruption that should jam any attempts to call for help. She couldn't have the Spectrum showing up. At least, not yet.

She resumed stomping across city streets, passing out of residential and into commercial and light industrial. The structures were larger and stronger here. She swept through a construction contractor's building, pulling the heavy machinery into her battle suit, followed by the office.

Then she lifted her gaze and looked ahead. In the distance, the Atherton skyscraper glimmered like a beacon. She would take that one next. And it would only be the beginning. With a voracious grin, she moved forward.

Mid-step, something caught her awareness, coming in from the right and moving far too fast. She turned to see another battle suit charging at her, this one a combination of vehicles. Just as she caught sight of it, the mech leapt and swung and smashed its makeshift fist into her flank with a resounding *crash*. Framework grunted from the heavy impact.

"Uh-oh!" Jim's voice blared through all the vehicles' speakers, his smaller suit squaring up with hers. "Looks like rush hour came early."

Framework gave a frustrated huff. "Jim, you know this is futile-*whoa!*"

Her brother dropped low and spun, sweeping her legs out from under her. As she clanked to the pavement, he rolled on top and grabbed her and kicked into a flip, using the momentum to send her tumbling down the street, back toward the rows of warehouses. Pavement buckled under the impact. Light poles and parked cars smashed beneath her. The few pedestrians in the area fled as fast as they could.

So, that's why he's pushing me in this direction, she thought. *Fewer casualties*. Well, she could use the warehouses, too, so his little gambit wouldn't matter in the end.

Climbing back to her feet, Framework absorbed the crushed cars beneath her and formed them into a hammer-like appendage.

As Jim darted in for another attack, she reconfigured her torso to add a spinning function, then whirled her top half like a lawnmower blade.

The hammer smashed into Jim, ripping off his mechanized right arm at the shoulder and tossing him through the air like a rag doll. He crashed through the foyer of a two-story building and the roof collapsed on top of him. She stomped her foot down on the wreckage, impacting it further, then turned to resume her trek toward Atherton Industries.

Only to face two more multi-vehicle battle suits, each wielding a light pole like a lance. Before she could react, they skewered her clear through the torso.

Jim's voice blared from both. "Oh, no! Which one is he in?!"

Still clutching the light poles, they dashed in opposite directions, spinning a circle around Framework until her top half sheared free of her bottom half and tumbled to the pavement. Then they leapt onto her legs and clawed at them viciously, reducing them to unusable scrap.

"Hate to say it, sis, but you're half the woman you used to be," Jim said. "Wait. That was a pun, and I kinda liked it. Does that mean I'm growing or regressing?"

"For God's sake, JUST SHUT UP!" Framework roared.

Snatching up Jim's machines, she smashed them together over and over until they flew to pieces. Then she flipped over and crawled, dragging herself toward the nearest standing warehouse. Her jamming pulse wouldn't hold the Spectrum off forever. She needed mass, she needed armor, and she needed them quickly.

With a great heaving motion, she scraped close enough to punch through the roof of a warehouse. It was practically an antique, but there was enough modern tech inside to give her control. Layer by industrial layer, the shell of the old place flew to pieces and joined her.

"*Alert*," a pleasant voice said inside her head. "*You have entered a Warded Zone. Please abide by-thurrrrrlllzzz . . .*"

The voice garbled and cut off as she finished absorbing the warehouse. Ignoring the warning—meaningless now that the building was hers—Framework stood while the battle suit reconfigured into a new, stronger form around her.

Feeling powerful again, she breathed a sigh of relief. If Jim came at her with yet another suit, their next clash would go much differently.

"If you're even still alive," Framework said aloud. Something deep inside her recoiled at that, a flash of regret. She shoved it down. "Not that it will matter soon."

"Aw, I love you, too."

Framework gasped as arms wrapped around her from behind—human arms of flesh and blood—and locked on with surprising strength.

"Hey, Summer," Jim said into her ear. "Let's catch up."

"But-but *how*?" Framework sputtered.

She struggled against his embrace. Jim clutched harder than he'd ever held anything before. It was darkly hilarious, knowing the fate of the world may depend on his grip strength.

"I was never in any of them," he said. "While you fought my suits, I drove to where they were herding you. Let me guess, you thought I was keeping you away from pedestrians? You never questioned why I brought you *here,* so you focused on replacing the mass I took away, and didn't stop to think twice about what you absorbed to do it."

She cursed under her breath. "It was Versus, wasn't it?"

"Yeah. You just ate my bar *and* my apartment—a sentence I never thought I'd have to say, by the way. And when you did, I was inside waiting for you."

He still barely believed his gamble had worked. As Framework reduced his building to components for her battle suit, he had ridden the fragments into the machine and climbed his way to her. With no time to plan something better, it had been the only way he could think to get close enough. For this to work, he had to be touching her.

"I love you, Summer," he said. "But you're wrong. You don't know *all* of human history—only what's on computers.

Too often, we record the darkness and forget the light, but that doesn't mean it's not there. The pure, the genuine, the self-less. A million little happy memories in even a single lifetime. Moments of kindness over cruelty, moments that go unno-ticed by the world but make all the difference to one person. The good that makes the bad bearable, the joy that carries us through the pain. The people we love and who love us. That was you and me, Summer, before all of this. It could be us again. You just have to stop."

She struggled against him, failing to break free.

"Please, Jim. I . . . I can't," she pleaded, on the verge of tears. "This is the only thing I'm alive to do." Then she grimaced and growled, desperation flashing into Framework's rage. "Release me *now*! You'll never stop me. I'll keep going until it's done, or until you kill me. If you have it in you."

Jim closed his eyes and sighed. It was the sound of his heart breaking all over again.

"All those moments we didn't record," he said, holding back tears. "That's what I'll choose to remember."

Framework cried out, straining against him with all her might. "How are you doing this?! I AM APEX!"

"You are." Jim's voice fell to a whisper. "But I'm a Vessel."

She turned her head in alarm, craning her neck to stare into his eyes. "You wouldn't."

". . . I already am." The first of Jim's tears fell. "I'm sorry."

He had started slowly at first, just a trickle so she wouldn't notice her power draining. But now that they both knew what was about to happen, Jim couldn't hold back. Inside, he released every limiter containing his ability and kicked the door wide open. Every scrap of his power focused on draining Summer of hers.

"No!" she wailed, shedding tears of panic. "Jim, please, *noooo*!"

"I'm sorry."

Her battle suit shuddered as she fought to keep control. Jim held on tighter, taking as much energy as he could from her. It felt like drinking the sun. Every cell in his body blazed. He kept going.

"I HAVE TO SAVE THE WORLD!"

"I'm sorry, Summer," he said through his own tears. "I'm sorry. I love you."

Her machine trembled. Then it collapsed.

Joined together, they tumbled as one to the destroyed pavement as heavy debris piled on top of them. Jim barely even felt it. He just held on to his sister, draining her of everything.

"I'm sorry," he said over and over. "I'm sorry."

The light inside her was flickering now. That glowing green orb was almost out. It wouldn't be long.

There was an eternal moment when all Jim could hear was their labored breathing. Then she shivered, and as she turned to look him in the eye, he saw something different in her gaze.

He saw his sister.

"Jimmy?" she said.

He worked to collect himself. "Yeah, Summer, it's me."

"Oh." Her eyes glazed over. Her head fell back, lolling against his chest. "I think I had a bad dream."

Jim choked back a sob. "Don't worry, it's over now. I'm here."

She groaned like she used to on lazy Saturday mornings, when she didn't want to wake up just yet. "I'm so tired."

"I know. You . . . had a busy day. And a long night."

"Oh. Did Mom make breakfast yet?"

"I'm sure she will soon."

"I hope it's pancakes. With . . ."

". . . with boysenberry syrup."

She nodded, smiling while her eyelids drooped. "Yeah. Why would–?"

"–why would anyone eat anything else?" Jim gave a little laugh that turned into a sob. He quickly suppressed it. "You can go back to sleep now. I'll come wake you when they're ready."

She gave a contented sigh. "Sounds perfect. Can't fight evil on an empty stomach."

"And if you could, why would you want to?"

Through the half-asleep haze, she laughed. Summer's real laugh, the amused little giggle, free of the weight of everything to come. With slow, languid movements, she reached into her pocket and withdrew something small and pressed it into Jim's palm. He looked down at it.

The Thunderous hero coin. The one he'd given her that night all those years ago, when she'd saved his life from their first enemy.

She had kept it. All these years, through all of this, Summer had kept the coin. Jim couldn't help flipping it over to read the inscription.

For Highreach. Always.

"You'll be here when I wake up?" Summer asked, almost gone now.

"Always. I promise." He kissed the top of her head. "Good night, Summer."

Her lips barely moved. "G'night, Jimmy."

Then, except for the smallest spark to keep her alive, Summer Riven went dark and Framework went with her.

Jim lost track of how long he lay there with her. Too long. Not long enough.

Eventually, the wreckage above shifted and a shaft of light illuminated them, while a team of heroes worked together to dig them free.

THIRTY

THE rain fell in sheets. A thick, gloomy night hung over Sydney in the aftermath of Framework's second attempt. A halo of ethereal silver light wreathed the Spike and the heavy mist around it, illuminating the shattered remnants of the terrifying machine.

Four shapes lay at the edge of the light. Moments before, the four heroes had been standing guard over this place, keeping vigilant until the Spectrum arrived tomorrow to inspect the wreckage and remove anything dangerous. Now they sprawled unconscious.

A figure hovered above them, keeping out of the light. A cloak like billowing smoke flowed off his shoulders, obscuring all but glimpses of his armored form. The space around him seemed to ripple and distort in response to his movements. He held up one shadowy, gauntlet-clad hand, and two lieutenants melted out of the darkness to stand at his side.

For a moment he kept silent and still, observing. Then he spoke in a voice like folded steel layered with whispers and screams.

"There is something here that we will need." He tilted his head. "Proceed."

"What do we search for?" one lieutenant asked.

"I will know when you find it. Recover what you can quickly, while the Spectrum licks its wounds. Destroy the rest."

"And the Spike?" said the other lieutenant.

A faint laugh of derision. "Not yet."

Turning toward the figure in shadow, the lieutenants bowed and spoke in unison.

"Yes, Chaos Merchant."

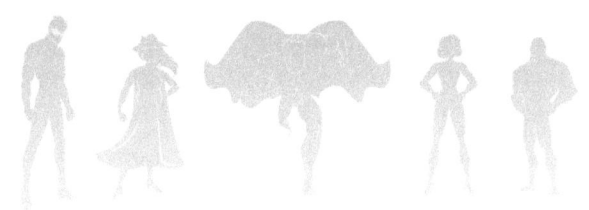

THIRTY ONE

"... QUESTIONS continue to mount in the aftermath of the disastrous new Dare and the reemergence of Framework, a villain long thought to be dead..."

"... various sources, speaking on the condition of anonymity, suggest that fatalities may have occurred on the Lighthouse. Though some details line up between their stories, there seems to be disagreement with regard to the nature of the Spectrum's involvement and their level of accountability for..."

"... responding quickly to rebuild what was lost in Sydney, as well as in Highreach. Though, thankfully, this attack by Framework appears to have been halted before any civilian casualties occurred..."

"... the object known as the Spike remains mysteriously unscathed..."

"... although none of the capes have yet to make public statements, Skypuncher did submit a written pledge to do so in the near future. In the meantime, the Spectrum has closed ranks in order to recover and reassess in the aftermath of what appears to have been a near-cataclysmic event..."

"... another in a long list of mysteries is the reappearance of Lode, who was a local Highreach hero more than a decade ago, *but whose last recorded action occurred around the same time as Framework's first attack on Sydney . . ."*

". . . footage captured in both Sydney and Highreach suggests that this small-time hero was present, and in fact a central figure, in the ultimate defeat of Framework. Lode, whose previous disappearance merited little more than a footnote in hero history, has now become the subject of fascination, with many around the world clamoring to know where he's been and why he chose now to return. However, he has not been seen since the recent battle in Highreach, and authorities remain unsure of . . ."

". . . and in other news, a rooftop explosion in New Beijinsk may be connected to a virus designed to target cybernetics, as well as the emergence of a new hero in the port city. Early reports indicate that . . ."

". . . yesterday a ninth victim fell into the same unnatural coma, and his condition is listed as critical. Investigators say a connection between these comas would not have been established—in fact, they would merely have been considered medical mysteries—if not for an anomaly present at these nine locations, which may suggest parahuman involvement . . ."

In his meditation chamber, Lord Neon watched and listened. Every written word, every frame of video—he absorbed it all.

As usual, there was much to do and little time to get it done. It would take work to restore confidence in the Spectrum, but it would happen. It always did.

The Chaos Merchant continued to elude him. He still hadn't puzzled out how that was possible. Everyone feared the villain, saw him as untouchable, and that led to assumptions about his power. Because if he continued undefeated, it must be because he is too strong to challenge.

Lord Neon disagreed. Whatever abilities the Chaos Merchant possessed, the hero believed they were far more subtle than everyone suspected. But that belief was not a source of comfort. If anything, it made the villain more dangerous.

An enemy who fought with fists was often predictable, but an enemy who fought with mind . . .

Well. The Chaos Merchant was a puzzle Lord Neon wouldn't solve today. He knew enough to recognize he didn't have all the pieces. Yet. He would continue devoting a corner of his mind to working on it.

In the meantime, the black cape had a bearer once again. The Spectrum needed Jim to go active soon, for both their sakes. Something told Lord Neon they would need each other.

And he prayed fervently that this Black Cape would work out better than the last one.

THIRTY TWO

Two Weeks Later

"SO, it turns out I'm *not* some all-powerful godlike being now."
Kelvin shrugged. "But Miss Atherton did say the Spike was basically a lottery, so I'll take what I can get. I would've settled for not dying, but this is a pretty cool bonus. All things considered, I guess I'd give my Spike experience five stars."

"Wow, five stars," Jim said. "That's high praise—take it from someone who owns a service business. Well, someone who used to own a service business and will own one again soon, after the rebuild. Yikes, that's a mouthful. Never mind, pretend I only said the first part."

Kelvin clapped him on the shoulder. "You got it, buddy."

Apparently, that flash of light when he hit the Spike had not been Kelvin vaporizing. Instead of killing him, the Spike had *remade* him. Gone were his Chaos Merchant implants and his wound from Jim ripping that tiny bomb out of his chest, and in their place was a fairly significant upgrade. Now, in addition to a higher Faraday rating and enhanced invisibility powers, Kelvin could phase himself and others over distance. There were one or two other new abilities, but he wasn't ready to talk about those yet. Even he wasn't totally sure what they did.

New Kelvin also came with an added bonus. The shedding of his implants, combined with a convincing new identity provided by one of Zoe's underworld contacts, might lead the Chaos Merchant to believe that his agent had perished amid the havoc. If all went as hoped, he would have a fresh start. The Spectrum still hadn't figured out what he uploaded to the Lighthouse, but they would keep looking.

With a contented sigh, Kelvin settled back in his chair and sipped his fancy cocktail. They sat side by side, lounging on folding beach chairs under an umbrella, while across the street the initial site work began for Versus 2.0. Big things were coming. What was old would be new, and Jim intended to put this place on the map again.

"I'll come back to visit, you know," Kelvin said. "But I need *new* while I figure out next steps, and it's about time I got reacquainted with a young gentleman by the name of *me*."

"You can crash on my couch anytime," Jim said. "You know, once I rebuild my living room. And the rest of my place around it. Besides, if you don't come back, I'll send my new assistant manager to hunt you down."

"Oooh, and she's scary," Kelvin said.

"You bet I'm scary!" Approaching, Natalie split a coconut open with her bare hands and poured the liquid into their glasses. "Anything else, boss?"

"You know the bar doesn't exist yet, right?" Jim said. "You can relax."

"Hey, you already started paying me. I'm on the clock."

"Then I command you to go find an apartment."

"You can give commands?" Kelvin asked.

"Sure. All bar owners can."

"Sweet. Up top."

Kelvin held up his hand to slap five, which Jim obliged.

"My own place?!" Natalie beamed. "Best day ever! Wait, no, the Skypuncher thing. Second best day ever!"

Right. The Skypuncher thing. Jim had to remind himself that they were allies now. He would get there, especially after seeing how happy the hero had made Natalie. She was too inexperienced to join a Prism right now, but that didn't stop him from offering to train her personally. Apparently, she had impressed him during their fight on the Lighthouse. Smashers were weird like that.

Kelvin gave another sigh and set down his glass. "Walk me to my car, Nat? Think it's time I hit the road."

"Totally."

Standing, Kelvin tossed Jim a little salute. Then, on the verge of leaving, he paused and his expression turned serious. "You saved my life up there. Thank you."

"You saved my life down here. Thank *you*." Jim returned the salute. "Don't be a stranger."

"Wouldn't dream of it."

Turning, Kelvin ambled away with a kick in his step and a friend by his side.

Two More Weeks Later

The basic shell was there now. Jim could see his grand design beginning to take shape. He hadn't known it was possible to anticipate something this much. Maybe when an old life ended, the new one just couldn't wait to begin.

He stood now in the bones of what would be his office, envisioning where the desk would go. And over *there* he would install bigger, thicker doors leading into the office closet. Because this closet was going to contain much more than boxes of old junk. A new workspace should reflect a new purpose, after all.

"Bold choice," Zoe said. "Building a bar with no walls or floor or bar."

Jim's heart leapt. He took an instant to gather himself, then turned.

He'd only seen her in normal street clothes once before, on the day they met. Now here she was, standing at what would soon be the doorway to his office in blue jeans and sneakers and a black babydoll tee that said *Don't Be An E=MC Square*.

Zoe wore a little grin. "Think I could get a drink?"

Jim feigned a severe look. "You got ID?"

"Yeah, quite a few from all sorts of places."

"Perfect. I don't want people thinking I run a respectable establishment."

Zoe laughed. Then she turned wistful. "Sorry I've been MIA."

"It's okay. Nat filled me in. Of all the excuses not to call a guy, being recruited for a Prism is a pretty good one."

Her cheeks reddened. "Apparently, I'm replacing Astro-Ninja. I still can't believe it."

"I can."

Jim stepped closer. He'd been envisioning this moment for weeks, going over what he would say. Now, though, as he fell into Zoe's dark eyes, he found he could barely remember his own name. He'd just have to wing it.

"We don't open for a while. Obviously. But when we do, we'll start with a soft launch. Basically an opening party, close friends and staff family only. With one exception—the owner made the rule that, as the owner, he can bring a date. So . . ."

Jim trailed off, the question dying on his lips. As he'd built toward asking, Zoe's eyes had cast farther and farther down until she was staring at the floor.

"I knew it," Jim said. "You're dating Royal Justice, aren't you? That guy's a charmer."

It would have made her laugh any other time. Today, she looked pained.

"It's not that I don't feel something. I do. I mean it." She made a helpless gesture. "But all these big changes I'm trying to make, building a whole new life in a new direction—I feel like it's going to take everything I have to make them work. At least for a while." She huffed and shook her head, as if frustrated with herself. "You matter to me, Jim. Is it horribly selfish to ask you to be my friend?"

Jim didn't want to answer emotionally. He gave himself a moment to process the disappointment.

Then he did what he does best.

"To inaugurate our new friendship," he said with a mischievous grin. "I'm going to say the exact opposite of what I feel. Ready?"

Looking puzzled, Zoe nodded.

"Okay." He put on a dramatic voice that announced *obvious performance*. "Zoe Blake, I do not find you beautiful. I am not impressed by what you're doing with your life. I am absolutely not intoxicated by how amazing you are at what you do. And furthermore, you are not welcome at Versus anytime you want, and you will absolutely not be having drinks on the house, so don't even bother asking. Have a made myself perfectly clear?"

By the time he finished, she was laughing. Going up on her tiptoes, she kissed his cheek. "You really are a good guy, Jim."

"Oof." Jim rocked back, hand on his chest. "And here I thought we were friends."

"I'm not going anywhere, you know," Zoe said. "You haven't seen the last of me, not even close. You can count on it."

Two More Weeks Later, Come On This Is Getting Ridiculous

"You're sure she's comfortable?" Jim said, unable to hide his concern.

"Cocooned in Lord Neon's meditation chamber," Eli said. "Sleeping like a baby while you build her a new home. As long as you absorb her power periodically, she'll stay dormant far more completely than with Arbiter's suppression. It's an effective solution." He cocked his head. "Speaking of Arbiter, did I hear correctly that you hired her?"

"Yep." Jim gestured to the ground under their feet, which would soon be his new battle arena. The skeleton of its primary structure was already in place, surrounding and towering over them. "I've got big plans. So stay tuned."

He let the quiet drag out for a moment, then hit Eli with a sneak attack.

"Tess Atherton is the White Cape, isn't she?"

The hero eyed him. "Why do you say that?"

"For one, she's a parahuman and the public doesn't know. And when I filed the insurance claim for the bar, they denied all coverage. But three days later, they said that not only am I covered after all, I'm basically getting a blank check to make Versus whatever I want. Turns out Atherton Industries suddenly bought their parent company. Coincidence?"

"Already figuring us out, I see." Eli wore a satisfied little grin, as if Jim had proved his faith to be well-founded.

"Just wait until the Black Cape starts finding out all your weaknesses. I'm betting *your* Price has something to do with scones. I'm just not sure whether it's blueberry or cinnamon." Jim narrowed his eyes in mock suspicion. "But when I find out, you'd better not turn evil during breakfast, or it's all over for you."

Eli chuckled "Only you could turn that part of the job into slapstick." He gave Jim a reappraising look. "I like this new Jim. He seems happy to be . . . well, participating in life."

Jim shrugged. "Dealt with some old issues, maybe picked up one or two new ones along the way. Life, basically. But overall? Yeah, you may be right."

Eli nodded. Then he looked away and cleared his throat. "I haven't told you how much I admire what you did. What you gave up for the rest of us. I do, Jim. I won't use the word you hate, but . . . well, there it is. And now I will enjoy watching you thrive."

"To be honest, I'm surprised I even survived. I mean, taking an Apex's power? Who does that and lives?"

"About that." Eli tapped his chin in thought. "I have a theory. More a gut feeling, really, but here it is. I believe that you, Jim, may have been Summer's Price."

Jim went quiet, taken aback.

"No one knows how random the weakness is," Eli continued. "I know a high-level hero who cannot ingest iodized salt, and salt and iodine are completely unrelated to their abilities. But it would explain how you were able to absorb Summer's full power without fatal consequences. If I'm right, you may be the only person on Earth who could have stopped her in time." He shook his head. "And therein lies the tragedy, I know. You came back into this world of ours to find her, and instead came face to face with your darkest hour. I will always be sorry for that. And eternally grateful you were there. The black cape *should* be worn by someone who makes the choices no one else can, and we need his help now more than ever . . ."

He peered at Jim with veiled hope, clearly not wanting to push too hard. They had agreed to give him time before activating, and apparently they were hoping that time was done.

Wow, they really are *desperate.*

Yeah. Let's have fun with that.

Jim held a neutral expression for as long as he could, enjoying the moment as he let Eli stew in uncertainty. Then he gave a mental command and his blue flannel shirt morphed into a bright orange suit with a floppy bowtie that was wider than his body.

"So, I was thinking this should be my new costume. A hide-in-plain-sight kind of thing. What do you think?"

Eli chuckled, his relief palpable. He pulled out a data pad and called up a file. "For your first mission, you may need something a little more subtle."

Jim perked up at that, orange suit shifting back to default. The black cape swayed as he approached and looked over Eli's shoulder. "What have we got?"

"Not much yet. The case is new, and the file is thin. We're hoping you can change that. A growing number of people, seemingly unrelated to each other, are falling into the same unexplained coma, and a parahuman is likely the cause. Wherever this happens, an unusual effect is left behind, which I'll let you see for yourself. We have no idea how or why someone is doing this, and to be honest, they may have continued to escape our notice if they hadn't escalated. We kept this next part out of the news, but it's why we're getting involved. Malachite—Bio Controller, a retired Prism healer—has gone missing, and we believe the person behind these comas has taken him."

"That's all we've got?"

"There is one more thing. A photograph." Eli swiped to the next page. "Sort of."

The photo of a man in a suit was blurry and grainy, from a distance and at a bad angle. Leaning closer, Jim could make out one unique detail—a scar on the man's right ear, as if the flesh there had withered.

So, he was starting with a mystery. One even the Spectrum couldn't solve. As Jim met Eli's eye, he flashed a grin.

"I've got you covered."

THE BLACK CAPE WILL RETURN

If you enjoyed
WORST TEAM-UP EVER
the story continues in . . .

AMATEUR VILLAINY
by
Archer Thorn

A hero is missing. Malachite, once a beloved healer for the Spectrum, now spends his retirement healing the world. Or he did, until he was abducted by a rogue parahuman who appears at random, cannot be tracked, and leaves his victims in unnatural comas. No one knows what he wants, or what dark fate he's planned for his captive.

Jim Riven is the Black Cape, and some heroes aren't happy about it. Okay, most aren't. He *is* the most dangerous villain in the world's brother, after all. So, when he's asked to find and rescue Malachite, it's a chance to earn some trust. Not that he cares what they think. He just wants a better discount at the Spectrum gift shop.

But Jim isn't the only one on the case. A gunslinging bounty hunter, a team of influencer heroes who care more about views than heroics, and Malachite's former apprentice all want to find him first, and things are about to get messy. If Jim's going to succeed in his first mission as the Black Cape, he'll have to do something no one sees coming.

He just has to figure out what that is.

Want a free short story set in the
BLACK CAPE UNIVERSE?
Get your copy here . . .
www.ArcherThorn.com/freestory

ABOUT THE AUTHOR

ARCHER Thorn was born in the same city as you, on the same day, in the same hospital. In the room next to yours, his mission began. He has hunted you day and night for your entire life. When you finish this book, he will be standing behind you.

Run.

GLOSSARY

Aethyr
Most people don't know, and the ones who do aren't talking.

Apex / "going Apex"
When a parahuman's power level exceeds the limits of the Faraday scale, literally going off the charts. Exceedingly rare.

Capes
No parahuman on Earth wears a cape. Except for the Spectrum. This is not official law, but hero and villain alike respect it as a cultural rule. Those who would prefer not to respect it still do so, lest they run afoul of other parahumans who don't take kindly to their attitude.

Faraday Parahuman Power Scale
The rating system by which a parahuman's energy output is measured. The higher the rating, the more powerful a parahuman is considered to be. This rating is independent of the energy's utilization, i.e. the powers that it fuels. The energy itself is not specific to any defined ability. A parahuman consumes this energy like calories, "burning" it as they wield their own particular powers (described in terms of class and sub-class). The

more energy there is to "burn," the more powerful those abilities become.

The scale is organized in a decimal system, with these generalizations:
0.0 – Normal humans
0.1 to 0.9 – weak parahuman
1.0 to 1.9 – from weak to low-but-capable
2.0 to 3.4 – from low-but-capable to somewhat respectable
3.5 to 5.5 – actually respectable to mid-range to moderately impressive
5.6 to 7.0 – impressive to very impressive
7.1 to 7.9 – formidable to don't-mess-with
8.0 to 8.9 – seriously, walk away
9.0 to 10.0 – we used to have a moon, but they blew it up

Power output increases exponentially as one moves up the Faraday scale. With each decimal point increase, the energy output multiplies. A 4.0 parahuman is not simply twice as powerful as a 2.0, they are orders of magnitude more powerful. The power growth between ratings also rises with higher numbers. A 4.1 is a certain percentage more powerful than a 4.0, but a 7.1 is a greater leap up from 7.0. In addition to their core abilities, the higher a parahuman's energy output, the tougher and more resistant to threats and damage they will generally be.

When referencing a parahuman's rating on the Faraday Parahuman Power Scale, it may colloquially be referred to as a Capacity, a Faraday rating, a power level, or simply a number. The terminology is pretty loose, but everyone will know what you mean as long as you don't get too weird with it.

Is it possible to exceed a 10.0 rating?
See definitions for **Apex*** and **"going Apex"***

Parahuman Class

The application of a parahuman's power, or the effects resulting from a parahuman consuming (or "burning") their parahuman energy. While that energy is the same for all parahumans, the effects of consuming it vary from person to person. In general, the "output" or manifestation of an individual parahuman's power can be slotted into a class (some manifest more than one class, typically at higher levels), and one or more sub-classes. While this system of categorization serves as a way to quantify the basics of parahuman ability, there are many more possible manifestations and permutations than the commonly known ones listed here. Powers, and power combinations, can vary as much as the wielders themselves, and more are being discovered all the time. As such, what is considered the standard definitions of the most commonly observed abilities is a shifting baseline, often changing and growing with each subsequent generation. New classes, sub-classes, and harder-to-quantify abilities continue to present themselves, and may do so at any time.

The primary parahuman classes are currently understood to be:

Blaster – Typically ranged attacks, with powers focused into beams or other concentrated output and directed at a specific target area. Most commonly emanate from hands or eyes, but are not limited to them. The quintessential Blaster is regarded as a "glass cannon," able to deal out enormous damage but withstand much less.

Controller – Specializes in manipulation, often at a distance and/or across a wide area of effect. These are not typically direct attackers or defenders, instead standing back and affecting elements of their environment on a larger scale, often to help allies and/or hinder enemies.

Sensor – Deals in information, absorbing unparalleled amounts of it through their specific medium. Able to parse, analyze, and interpret absorbed information quickly, often drawing conclusions that elude non-Sensors. Typically, they also have greater access to the information noted by their unconscious minds, and can factor all of that seemingly unperceived data. Some Sensors don't only absorb information, they can also transmit it (such as with telepaths or faunapaths).

Smasher – The tanks of the parahuman world. Typically very strong and very tough, with the ability to absorb tons of punishment. Damage output tends to be less than a Striker of similar power level, but constitution is higher. Abilities tend to manifest in close proximity to the wielder. In contrast to Blasters or Controllers, who are more likely to apply their power across a wide area, Smashers tend to sheathe themselves in their ability, becoming human shields / battering rams / living weapons / bullet sponges, etc. While their abilities don't typically extend far beyond their person, the intensity with which they manifest is formidable.

Striker – Fighter class, dealing out lots of damage while being able to withstand a respectable amount. General toughness (constitution, damage resistance, etc.) is higher than Blasters, Controllers, and Sensors, but lower than Smashers. With the exception of the Sniper sub-class, abilities tend to be up-close and personal, melee-oriented, usually quick and hard-hitting.

Traveler – Travel abilities are often considered a secondary power. But for parahumans with a strong enough affinity, and the will to learn and use it creatively, a travel power can be capable as a main. The stronger a Traveler power is, the more pronounced the parahuman's ancillary enhancements will be in order to support it. For instance, an especially fast Runner will find that in addition to being fast, their body is able to withstand the force and strain of moving at incredibly high speeds (wind sheer, gravitational pull, etc.), while their mind is able to process information quickly enough to keep them safe while in motion.

Parahuman Sub-Class
A more specific definition of a parahuman's ability, describing the particular aspect of a power class that manifests when they expend energy. Like classes themselves, sub-classes are highly diverse, always changing and growing, and many defy casual classification when all of the nuances specific to each parahuman are considered. As such, what's considered common is expected to shift over time.

Blaster
Aethyr – considered theoretically possible, but never documented
Energy – Radiant, Solar, Thermal/Heat, Nuclear, Cosmic, etc.
Elemental – Air, Ice, Fire, Lightning, etc.
Force / Kinetic
Psionic – sometimes called Mindsnipers
Sonic

Controller
Aethyr
Bio / Organic – areas of influence can include plants, animals, themselves (such as shapeshifters), and other people. Most healers are a variety of this class.
Booster – specializes in Buffs, elevating or augmenting a target's natural attributes and abilities. Can be used on parahumans or normals.
Digital / Technological
Electrical / Electromagnetic
Elemental – Air, Water, Ice, Earth, Fire, Lightning, Solar, Thermal/Heat, etc.

Gravity

Force / Kinetic

Psionic / Mind / Emotion – sometimes called Dominators

Suppressor – specializes in Debuffs, dampening or negating a target's natural attributes and abilities. Can be used on both parahumans and normals.

Time / Temporal

Weather / Climate

Sensor

Telepath

Empath

Enviropath – sense and absorb information about the immediate environment

Intellect / Genius – super-genius, process information with superhuman speed

Mediapath – sense and absorb information from sources of media

Florapath – communicate with, and sense information from, plant-life

Faunapath – communicate with, and sense information from, non-human creatures

Striker

Brawler – enhanced hand-to-hand pugilism

Duelist – enhanced proficiency with martial weapons (swords, staffs, shields, etc.)

Sniper – enhanced proficiency with ranged weapons (bows, guns, shuriken, etc.)

Stalker – the ninjas of the parahuman world, able to operate with enhanced stealth

Smasher

    Aethyr
    Bio
    Energy – Solar, Thermal, Electrical, etc.
    Elemental – Air, Ice, Fire, Lightning, Earth, etc.
    Mega-Strength
    Stoneskin / Steelskin

Traveller

    Dodger – typified by hyper reflexes and escapes from danger
    Flyer
    Leaper
    Phaser – can pass through and travel within solid objects
    Runner
    Teleporter

Parahuman Power Augments

Some abilities manifest, not as core powers, but as augmentations or complements to core powers. For instance, a Striker with a Brawler sub-class is typically considered a pugilist, some variety of hand-to-hand fighter. A Striker Brawler who can sheathe their hands in flame and deliver fire punches would be described as a Striker Brawler with a Fire augment. Fire is not a power that the Striker wields or controls as its own thing. It only manifests as an addition to the core abilities of the Brawler sub-class. Sensor augmentations are perhaps the most common. For instance, an Electric Controller will likely also possess some level of Electric Sensor ability, allowing them to perceive in greater detail what they control.

The Price

A secret weakness associated with high-level parahumans, like the universe's way of balancing such great power. As this is their least favorite subject, little is known about the level of randomness when it comes to someone's Price. However, when a parahuman encounters theirs, no matter how high their level, they will almost certainly drop them like a rock.

Prism
A team of heroes working directly for the Spectrum. While not as revered as the Spectrum seven, they are also highly regarded and respected. There are seven Prisms in total, each one under the direct supervision of a Spectrum member. Every Prism is also a team of seven heroes.

The Reaches
The twin cities of Highreach (yay) and Cloudreach (ugh).

The Spectrum
The world's most famous team of legendary heroes. Always seven members, each wearing one of only seven capes in the world. Each cape represents a color from the visible light spectrum. Three original members remain on the team–Skypuncher, Millennia, and Lord Neon–while the other positions have changed over the decades due to death, retirement, or other circumstances.

Warded Zone
Safe areas where no battle will occur unless agreed upon by both sides. Any parahuman crossing into the shield's radius will receive a small psionic burst, alerting them telepathically that it is time to behave. Even when battle is agreed upon, no major damage or fatalities are allowed in a Warded Zone. These areas are marked by a copper shield. This agreement is honored by heroes and villains alike, and even the worst of them abide by it. Some codes you just don't break.

Velocity
Parahumans are not allowed to play in normal people's sports, as their abilities grant them an unfair advantage. So a new team-

based game was invented specifically for parahumans only, to showcase and leverage their unique abilities. It quickly became the most popular sport in the world. A high-octane combination of football, dodgeball, and insane obstacle course.

Vessel

An ability so rare, some believe it is mythical and doesn't actually exist. Once a child's parahuman power manifests (most commonly between ages 8 and 11), their energy output will grow as they age, and will typically stop growing as they reach adulthood (most commonly between 19 and 22). That final Faraday rating will be theirs for life, and generally considered to be "their power level." Though a parahuman can cause minor fluctuations in their energy output, it will remain mostly constant.

Not so with a Vessel. Their Faraday rating is often on the lower side, but it is considered only their *base resting* power level. Vessels are able to absorb energy and use it to boost their power level temporarily, essentially becoming a stronger version of themselves until the absorbed energy is expended.

It is theorized that Vessels must absorb the type of energy related to their core ability in order to boost their power. For instance, a Solar Blaster who is also a Vessel would have to absorb sunlight in order to increase their power level, while attempting to absorb electrical energy would do nothing. However, due to the extreme rarity of the Vessel ability, and the unwillingness of Vessels to identify themselves for study, most suppositions about how the ability works come from anecdotal observation.